Any Given
DOOMSDAY

St. Martin's Paperbacks Titles
by Lori Handeland

Any Given Doomsday

Thunder Moon

Hidden Moon

Rising Moon

Midnight Moon

Crescent Moon

Dark Moon

Hunter's Moon

Blue Moon

Any Given DOOMSDAY

Lori Handeland

St. Martin's Paperbacks

This is a work of fiction. All of the characters, organizations, and events portrayed in this novel are either products of the author's imagination or are used fictitiously.

ANY GIVEN DOOMSDAY

Excerpt from *Doomsday Can Wait* copyright © 2008 by Lori Handeland.

Copyright © 2008 by Lori Handeland.

For information address St. Martin's Press, 175 Fifth Avenue, New York, NY 10010.

ISBN: 0-312-94919-7
EAN: 978-0-312-94919-8

Printed in the United States of America

St. Martin's Paperbacks edition / November 2008

St. Martin's Paperbacks are published by St. Martin's Press, 175 Fifth Avenue, New York, NY 10010.

10 9 8 7 6 5 4 3 2 1

Acknowledgments

Grateful thanks to:

My editor, Jen Enderlin, a brilliant talent and a great cheerleader. Thanks for letting me go where the muse takes me.

My sons, who turned into such lovely young men. I'm so proud.

My husband, for singing "You are my sunshine," in answer to my every snarl. (Yep, he's a keeper.)

My first-Thursday-of-the-month breakfast group—without you I'd go stark, raving nuttier.

Chapter 1

On the day my old life died, the air smelled of spring-time—budding trees and just-born flowers, fresh grass and hope. I should have known right then that something was coming.

I've always been psychic. I've never once been happy about it. In fact, I did everything I could to drown that gift in the realities of a normal life.

But normal went out the open doorway that morning in early May, and I never got it back again. I'm not sure I ever really had it in the first place.

I went to work as always. I'm the first-shift bartender at Murphy's, a cop bar on the east side of Milwaukee. Twenty-five and still a bartender. I'd be more concerned about my career arc if I hadn't already tried being a cop—and failed.

Cops and psychics don't mix. Go figure.

Not that I'd ever broadcast what I could do. I wasn't a complete moron. However, sometimes those flashes were impossible to hide. Sometimes hiding what I knew would have been more criminal than what I'd seen in the first place.

Of course I'd tried to downplay it; I'd tried to invent excuses for the information that came to me in a way I couldn't explain. But what excuse is there for something like that? I was never able to come up with one that made any sense.

The cops I worked with didn't trust me because they didn't understand me. They avoided me as much as they could, unless they needed my help. When they asked, I had little choice but to answer, if there was any answer to be had. Eventually my too accurate hunches had led to a disaster, and I'd had no choice but to leave the force.

Thank God for Megan Murphy. Without her, I don't know what I would have done.

Luckily Megan had been in my situation before—without income, alone in the world, and desperate. Just because I was the reason she was a widow didn't mean she wasn't going to help me.

A lot of cops become private detectives when they leave the force. I had the training; I even had a gun. All I would have had to do was get my license and hang up a sign.

ELIZABETH PHOENIX — DICK FOR HIRE.

Can you imagine the business I'd get just from the walk-ins?

In the end, I'd taken the job at Murphy's. I figured I owed Megan, and at the time I'd wanted nothing more than to be flogged daily for what I'd done. Becoming a bartender in a cop bar after getting my partner killed was a good place for that.

That morning I had customers pounding on the door before eleven A.M. There's a reason beer made Milwaukee famous. When the sun shines and the temperatures climb above freezing, people in my hometown make a beeline for the Miller Lite.

I propped the front door wide open, all the windows, too, and watched the just-sprouted tree limbs waver, sending dappled shadows dancing across a sidewalk the shade of storm clouds. The spring wind stirred my hair, and goose bumps sprang up all over my body despite the uncommon heat of the day. I was possessed with a sudden and undeniable urge to—

"Leave."

The five off-duty cops at the bar glanced up from their beers and sandwiches. They looked at each other, then back at me.

"Not you," I said.

They returned to their meals, but not without a few eye rolls and one derisive snort.

Why on earth had I said that out loud? No matter how hard I tried to be normal, the truth remained—I wasn't.

The lunch help hadn't arrived yet, but that didn't matter. Everyone at Murphy's was a regular. Often, when Megan had a problem late at night with one of her kids, she'd toss the keys to the top cop in the place and go about her business.

"Kenny." The man looked up from his Reuben with a scowl. I was already headed around the end of the bar. "Got an emergency. I'll be back as soon as I can. The lunch shift will be here in ten."

Kenny's scowl of annoyance became a frown of confusion. "What emergency? You didn't even get a call."

What else is new? I thought.

I did use my cell phone once I got into the car, but Ruthie didn't answer, which wasn't surprising. Sometimes I wondered how she juggled all the responsibilities in her life without two extra sets of hands.

Ruthie was an ancient black woman who ran a group home on the south side of Milwaukee amid an explosion of ranch houses built in the 1950s. Nice yards. Good schools. A lot of last names that ended in *ski*.

Back in the old days, Ruthie had been the only African

American within thirty miles. She hadn't cared. Amazingly, no one else had either. Ruthie was like that.

People who would have walked across the street to avoid a . . . well, let's not say the word, took to Ruthie like a long-lost auntie.

Nowadays a few more colors had popped up amid the Caucasians, though the majority of the names still ended in *ski*.

Twenty minutes later, I parked at the curb and contemplated the only two-story house on the block. Things appeared quiet. Why wouldn't they? At this time of day, the kids were in school. Ruthie might not even be here.

However, I'd learned over the years that whenever I felt the urge to see Ruthie there was always a damn good reason.

I got out of the car and headed up the walk.

Ruthie was a no-nonsense throwback to a time when parents ruled with love and an iron fist. Once Ruthie took you in, she never gave you up. She understood that part of the problem for throwaway kids was the being thrown away. She was the only mother I'd ever known— or perhaps the only one I allowed myself to remember.

I reached the porch before I saw it—that tiny sliver of shadow creeping onto the cement through the half-open door. My hand automatically went to my hip, but my gun hadn't been there in months. I missed it then more than I ever had before.

Though I knew better, I pushed open the door and began to call her name. "Ruth—"

The scent and sight of blood caused the word to stick in my throat.

I found her in the kitchen, lying in a puddle of sunshine and blood. She'd always loved the sun, really hated blood.

I dropped to my knees. I wanted to check for a pulse but her throat . . . She didn't have much of one left.

"Lizbeth." Her eyes opened. "I knew you'd come."

"Don't try to talk." How *could* she talk? "I'll call—"

"No." She closed her eyes, and for an instant I thought she was gone. What would I do if I lost her? She was the only person who truly loved me on this earth.

"Ruthie!"

"Shh." She patted my knee, leaving a bloody splotch. Strange, but her hand looked as if it had been bitten, mangled. For that matter, so did her—

"I've been waitin' for you to come around, but you haven't."

I winced. I'd been working a lot of hours. What else did I have to do? Except visit the woman who'd taken me in off the streets.

"I'll come more often. I promise."

Her gaze suddenly bored into mine. "When I'm gone, it's up to you."

"Ruthie, don't—"

"The final battle," she managed, though her voice was fading, "begins now."

She grabbed my hand in a surprisingly strong grip for a dying old lady, then my skull erupted in agony and everything went black.

Chapter 2

When I awoke from the coma more had changed than the weather. I distinctly recalled going to Ruthie's house on a clear, spring day.

Post-coma, the windows of the hospital room revealed swirling snow. I experienced a moment of panic, thinking I'd lost nearly a year, then remembered where I lived.

In southern Wisconsin, April sunshine sometimes brought May blizzards.

A movement in the room caused me to turn my head. A blinding flash of pain made me close my eyes, and what I saw when I did made me open them again.

"Whoa," I muttered. "That's new."

Sure, I was psychic, but I'd never had a vision. If that's what the horrific scene I'd just flashed on had been.

No. Couldn't be. I'd seen monsters. Tooth and claw, lots of blood and death—and I'd seen them at Ruthie's place.

That hadn't happened, couldn't happen except in a—

"Nightmare," I mumbled, my tongue dry and thick. Who knew what meds they'd been giving me. There was no such thing as monsters—unless you counted those who preyed on the weak and the innocent, which, of course, I did.

I tried to remember what had happened when I'd gone through that open door, seen the blood, started screaming Ruthie's name. But I couldn't remember, and trying only exhausted me so much I slipped back into the soft, dark place where safety beckoned.

Funny, I hadn't needed a safe place since before I'd come to Ruthie's.

When I awoke again, Laurel and Hardy had drawn two chairs next to my bedside.

Their names were really Hammond and Landsdown, but one was tall and thin, kind of dopey-looking, the other was shorter, fatter, even dopier. They were homicide detectives and about three thousand times smarter than they appeared.

"What do you want?" I reached for the bed controls to raise my head and shoulders. If there were anything seriously wrong with me, the doctors wouldn't have let these guys darken my door.

As soon as I was upright, my mind flashed on what had happened to put me here. Suddenly I remembered everything, or almost everything.

"Who in hell hit me?" I demanded.

Hammond's eyes widened. "Hit you? When?"

"I went to Ruthie's. The door was open—" Very un-Ruthie-like, as was the blood all over the walls.

The significance of these two being homicide detectives reached me at last. So I wasn't firing on all cylinders; I blame the coma.

"She's dead, isn't she?"

"Yes," Landsdown said simply.

I wanted to cry, but I wasn't sure how. People like me have the crying beat out of them pretty early.

They waited a respectable amount of time for me to shed a tear, and when I didn't, they moved on.

"What did you see?" Hammond asked.

I took a deep breath, closed my eyes, and experienced again the flashes of tooth and claw, the strange, nightmarish beings that couldn't be real. What had they been putting in my IV?

I shook my head, opened my eyes and met Hammond's steady gaze. "Ruthie on the kitchen floor. I went to her."

"Was she alive?" Landsdown prompted.

They seemed to follow the tag-team method of questioning—first one, then the other, no good cop/bad cop for these guys. They were almost interchangeable.

"Yes," I answered.

"Did she speak?" That was Hammond.

"She said 'I knew you'd come.'"

"Why would she know that?"

I hesitated. Why had she? I'd gone there on a whim, beset with an irresistible urge to see her.

"I have no idea," I said, then frowned. "What about the kids?"

Ruthie's was always filled to capacity, which meant there were up to eight children living in that house along with her. I hoped to God none of them had come home and found us.

"They're fine," Landsdown assured me. "All at school. Didn't see a thing."

"Good." I let out the breath I was holding. "Where are they now?"

"Back in the system."

I winced, but there wasn't anything I could do about it. Even if I were capable of mothering eight problem kids, the state would never let me.

"You think someone hit you?" Hammond asked.

"Someone did. Ruthie grabbed my hand and then . . . wham! Next thing I knew I woke up here."

The two of them exchanged glances.

"What?"

Landsdown nodded and Hammond spoke. "According to the doctor there wasn't a mark on you. No head trauma. No gunshot or knife wound. No drugs in your system."

"But—" I lifted my hand, trailing tubes and sensors. I didn't feel any bumps. "How long have I been out?"

"Four days."

I glanced at the window where snow still swirled. I'd been right about the weather. Still springtime in Wisconsin. Gotta love it.

"Someone hit me," I insisted stubbornly.

"Maybe you fainted."

I glared at Landsdown. I did not faint at the sight of blood like a swooning maiden.

"If no one conked me on the head," I pointed out, "then why was I in a coma for four days?"

Hammond shrugged. "No one knows."

The two detectives shifted in their chairs, then twitched their necks as if their ties were too tight. Considering that the offending pieces of clothing appeared to have been loosened hours ago, perhaps when they'd slept in those suits, I didn't need a psychic flash to understand they wanted to ask me something, and then again, they didn't.

"We need a favor." Hammond actually tried to smile. He must have needed a favor bad.

"Mmm," I said noncommittally.

Without even a *do you mind?* Hammond tossed something at me, and I caught it. The instant I did, I murmured, "Jimmy."

"Jesus," Landsdown muttered. "How do you *do* that?"

I wish I knew. Because if I did maybe I could quit doing it.

If wishing could have made the bursts of intuition disappear, they'd have been gone shortly after I was able to voice what I'd been seeing all my life. That was when everything pretty much went to hell.

"Where is he?" Landsdown demanded.

"What?" I shook the cobwebs from my mind, peered at the baseball cap gripped desperately in my fingers. The Yankees. I hated the Yankees. Doesn't everyone?

"Do you see where he is?" Hammond murmured.

My heart picked up in panic. These guys were homicide. However, if they wanted me to tell them where Jimmy was, he couldn't be dead. Or at least I hoped not. I might have kicked him out of my bed a long, long time ago, but I'd had a much tougher time kicking Jimmy Sanducci out of my heart.

"No." I pitched the cap into Landsdown's ample lap. "What do you want with him?"

They exchanged glances again. The two of them were like an old married couple, which is what most longtime partners were. They squabbled, made up, shared jokes, and spoke without having to speak.

My partner and I had been like that, which was why he'd listened to me when I said I had a "hunch" where we could find the strung-out junkie who'd killed his supplier. Because of me, that strung-out junkie had also killed Max.

"You're acquainted with Sanducci?" Landsdown's voice brought me back to the hospital.

"You know damn well I am."

They might be annoying, but they were thorough. They knew about Jimmy and me—at least what was fit to print in the records of social services.

"When was the last time you saw him?"

I didn't bother to be nice. I rarely did—especially when the conversation involved Jimmy Sanducci.

"I believe it was right after I told him not to let the door hit him in his incredible ass on his way out of my life."

Hammond coughed, but his lips quivered as he tried not to laugh.

"You had a relationship with Mr. Sanducci?" Landsdown asked.

"No."

What Jimmy and I once had could by no stretch of the imagination be called a relationship. Jimmy didn't understand the meaning of the word. In truth, neither did I. I shouldn't be angry with him, but I was.

"Why are you looking for him?"

Hammond met my eyes. "Why do you think?"

For several beats I still didn't get it. When I did, I straightened so fast Hammond reared back and nearly upset his chair.

"Jimmy wouldn't hurt anyone."

"He wasn't so particular about hurting people when he was a kid."

My eyes narrowed. Juvenile records were sealed. They couldn't know about Jimmy and—

I cut that thought off before it could drift through my mind and show on my face. But I wasn't fast enough.

"You know Sanducci is capable of murder," Landsdown said triumphantly.

I did. But I wasn't going to tell them that.

"He'd never hurt Ruthie. Never."

Hammond shrugged. He didn't seem convinced.

"Why are you so sure he did it?"

"Smoking gun."

"Gun?" That definitely didn't sound like Jimmy.

"Figure of speech," Hammond said. "Knife. Pure silver."

I winced. *That* sounded more like Jimmy. He'd always been weird about his knives.

"He fled the scene."

"You're gonna need more than that."

"Fingerprints on the knife, hell, every old place."

"Too dumb for Sanducci."

Landsdown lifted a brow. "Why would a photographer be so savvy about evidence?"

Jimmy was a globe-trotting portrait wizard. Annie Leibovitz with a penis. An artiste of epic proportions. Everyone who was anyone wanted their picture taken by the great Sanducci.

"Any moron knows better than to touch everything," I said.

"Maybe he was pissed. Maybe he'd just found out Ruthie was going to leave you all that she had."

I frowned. "Ruthie doesn't have anything."

"According to the neighbors, they were shouting at each other. Then Ruthie's dead; Sanducci's running. Open and shut."

Not so much. Jimmy never yelled. Unless it was at me.

"Do you know where he is?" Landsdown pressed.

"Give her the hat again," Hammond ordered.

I held up my hand. "It doesn't work like that. You can't tell me what you want to know then expect an answer. I'm not a crystal ball."

"What are you?"

Though Landsdown's voice was neutral, his face gave him away. He thought I was an aberration, if not a con artist.

"I've never been quite sure of that myself," I murmured. "I get flashes sometimes when I touch things or people."

"But not always?" Hammond asked.

"No."

"And not now." Landsdown sighed. "Let's go."

I didn't bother to say good-bye, just listened to the

door shut behind them, then, seconds later, listened as another opened behind me.

"Why didn't you tell them?"

The voice came out of the darkness, flowing over me like a warm summer wind, making me remember things I'd spent years trying to forget.

"You knew I wouldn't, Jimmy. Otherwise you never would have come here."

Chapter 3

I could smell him from across the room—cool water, tart soap, and a hint of cinnamon to his aftershave. Jimmy always smelled like he'd just stepped out of the shower. Usually because he had.

No doubt a remnant of a childhood without abundant water and scented toiletries, his teen years had been full of both. Sometimes he took three or four showers a day. I wondered that his skin didn't peel off.

I bit my lip to keep from saying something I'd regret. I hated him, but I loved him too. Talk about a gift and a curse.

He hovered in the shadows; I reached for the light. "Don't," he murmured.

I swung my legs over the edge of the bed. I couldn't lie here any longer. I felt fine. Better than fine, in fact. Rested, jazzed, ultra-alert—not at all the way I assumed I'd feel after a four-day sojourn in the land of coma.

The tubes and wires prevented me from getting up, so I yanked them out. The IV hurt like a bitch anyway.

As I got to my feet, I flicked the switch on my bed-side lamp. I never had been very good at taking orders, especially from Jimmy.

The muted glow spread across the faded tile, lending just enough light to see. He had one helluva shiner.

"Ah, Jimmy." I lifted my hand toward his face.

He had the good sense to step away. "Baby, if you want to go back to where we were when you threw me out, I'm all for it. But right now I'm a little busy running for my life."

"Do *not* call me 'baby.' " My hand, which had been hovering in the air, clenched into a fist. "You don't ever get to call me 'baby' again."

The pain in my voice surprised me. I'd thought I'd gotten over his betrayal. Guess not.

"Fine." He sighed. "Just don't touch me. I—" He broke off and ran a hand through his hair. Longer than I remembered, but just as sleek and black. "Never mind."

Everything about him was dark—his eyes, his clothes, his heart. His complexion, tan even in the middle of winter, pointed at several heritages, but he didn't know any for certain. Like me, Jimmy had been dumped. He hadn't a clue who his parents were any more than I did.

Despite the shiner—or perhaps because of it—he still looked the same. Too good. Jimmy Sanducci was major eye candy, always had been. It was how he'd survived on the streets for so long.

There were things he'd done even I didn't know about, and I didn't want to. I'd done things too. Until you're so hungry you'd wrestle garbage away from a rat, you have no idea what you're capable of. Jimmy and I knew. We were two of a kind.

"Did you do it?" I asked.

His black eyes flicked to mine. "Fuck you."

"Not in this lifetime. Or at least not again."

"What the hell did I come here for?"

He started toward the door; I blocked his way. "What *did* you come here for?"

"Lizzy," he warned.

Jimmy was the only one who dared call me that. To everyone else I was Elizabeth—Liz if you were really trying to be my pal. But Lizzy? Just try it, and Jimmy's shiner would look good to you in the morning.

"Did. You. Do. It." I punctuated each word with a step forward; with each one he took a step back until his shoulders slammed against the wall.

He wanted to deck me; I saw it in his eyes. But while Jimmy might have done things he couldn't forgive himself for, he would never hit a woman, especially me. I hit back. He'd learned that the hard way when we were twelve.

I smiled at the memory of the first day we'd met. He'd been living at Ruthie's for two years; I was brand-new. Fresh from another foster home that hadn't wanted to keep me.

I was an angry twelve-year-old. Taller than the other girls, already developing and mortified by it. I wore shapeless clothes, hunched my shoulders, let my hair cover my face. On the streets, in the system, you didn't want to be noticed. And a girl like me, with my special talents, wanted to be noticed even less than most.

"What's so funny?" Jimmy slumped against the wall as if he needed it to hold him up. Were there more bruises than the ones I could see?

Always.

"I was remembering the first time I had to kick your ass."

He tilted his head and his too-long hair slid over his injured eye. "And that was funny?"

"Hilarious."

Jimmy was the big cheese at Ruthie's place. He'd had

to move in with one of the other boys so I could have his room. He wasn't pleased, so he'd put a grass snake in my bed.

I'd named the snake James, found him a cage, then loosened Sanducci's teeth the next morning. He hadn't messed with me again.

Until we were seventeen.

And there was a memory I didn't want to revisit. Not now with him so close and me naked beneath my thin, gaping hospital gown.

"Who hit you?" I asked.

"Does it matter?"

"If you want me to help, you need to tell me everything."

"Who said I wanted help?"

"Why did you come here if not for that?"

He looked away, out the window where the snow still swirled. "Maybe I wanted to keep an eye on you."

I recalled waking up once, the sensation that I wasn't alone, then that weird flash of monsters.

"How long have you been here?" I asked.

He shrugged.

"How long?"

I could just see him hiding in the bathroom, watching me. Hell, he'd done it before. Back when peeping at me was his idea of foreplay.

"Not long." He flicked a finger at my hair. "When did you cut it?"

I blinked at the change of subject. What did my hair have to do with anything?

"Years ago," I snapped, the amount of time reminding me that when I'd thrown him out, he hadn't returned. Why was that almost harder to forgive than his betrayal had been?

"You had really pretty hair."

Everything seemed out of sync. Jimmy in my hospital room, talking about my hair when the cops wanted to arrest him for Ruthie's murder. I'd had dreams like this before—so full of mundane activities that they must mean something, though I never could figure out what.

The reality of Ruthie's loss hit me, making me a little dizzy, causing me to snap out an answer. "Having hair down to your ass causes too many problems when you're a cop."

"I heard you weren't a cop anymore."

As if I needed to be reminded.

"The third time some dickhead spit his gum into my hair through the wire cage in the squad car, I hacked it off. It was so much easier, I never went back."

"Seems even darker short."

"My hair's the same color it always was."

Dark brown with a twinkle of red—mahogany in certain lights. My skin was also darker than the average Caucasian. I was part something else, but what that could be was anyone's guess. My blue eyes were as much a mystery as the rest of me.

"What happened at Ruthie's?" I asked.

"According to your cop pals, I killed her." He stared at me for several seconds. "You seem to think I did too."

"You wouldn't."

His brows lifted. "Such faith. I'm touched."

"I'm the only friend you've got right now, Sanducci. *Don't* piss me off."

"I doubt I'll be able to manage that," he muttered.

"Just tell me what happened. Why would you and Ruthie argue? Who came to the house? Who killed her? And how could they if you were there?"

Jimmy would fight for Ruthie. He'd die for her. So then why was he here and she wasn't?

"Lizzy." He sighed. "There are things going down you don't understand."

There always were. Despite having "the sight," as Ruthie said, I was a bit slow on the uptake when it came to people. I'd certainly been a dimwit when it came to Jimmy.

I'd believed in him, in us; then I'd seen him screwing someone else only hours after he'd screwed me. At the time, I'd thought we'd been making love. At the time, I'd thought what we had was love. But when I touched him, I'd learned differently.

"I don't trust you," I said.

"You believe I'd kill someone?"

"You have been known to stick sharp implements into people who annoy you."

He scowled. "I haven't stuck one into you yet."

"No, but I'm sure you've dreamed about it."

His lips turned upward. "When I dream of you, I don't dream of knives. More like whips, chains, some rope, a little whipped cream."

"Funny, when I dream of you I *do* dream of knives."

His half-smile faded. "The cops told you Ruthie died from a knife wound?"

"I thought you were listening at the door."

"I only heard snatches. Good door."

"They said they found a knife and from the description, it's yours. Combined with your fingerprints on everything and the screaming match you had with Ruthie, you've landed at the top of their most-wanted list."

"I hope you didn't tell them about my childhood fascination with sharp, shiny things."

"They seemed to already know."

He muttered several curses that would have singed the ears off most people, but not me. I'd heard every one of them before my fifth birthday.

"Maybe you should turn yourself in—" I began.

"No."

The word was clipped and just a little desperate. Jimmy never had gotten over the time he'd spent in jail as a kid. I couldn't really blame him. Still—

"If you didn't do it—"

"I'm going to have a hard time proving that, considering the knife." His head tilted, as if he'd heard something far away. Before I knew what he meant to do, he crossed the room and slipped out.

I followed, reaching the door only seconds after it closed. But when I opened it, the hall was deserted.

"How does he *do* that?" I muttered.

The guy should be in covert operations the way he went Houdini at the drop of a hat. I suspect being raised the way we were—basically raising ourselves until Ruthie—had made both Jimmy and I adept at disappearing.

Even in a crowd, I knew how to become invisible. And while Jimmy had made an art out of garnering attention for himself and his work, I doubted he'd ever lost the talent for avoiding attention when such avoidance was the best course of action.

"What are you doing out of bed?"

A nurse had appeared almost as mysteriously as Jimmy had disappeared. She shooed me inside and tried to hustle me back to bed.

"Did you see anyone leave my room just now?" I asked.

"The detectives."

"After that?"

She shook her head, distracted by a call button dinging down the hall. I couldn't take what she'd seen or not seen as gospel. She had other things to worry about besides me and my visitors. Although she didn't have me for long.

The doctors could find nothing wrong with me, and though they weren't wild about my leaving, they couldn't stop me.

Within the hour, I'd checked out and headed for home.

Chapter 4

Friedenberg was a yuppie paradise. Located directly north of Milwaukee, the village had once been the oldest German community in the county, which was why we were overrun with Lutheran churches built of stone.

For centuries the area surrounding the place held nothing but cows; then the city got dangerous and those with money went north.

They discovered a quaint town with a main street that ran parallel to the Milwaukee River, making the real estate prime for any business that might profit from water flowing past an eastern exposure.

But what really made Friedenberg grow was the vast amount of farmland that surrounded it. Once the bottom fell out of milk and cheese, the farmers sold what they had left—the land—and a subdivision was born. A very wealthy subdivision. Houses around Friedenberg started at half a million dollars.

However, the town proper—where I lived—was jokingly referred to by locals as the ghetto. I didn't find it funny, but at least my building didn't boast property taxes that equaled the gross national product of a small African nation.

The cab let me out in front my place—a two-story,

business-residential combo I'd purchased after leaving the force. I'd wanted to get as far away from my previous life as I could without being too far from Ruthie to visit.

I rented out the first floor to a small retail establishment that sold useless knickknacks to the wealthy hausfraus in the area.

These women made a career out of raising spoiled children and spending wads of their doctor, banker, lawyer husbands' money. They hired full-time nannies so they could shop, order salad at the ridiculously expensive local lunch spot, then work out until they were as slim and hard as their French-manicured nails. It was a weird, weird world.

I lived in the efficiency apartment on the second floor, which worked out well since the store opened at ten and closed at five. The rest of the time, which conveniently encompassed the hours I was home, the place remained dark and silent.

Like now, thank goodness. All I wanted to do was sleep. My earlier burst of energy had faded into the exhaustion that follows an adrenaline rush.

The ground was covered with snow. According to the radio, tomorrow had a predicted high of sixty-four degrees. Welcome to Wisconsin. By tomorrow night, everything would be a sea of mud.

The moon had come out from behind the clouds, bright and eerily silver, casting cool blue shadows across the pristine white carpet.

I stumbled upstairs and locked the door behind me. The place already smelled closed in, musty. Didn't take long.

I left the mail in the mailbox—one more night wouldn't hurt—and ignored the blinking red light on my message machine. I was certain at least one if not more of the messages was from Megan. According to the nurse, she'd been a frequent visitor while I was unconscious.

She'd left a *Get Well Now* card. At the bottom she'd scrawled: *Come back as soon as you're up to it.* I planned to be up to it by tomorrow.

My apartment was sparse. The kitchen lay to the left, my bed to the right, a bathroom in the far corner next to the only window. I didn't need much; I spent most of my life at Murphy's anyway.

I didn't bother with a light, just dropped my clothes in a trail that led to the bed. Then I crawled in, pulled the covers over my head, and dreamed.

I was at Ruthie's, but in the way of dreams the house was different—white with green trim and a picket fence. Too hokey for Ruthie, but nevertheless I still knew it was hers.

A rugrat in ringlets opened the door. I'd never seen her before, though I'd seen a thousand just like her. The eyes were far older than the childish face and doll-baby hair.

Had I looked like that? I knew damn well I had, even without Jimmy's never-quite-amateur photography to remind me.

"Who you?" the child asked.

"Elizabeth," I said. "I need to see—"

"Lizbeth?" The door opened wider and there she was, her appearance exactly the same as it had been for as long as I could remember.

Ruthie Kane was sharp—from her all-seeing dark eyes, past her razorlike elbows, to her spiky hips and knobby knees. The only soft things about Ruthie were her steadily graying Afro and her great big heart.

"Run along," she said to the girl. "Others are out back playin' at somethin'."

As the woman-child turned away, Ruthie ran her weathered hand over the youngster's head. "Sweet baby," she murmured.

The kid left skipping.

Ruthie headed for the kitchen. "I figured you'd be by."

I followed, uncertain. My conscious mind knew Ruthie was dead, knew I was dreaming, yet this all seemed so real, and Ruthie very much alive.

"Figured?" I echoed as I stepped into the sun-bright room.

"I know I'm dead, honey."

I'd always wondered if Ruthie were a bit psychic herself. She'd been the first to talk to me about my "special gift." And while most people as religious as Ruthie might have taken me for an exorcism, or at least laid on the hands to rid me of my whispering demon, she had introduced me to someone who understood. Someone who had helped me learn how to deal with what I was.

I fingered the tiny piece of turquoise I'd worn around my neck since I was fifteen.

Someone who had scared the living hell out of me, but that was another story.

"Is this heaven?" I wondered.

"Sure enough."

Why had I asked? Where else would Ruthie be?

"Why are you still taking care of kids?"

I heard a bunch of them through the open window, laughing, running, being kids.

"How could I be happy without little ones to care for? These here had their lives ended too soon. They need somethin' extra."

Trust Ruthie to find lost souls to mother even in the afterlife.

"Ah, Ruthie," I whispered. "What am I gonna do without you?"

"Go on. That's what everyone does."

"Not sure I can."

"You have to. Jimmy needs you."

My head, which had been sagging with grief, jerked

up. "Jimmy's never needed anyone but himself." And a little sugar on the side.

"That's not true. He's always needed more than any of the others. He just refuses to say so. Doesn't think he deserves happiness. Anything that might be good in his life, he makes sure he ruins, because he hates himself more than anyone else ever could."

"I doubt that," I muttered.

Her eyes narrowed. "You *will* help him, Elizabeth."

She'd put the *E* in my name. I didn't have much choice.

"Yes, ma'am."

She nodded, satisfied. "I gave you all that I had."

I remembered what Hammond and Landsdown had said about Ruthie and Jimmy arguing. Had she really left me her house, her bank account, her everything?

"What about the kids?" I blurted. "They should get something."

She smiled softly. "You probably won't want this gift, but I've known it would be yours from the moment I met you."

Not want it? Whatever *it* was, if it came from Ruthie, I definitely wanted it.

"You'll hate me for this—" she began.

"Never."

"You don't know yet what I've done to you."

To me?

"I don't understand," I said.

"You will." She looked up, and then past me, as if someone had called her name. Fear crossed her face and I spun around, but nothing was there.

"They saw you," she whispered. "They know who you are."

"Who's they?" I asked, but suddenly I understood. "Who killed you, Ruthie?"

She shook her head, still gazing past me. "Doesn't work like that. I can guide you, but the truth is something you must discover for yourself."

"Great," I muttered, although it would have been too much to hope for to have Ruthie's ghost—or whatever she was—tell me her murderer's name so I could tie this all up neatly by sundown.

"You have to go," Ruthie insisted. "They're coming."

"The people who killed you?"

Her gaze met mine, and what I saw there scared me.

"They aren't people," she said.

Chapter 5

My eyes snapped open. I was in my room, my bed. The covers were still pulled over my head, and there was someone moving around in here besides me.

My Glock resided in a small gun safe beneath the kitchen sink. I left the weapon there unless I had a damn good reason to take it out. In retrospect, not the best decision I'd ever made. Right now, I wished I kept the thing in my nightstand.

If I chose to believe dream-Ruthie, the people who'd killed her had come after me. Except they weren't people.

What in hell did that mean?

And what did they want? I hadn't seen them. I had no idea who they were. Unless they thought Ruthie had told me something before dying.

Shit.

I was starting to get twitchy. They could shoot me, stab me, pretty much anything me, and I wouldn't know about it until too late. I could feel the bull's-eye on my back already.

Slowly, trying not to rustle the covers, I crooked a finger in the sheet and drew it downward.

A man knelt by my bed, or at least I thought he knelt. Either he was extremely short and standing, or freakishly tall and kneeling. From the breadth of his shoulders, which blotted out most of my room, I figured the latter was a better bet.

He was also naked, at least from the waist up, and that piece of info disturbed me almost as much as his being here in the first place.

Despite the shadows, his hair shone eerily white, a towhead at an age when most had darkened to muddy blond. His eyes were spooky too, seeming to reflect the silver light of the moon when the moon had already risen past the apex and started to descend on the windowless side of my building.

In other words, no possibility of a reflection. His eyes appeared to glow from within.

The cops were not going to believe any of this—if I lived long enough to tell them.

The intruder grinned, and I saw something else the police wouldn't believe. His teeth had been filed to spiky points. What a nut.

I erupted from the covers, reaching for the lamp on the bedside table, a book, a paperweight, anything to bonk him over the head with.

He grabbed my wrist, moving quicker than anyone I'd ever known. I froze as images tumbled through my mind—what he'd done to people, what he was.

A monster.

And not the Ted Bundy, Jeffrey Dahmer type of monster, not even Hannibal Lector; he was a . . .

Berserker.

The word whispered through the air in Ruthie's voice. I was so surprised I almost didn't duck when he swung a hamlike fist at my head.

I'd been a state champion in high school gymnastics, and a few times a month I still practiced at the Y. I was nimble and quick. I did all sorts of cool things.

Back flips, kips, round off after round off. I could swing on a parallel bar and walk across a very thin balance beam. Sadly, none of that was going to do me much good here, so I snatched up the lamp.

Yanking the cord out of the wall, I smashed it into his face. He bled, but he didn't go down. He did let me go, and the horrible images stopped.

Then he rose. And rose, and rose. Yep, naked all the way from his head down to his toes—a particularly long distance since I put him in the vicinity of six seven. And that adage about big feet, big—well, you know the one—this guy appeared to have invented it.

He started toward me. I backed away. He didn't have a weapon, but then a guy his size had a pretty good weapon in his fists.

I bumped against the nightstand, set my hand down, and felt something sharp and cool and foreign. A knife when I was a gun kind of girl.

"Jimmy," I whispered, and the mammoth tilted his head like a dog that had heard a word it recognized amid so many it did not.

"Sanducci," he snarled, then threw back his head and roared. The sound was so loud, so feral, it made me cringe. I wanted to put my hands over my ears, but then I'd have to drop the knife, and that wasn't happening.

But something else was. The man in front of me had begun to change.

The first indication was the shift in the tenor of his voice, lowering from a man's wordless anger to a beast's primal growl.

He dropped onto all fours, hunched, shook his huge head, and fur sprang out everywhere.

I blinked, and when my eyes opened a man no longer stood in front of me but a bear.

He opened his mouth and emitted a bellow that should

have shattered my window, maybe my eardrums. Then
he rose onto his hind legs and swiped at me with one
massive paw.

He wasn't as quick in this form as he'd been as a human and I jerked out of the way of his sharp claws. Of
course if he caught me with one of those blows I'd be
dead, so I couldn't take the time to pat myself on the back
for my agile avoidance. Instead, I scurried away, clutching the knife. He lumbered after.

As I watched him waddle, I got a sense of déjà vu so
strong I wavered with it. I'd seen this very thing in the
dream I'd had at the hospital. This man-bear had been at
Ruthie's.

Of course she *had* said they were coming.

They? Hell. I hoped there weren't more of these hanging around.

He swiped at me again, and I realized it didn't matter
how many there might be. This one was going to kill me
if I didn't do something.

All I had was the knife, so I gripped it tightly, waited
until he took another swing, and after I ducked, I came
back up knife first.

The instant the tip entered his body he erupted outward, covering me with a fine layer of ash, the rest floating in the gray-tinged darkness like dust motes in the
sun, then cascading downward to coat the floor.

I stood covered in fine gray powder, uncertain what
to do. No reason to call the cops. There was nothing left
to arrest, and I really didn't want to talk about how the
big, naked man had turned into a huge, snarling bear.

Something weird was going on—something much
weirder than anything that had ever gone on in my life before, and that was saying a lot.

I threw on my clothes, grimacing at the feel of ash on
my body. To be on the safe side, I removed my gun from

the safe and then, keeping tight hold on both it and the knife, I crept downstairs and took a tour of the area surrounding my building. Neither man nor beast lurked about. Apparently "they" had only sent one assassin after me tonight.

Back inside, I locked up and went directly to my laptop, connected to the Internet, typed in *berserker*.

"Old Norse for bear shirt," I read. *Got that right.* "Germanic warriors who, in the frenzy of battle, literally became an animal, usually a wolf or a bear."

I paused, trying to take this all in, but I was still having a hard time believing what my eyes had clearly seen. A man turning into a bear—then disintegrating into ash. I forced myself to read on.

"Since the only way to kill a berserker was with pure silver, and silver was a rarity at that time, these warriors understandably gained the reputation of being indestructible."

I picked up the knife. Must be silver, which meant it was Jimmy's.

I needed to find him. He had a few questions to answer.

For instance, why had the man-bear known his name and really seemed to hate it?

Why had Jimmy thought I might need a solid silver knife?

Why had that thing, and a whole lot of others if my bizarre post-coma vision were true, been after Ruthie, and why did they now appear to be after me?

And, most importantly, just what in hell had happened to make me see monsters when all I'd seen before was the truth?

Unfortunately, Jimmy was hiding. Conveniently, I was very good at finding the missing.

I needed to talk to Laurel and Hardy—I mean Hammond and Landsdown—and find out what, if anything, they'd learned since our last encounter.

I swept up the remains of my attacker, tossed him into a plastic garbage bag and deposited everything in the Dumpster. Then I washed that man right out of my hair. It took a lot of shampoo.

By nine A.M. I was headed past the heart of the city.

Like most ethnic towns, Milwaukee had sections— what had once been called boroughs or ghettos; hell, they still were. But along the river, the same one that divided Friedenberg from the rest of the world, the ultrarich occupied brand-new condos.

The only thing more expensive than living in one of those was living in a high-rise on Lake Michigan. Water—even water that's icy eight months out of twelve—does a number on the real estate values.

I cruised by the courthouse, glanced at the Bradley Clock—the largest four-sided clock in the world—caught a glimpse of Miller Park to my right, and drove over the Hone Bridge. Ten minutes later I left my Jetta in the visitor parking lot and walked into the police station where I'd once worked.

At the desk I asked for Landsdown and Hammond. Just my luck, they were in.

"If it isn't Sixth Sense," Landsdown greeted, using the nickname I'd come to loathe.

I ignored him. Sometimes it helped.

"Have you been in contact with Sanducci?" Hammond asked.

"Not lately," I said, skirting the truth with a lie.

His face fell. "Why are you here?"

"Maybe she saw him," Landsdown murmured, "with her X-ray vision."

"Why did you ask me to help if you think it's all BS?" I demanded.

"You've come up with some extremely convincing BS."

I had, at that.

"Either way," Landsdown continued, "if you're the real thing, which I doubt, or you're bogus, which gets my vote—you've got a history with Sanducci. Even if you can't tell us where he is, maybe we'll stumble over him coming out of your place after a long night of the horizontal bounce."

I hadn't horizontal-bounced in so long I got distracted a minute just thinking about it. Sanducci had been a damn good bouncer.

"I wouldn't hold my breath waiting for that," I said. "I've got a few questions."

The two men glanced at each other and together they shrugged, which I took as a green light.

"Any word on the autopsy?"

"Not yet."

Rats.

"Do you know why Sanducci was in town?" Maybe knowing that would help me find him.

"According to his manager," Landsdown said, "Sanducci was here to do a shoot with Springboard Jones."

"The basketball player?"

"You know a lot of guys called Springboard?"

Excellent point.

Springboard—given name Leroy—was Milwaukee's own Michael Jordan. He'd taken City High to the state championship at the Kohl Center, dragged the Badgers along with him to the Final Four, then been picked number three in the draft and would soon begin playing for our very own Milwaukee Bucks. Springboard had made good, and everyone loved it. However—

"Jimmy's not a sports photographer."

"Assignment was a portrait for the cover of *Sports*

Illustrated," Hammond explained. "Man of the year or some such shit. They wanted the best."

Jimmy was that—in more ways than one.

"Did he take the picture?"

"No. It was scheduled for tonight at eight."

"Where?"

"City High."

I frowned. Only a few miles north of the bright lights and little city, the neighborhood changed—a lot. Tenements. Burned-out houses. Scrabbly grass, broken sidewalks. Boarded windows if they didn't have steel bars. I had a hard time believing Jimmy would cart his precious cameras past Third and North after dark, even for *Sports Illustrated.*

"I thought they tore that school down."

Asbestos in the ceiling and floor tile—a common occurrence in buildings constructed in the fifties and sixties—was making a lot of contractors a lot of money.

"Next week. I guess Sanducci wanted to work his magic in the gymnasium where it all began."

I could see it—dusty faded court, broken wooden bleachers, old school uniform, the photo in black-and-white. Stark, beautiful, as only Jimmy Sanducci could make it.

Hammond studied me. "You don't think he'll actually show up there, do you?"

I shook my head. Jimmy wasn't that dumb. But if not there, then where?

"Anything else I should know?" I asked.

Hammond tensed. Landsdown scowled.

"What?"

"There've been odd disappearances in some of the cities he's frequented," Hammond said.

"There are always odd disappearances in cities. You know that as well as I do."

Joe Citizen had no clue how many people disappeared each year and were never seen again.

"You know why there might be ash residue at Ruthie's?"

I kept my face carefully blank. "She didn't even have a fireplace."

"Right. Looked like someone tried to clean up in a hurry, but they didn't do a decent job."

I knew exactly where the ashes had come from. The bizarre shape-shifting monsters I'd seen in my coma. But who had killed them?

I had a pretty good idea.

Chapter 6

"Thanks for your time, Detectives." I rose. "Could you let me know when you get the autopsy report?"

"Anything special you're interested in?" Hammond asked.

"Cause of death would be nice."

"Considering the state of the body and the presence of the knife, we're going with knife wound."

I nodded, but I didn't believe it. Not anymore.

"This is an ongoing homicide investigation, Phoenix. We aren't going to give you any autopsy results, and you know it."

I had, but it never hurt to try. I had my own sources anyway.

As I headed out of the police station I caught sight of the Yankees cap, encased in plastic as all evidence should be and perched on a filing cabinet.

I knocked it to the ground, then knelt to tie my shoe. Shielding my movements with my shoulders, I slipped a finger into the bag and brushed the bill. Then I rose and continued on my way, leaving the cap on the floor. Better for someone to find it there later and think the evidence had fallen than for them to see me picking it up, wonder if I'd touched the thing, decide I had and start to follow me.

Where I was going, I didn't need an audience. Just in case I gave in to temptation and kicked the living hell out of Sanducci.

I should have known where he'd run. If I hadn't been off my game—between the coma and the cops, the visions and the berserker, being off was kind of understandable—I'd have figured it out on my own. Jimmy had gone to *his* safe place.

I jumped in my car and took the grand tour of the town to make certain I hadn't picked up a tail. Sliding slowly past City High, I noted several unmarked cars. Even if Jimmy was dumb enough to show up, he'd never be blind enough to miss the stakeout.

I waved at the detectives, earning a scowl, and in one case a rude hand gesture, before I headed west.

While at Ruthie's, each of us had spent a month every summer between the ages of thirteen and eighteen working for someone or learning something. Ruthie believed in that almost as much as she believed in reading the Bible before bedtime.

I'd been sent to New Mexico, to the edge of the Navajo Reservation, to learn more about what I was and how to use it.

Jimmy had been sent only an hour away, to a dairy farm between Milwaukee and Madison. He had loved it.

Not so much the milking, the plowing, the planting, but the place, the people and the animals. The photos he'd taken at that farm had been some of his best, and had led to his receiving a scholarship in photojournalism from Western Kentucky.

Not that he'd ever used it. When he'd left, I don't know where he'd gone, but it hadn't been to college. The lack of a degree didn't seem to have hurt him any.

He'd always had an unbelievable way of looking at

things, and when he'd looked at me, I'd wanted to give him everything I had. Back then all I'd had was me.

Shaking off those memories, I accelerated around a semi and set my cruise control at seventy. I wanted to get there fast, but I wanted to get there in one piece, without a ticket that would broadcast to every last cop in the land where I was.

Though I hated to, I called Megan and left a message. "I won't be able to come back to work right away." I paused, unwilling to ask for a favor, but I had to. "Would you get me a copy of Ruthie's autopsy report?"

If anyone could do it, Megan could. Max had been a highly decorated officer, a stunning loss to the community and the force. I didn't think there was a cop in the city who'd deny Megan anything that she asked.

I reached the farm just after noon. No one was there. I hadn't realized the Muellers had packed up their cows and sold the place.

I got out of the car. "Hello?" I shouted, though I really didn't expect anyone to answer.

The house was locked, the windows unbroken. Such would never have been the case any closer to town.

Everything was gone. Not a stick of furniture or even a stray newspaper had been left behind.

The barn wasn't much different. No hay. No straw. No manure. These people were freakishly clean.

Until I reached what had once been the tack room but had morphed into a hired hand's apartment. The hired hand appeared to be in residence, if the bedding and the duffel bag were any indication.

"Hello?" I tried again. Still nothing, so I checked in the bag. I didn't need my sixth sense to know whose it was. The scent of cinnamon and soap wafted up as soon as I tugged on the zipper.

Nothing but clothes inside—no ID, no camera equipment, no knife, no gun, nada.

I stepped to the back door of the barn and let my gaze wander over the rolling pastures just beginning to sprout with green and gold, wildflowers tangling with the weeds, a patch of snow here and there on a hill. No sign of Jimmy. I'd just have to wait.

I sat on the mattress. An hour later I rested my head on his pillow. The last thing I remembered was the sun beginning its fall toward the end of the earth.

Whir-whir, kaching-kaching-kaching.

My eyes opened. The room had gone gold with fading sunlight, illuminating a hundred million dust motes invisible at any other time of the day.

I lay on the cot. Jimmy stood in the doorway, camera attached to his face. A quick glance revealed I still had on all my clothes. Maybe he had learned something after I'd slugged him the last time.

"You know, most women might call a cop if they found some guy taking pictures of them while they slept."

He didn't even lower the camera. "You're not most women, and I'm not some guy."

Kaching.

I sat up. His eyes appeared above the lens. "Come on, Lizzy, I'm almost done."

"You *are* done." He sighed and set the camera aside. "Where are the Muellers?"

"They sold out a while back."

I had a sudden bad feeling. "Sold out to who?"

His lips curved.

I leaped to my feet. "Dammit, Jimmy. You think cops are stupid? I'm surprised they didn't get here ahead of me."

"I didn't buy it outright. You nuts? No one will find me, at least not yet."

"What are you doing here? If you mean to run, then run. If not, then turn yourself in, get this settled and go back to your life."

"It's not that simple."

Something in his voice made me pause. He sounded old. Tired. Sad. Defeated. Jimmy was a lot of things, but none of *those* things.

"What's the matter?" I asked, taking a better look at him. He was thinner than normal, pale too. I hadn't noticed until now because the usual shade of his skin was so much darker than most.

He glanced away, hesitating just long enough that I knew whatever he said next was not what he'd planned to say first. "I've been sick."

"You?" Jimmy didn't get sick. Probably because he'd been exposed to every germ on the planet before he turned ten.

Concern flickered, but I refused to let it show. He did *not* need me. He never had.

"You're better now?"

"Yeah. I was pretty out of it for a few days—worst I've ever been—but a little rest, a lot of fluids, good as new."

He didn't sound good as new; he sounded ancient as Methuselah, one of those Old Testament patriarchs who'd checked out at the age of nine hundred and sixty-nine.

"What's the matter?" I repeated softly.

He remained silent for so long, when he finally answered, I no longer expected him to.

"Ruthie's dead. Isn't that enough?"

I hadn't forgotten. But I didn't feel as though Ruthie were really gone, perhaps because I'd talked to her in my dreams.

However, the woman who'd raised us had been murdered—horribly—and Jimmy was accused of it.

Though in light of recent events, I knew the accusation wasn't true.

"What did you see at Ruthie's?" I asked.

He gave me a sharp glance. "Why? Had a news-flash?"

"You might say that."

Jimmy inched into the room and closed the door. I frowned. There was no one here, so why close the door?

I'd left my gun in the safe—not that I'd use it on Jimmy. Maybe. But I'd brought along the knife, concealed it in a fanny pack I'd had around my waist until I'd decided to lie down. The thing was tangled in the sheets, too far away for me to retrieve without making an issue of it. Did I want to make an issue of it?

Jimmy stopped several feet from me. *Not yet.*

"What did you see?" he asked.

"Why did you leave a silver knife on my nightstand?"

His eyes widened. He didn't bother to deny he'd left the weapon. "Did you need it?"

"Yes."

"What came for you?"

"Berserker."

"Wolf or bear?"

My mouth fell open at his knowledge of the word. Jimmy hadn't exactly been a brainiac in school.

"Bear," I said. "And how did you know that?"

He shoved a hand through his hair. "I didn't want you involved. I told Ruthie you weren't ready."

"For what?"

He hesitated, face set, mouth tight, then threw up his hands. "It's too late now. She gave you the power. You're going to have to deal."

"With what?"

"Ruthie was special."

"You're just figuring that out now, Sanducci?"

He ignored my sarcasm. "She had a gift."

I stilled. "She said she'd given me a gift."

"You talked to her before she died?"

I had, but not about this.

"Not exactly," I murmured.

He moved closer, the tense way he held himself making me move back. "What, exactly?"

"After."

His brows lifted. "You talk to dead people now?"

"Just Ruthie."

Over the years I'd done a bit of research on psychic phenomena. According to the "experts" I was psychometric, which meant I could pick up information and images from touching objects—inanimate and animate. Considering my sudden ability to see, hear, and talk to a dead woman, I appeared to have latent channeling abilities too.

Jimmy had gone silent, thinking. "The gift is different for everyone. Ruthie said she got her tips from God." He shook his head. "Hell, she probably did."

"What are you talking about?"

Jimmy lifted his gaze to mine. "The world is full of monsters, Lizzy, and someone has to kill them. That someone is me, and the someone who tells me what they are, where they are, and who they are was Ruthie, but now . . ." He spread his hands. "Baby, it's you."

Chapter 7

I didn't bother to chastise him for calling me "baby." I had bigger problems than that.

I hadn't ever wanted to see Jimmy Sanducci again, and now I was supposed to work with him to save the world from monsters? Talk about a bad day in supernatural fantasyland.

"What if I don't want this power?" Hell, I didn't want the one I'd been born with.

"Only death releases you from it."

My fingers curled into fists. Jimmy took several steps back. "Don't be mad at me; I was against it. Ruthie called me to town. She wanted us to tell you together."

"Oh, that would have gone well," I muttered. At the first sight of Jimmy, I'd have been out of there.

"There wasn't time to prepare you. If she'd died before she passed on her power it would have been lost."

I could understand Ruthie's desperation, but I wasn't exactly thrilled to be infected against my will.

"She'd been waiting years for you to accept who you are."

My chest went tight. Ruthie had always encouraged me to be happy with my gift and use it to help others. I'd become a cop so I could fulfill the latter without using the former. My psychometry had always creeped me out nearly as much as it had creeped out everyone who'd ever witnessed it. Except for Ruthie.

"She thought it would be easier for you to accept this"—he made a gesture with his hands to encompass the fine mess I was already in—"if you'd accepted that."

I had to say, the odds didn't look good.

"Wait a second," I said. "You and Ruthie were arguing *before* she was . . . hurt. How could she have been planning to give me her power, when only death releases it? Makes no sense."

"She knew her time was near. Seers have to be aware of the end or risk taking their powers with them to the grave."

"What if I hadn't shown up when I did?"

"You didn't just show up accidentally. When I said Ruthie called me to town, I didn't mean by phone. Didn't you often feel sudden, irresistible compulsions to see her?"

My eyes narrowed and he shrugged. "Ruthie had skills of her own, even before she became 'the one.'" Jimmy made quotation marks in the air around the last two words.

"I'm going to smash your *Matrix* DVD into itty-bitty pieces."

"I'm not kidding, Lizzy."

"Neither am I."

"She said she dreamed of me. Maybe that's how she sent out those vibes; I don't know. But I came, and so did you."

I understood now the urgency of the need that had overcome me at Murphy's. When Ruthie had sent out whatever vibes she had, she must have already been dying.

I tried to focus. There was so much I needed to know. "Ruthie was the only one?"

"Figure of speech. There are dozens like her, hundreds

like me. You don't think two people could counteract all the supernatural evil in the world, do you?"

"Until last night I didn't know there *was* any supernatural evil."

"Don't tell me you didn't suspect it. Not with your gift."

I'd known there was evil—hell, everyone did—but supernatural? Hadn't seen *that* coming.

"Ruthie raised you for this. Me too."

"What?" My voice was so loud I startled a few doves out of the rafters.

"She chose us for what we were, raised us to be what we were meant to be. Ruthie was a general in a war that's been raging for aeons."

If I thought my mind had been spinning after the berserker's visit, that was nothing compared to now.

"Ever since the angels fell," Jimmy continued, "there've been monsters on this earth. It was part of the plan."

"What plan?"

"The big plan." Jimmy spread his arms. "Good versus evil. We need to win for the human race to survive."

I sat on the cot and put my head in my hands. Jimmy just kept on talking.

"Ruthie's duty was to make certain the fight continued after she was gone. She had to find people like us to do that."

"She chose us because she loved us," I whispered.

Jimmy snorted. "We were delinquents. Foulmouthed, smelly little rats."

"Speak for yourself."

"She came to love us. But we found a home with her because she needed us. The whole world does."

"How can there be monsters everywhere and no one knows about it?"

"I wouldn't say no one. There's always the odd truth in every other *National Enquirer*."

I shot him a glare but, once again, he was serious.

"The problem is, they look just like you and me unless they decide to change—and then they're hell to kill—and some of them *always* look like you and me. Without Ruthie, without you now, they'll own this world, and the humans will just be—" He broke off.

"Be what?"

"Food, amusement, slaves. Nothing good."

"What did Ruthie do? How did she know?"

"She would have a vision, which would reveal the type of demon along with its human face."

"Demon." I seemed doomed to repeat most of what he said.

"For lack of a better word. How familiar are you with the story of the fallen angels?"

"Satan?"

"He got the kingdom he coveted." Jimmy pointed to the floor. "But the rest . . ." He swirled his finger in the air.

"You're telling me the fallen angels are still on earth in the form of demons?"

"In a way. Ever heard of the Grigori and the Nephilim?" I shook my head. "The Grigori were known as the watchers. They were sent to earth to keep an eye on the humans. They lusted after them instead and were banished by God to Tartarus, the fiery pit where all divine enemies are thrown." He shrugged. "Basically the lowest, locked level of hell."

"I don't remember this story in the Bible."

"Book of Enoch."

"Once again—"

"Not in the Bible," Jimmy finished. "But it was. You're aware that over the centuries, several books and gospels were removed?" I nodded. "Enoch was beloved by Jews and Christians alike until it was pronounced heresy and banned. The text disappeared for nearly a thousand years until a copy was discovered in Ethiopia."

"So why isn't it part of the Bible now?"

"People don't like change."

"Or maybe Enoch is just a fairy tale."

"Then why are there over a hundred phrases in the New Testament that are also found in the Book of Enoch? Considering that Enoch was written two centuries before the birth of Christ, to me that means it was studied as carefully as Genesis. I highly doubt Jesus would have bothered to quote a book he didn't believe told the truth."

I kind of doubted it too.

"The offspring of the watchers and the daughters of men were known as the Nephilim. They became every type of supernatural being you can imagine."

"Like vampires and werewolves and berserkers?"

"To name a few. God destroyed ninety percent of the Nephilim in the flood, but allowed ten percent to remain on earth to challenge mankind."

"By challenge you mean kill, enslave, and eat?"

"Life wasn't supposed to be easy."

I had so many questions, but uppermost in my mind was—"Why didn't they ever come for Ruthie before?"

"They didn't know who she was. The identities of the seers are known only to their DKs, or demon killers."

My eyebrows lifted. "I can see why you use an acronym. Running around using the term *demon killer* just might buy you an all-expenses-paid trip to a little white room."

He rubbed a hand over his face. "Someone broke the number-one rule—protect the seer. I mean to find out who, then make certain they never do it again."

From his expression, that person would never be doing

anything again once Jimmy finished with him, which was fine by me.

"Gonna start with Springboard," he muttered. "Although he idolized Ruthie."

"Springboard Jones is a——"

"Yeah. A lot of DKs have jobs that take us from city to city. Good cover."

As was the fact that their kills turned to ashes. Not much evidence that way.

"I plan to personally dust every single Nephilim who crossed Ruthie's threshold," Jimmy continued. "And you're going to help me."

"You say that as if I mean to argue." I wanted them dead too.

His face softened. "I know this has been tough. It's hard enough coming into our world prepared. This isn't like anything you've ever faced before."

"I figured that out when the big blond guy turned into a bear."

Jimmy shifted his shoulders, rolled his neck. He had something else to tell me.

"There's a little more to this than you know," he said slowly. "Ruthie was the leader of all the seers and DKs."

"Okay." I could understand that. Who wouldn't follow the woman to hell and back?

"There are legends, prophecies, beliefs that have been handed down through the ages to guide us. One of them states that when the leader of the darkness destroys the leader of the light, doomsday is the result."

"Doomsday," I repeated. I didn't like the sound of that.

"A time of catastrophic destruction and death leading to the final battle between good and evil."

My neck prickled. "She said that." I tilted my head, remembering. "Ruthie said, 'The final battle begins now.'"

Jimmy's face tightened; fine white lines spread out from his mouth. "It has."

"So not only do I have to be a seer when I have no idea how, but we've got Armageddon coming down on us?"

"Pretty much."

"Who in hell is the leader of the darkness? The Antichrist?"

"I don't think so."

"Why not? If I remember correctly, he's the leader of the whole end-of-days dance."

"True. But according to prophecy, he'll be a huge international figure. We don't have that. Yet."

Yet. Hell.

"Leading up to the appearance of the Antichrist," Jimmy continued, "is a period of chaos."

"Doomsday."

"Bingo."

"So who do we blame for starting this mess?"

"I wish I knew."

Add not knowing who our enemy was to the list of things I hated about my new life. Right below the sudden appearance of creatures that wanted to kill me.

"Your knife came in handy the other night," I murmured. "Thanks."

"It was a precaution. I—" Jimmy paused and several expressions flitted over his face—sadness, confusion, fury. "I killed all that I could at Ruthie's, but there were so many, and a few of them—"

He fluttered his hand to indicate . . . I'm not sure what. Running? Lumbering? Flying? Maybe a bit of each.

"No one noticed zoo animals streaking through a suburban neighborhood?"

"Most of the people around there work for a living. And the beasts that attacked Ruthie were shape-shifters.

I doubt they were beasts very long. Once they were men and women—"

"They blended right in."

Jimmy nodded.

"Silver works on all of them?" I asked.

"Most," he clarified. "Not all. But it's always worth a try." He took a deep breath. "I didn't think they'd seen you, or I never would have left you alone."

"I can take care of myself."

"Against human opponents, probably." I scowled and opened my mouth to argue, but he kept right on talking. "These are beings beyond anything you can imagine. If we had the time you'd be studying the ancient texts, becoming familiar with every known type of monster."

"But we don't have time. The final battle is now. So what do we do?"

"The best that we can."

That never worked out half as well as people hoped.

I hadn't noticed Jimmy moving closer as we spoke, but now he was too close, trapping me on the cot. If I stood, my entire body would slide against his. If I stayed where I was he'd continue to loom over me, his crotch level with my mouth. I licked suddenly dry lips.

"There's something I have to tell you," he said, and his voice was rough, as if he'd been running several miles through ice and snow.

I lifted my gaze to his, the movement brushing my chin across the suddenly bulging zipper of his pants. I had a flash of wine as rich as blood. "Tell me."

He winced as my mouth moved, my breath cascading over him. We'd always been like this—one stray movement, a single glance and we were so hot for each other we couldn't think straight.

Talk about doomsday.

I could smell him; I could almost taste him. All I had to do was reach forward, flick open the bronze button, draw down the zipper tab, reach in and trace a finger along his length, then take him in my mouth and—

Jimmy cursed and grabbed me by the elbows, hauling me to my feet and dragging me along his body just as I'd imagined.

Our mouths melded, tongues searching, teeth scraping. I yanked his shirt out of his waistband, ran my thumb across the ridges of his abdomen, spread my palms over his chest and allowed my nails to trace his nipples. He moaned my name; lust shot through me, enticing and familiar.

Behind my closed eyelids, images wavered. I caught a flicker of fangs, the tangy, metallic scent of blood, and then a single word in Ruthie's voice.

Dhampir.

I tore out of Jimmy's arms, stumbling away when he tried to drag me back. "Don't touch me."

He froze. "It isn't what you think."

What was it then? I knew what I'd seen, what I'd heard, and I knew the truth about Jimmy as surely as I'd known the truth about so many others.

He wasn't human.

Chapter 8

My eyes flicked to the closed door, which had taken on a sinister aspect as quickly as Jimmy had. Suddenly I wanted that silver knife I'd left in the fanny pack as badly as I'd wanted him. I should have followed my instincts and grabbed the weapon as soon as he'd come in the door.

He stepped toward me again.

"You need to stay the hell away," I snapped.

"We don't have time for this."

"I always have time to kick your ass."

His lips twitched. "You can try, but it won't be as easy as it used to."

"Back off," I ordered, and he did, slowly moving toward the door, then leaning against it. The movement was casual, but I knew better. He'd just put himself between me and any possible escape.

He folded his arms over his chest. His dark shirt, which I'd managed to unbutton halfway down, gaped, revealing a thin slice of skin I had once spent hours tasting.

Keeping my eyes glued to his, I reached over and retrieved the fanny pack from the cot, secured it around my waist in case I managed that quick getaway I was fantasizing about, and withdrew the knife. He didn't appear

concerned, which made me suspect that silver didn't
kill a—

"What in hell is a dhampir?"

Jimmy sighed. "Touching you has always gotten me
into trouble."

I suddenly remembered the hospital, his black eye.
Now, there wasn't a mark on him.

But yesterday, the sight of the bruised skin had made
me lift a hand toward his face and he'd said—

Just don't touch me. I—

I'd thought he was refusing sympathy. He always
had. But what he'd wanted was to avoid letting me know
the truth too soon.

"You thought we could go indefinitely without touching?" I asked. "I take it that stupidity is one of your superpowers."

A short burst of laughter escaped him. I nearly laughed
too. One thing we'd always shared, besides ourselves, had
been a strange sense of humor.

But nothing was funny about this. Ruthie was dead,
and Jimmy wasn't human. How was anything ever going to be funny again?

"I wanted you to trust me before I told you."

Now I was the one emitting a short burst of laughter,
although there wasn't a hint of amusement in mine.

His lips tightened, something flickered in his eyes,
but he let it go to reiterate, "It's not what you think. *I'm*
not what you think."

"Like I haven't heard *that* one before. Sing a new
tune, Sanducci." I waggled the knife. "Spill your guts before I spill them for you."

"You think I'd give you a weapon that would work
on me?"

My eyes narrowed. "What kills a dhampir?"

He didn't answer.

I tightened my fingers around the hilt of the dagger. My palm was slick; I'd have a hard time getting any leverage, even if I found the courage to use the blade. Silver might not kill him, but I'd bet a good portion of my life savings that it would sting like hell.

"If this isn't what it seems," I asked, "then what is it?"

He opened his mouth, shut it again, looked away, then quickly looked back, his gaze flicking to the knife, then to me as if gauging how serious I was about sticking him. He should know me better than that.

"I'm not sure where to start," he murmured.

"How about when you turned into one of the things you're supposed to kill?"

The words caused an involuntary flinch. I might have wished him dead a hundred and one ways, considered doing him in myself on many a long, lonely night—a girl had to have some fun—but I didn't really want him dead. I didn't really want to be the one to kill him. Too bad what I wanted had never once been something I could have.

"I didn't turn," he said, "and I'm not one of them."

"Then why did Ruthie say you were a dhampir?"

"Because I am!" he shouted.

The fury in his voice startled me, and the knife I'd let drop to my side came back up.

He slumped against the door, as if needing the support rather than blocking my way. His gaze lifted from the weapon to my face. "You've never heard of a dhampir?"

"How would I? You think bizzaro legends from the land of crazy are something I keep up on?"

"You will." He took a breath, then another before beginning. "I was born of a human and a vampire."

"I didn't think you knew who your parents were any more than I did."

"I don't. All I know is human plus vampire equals dhampir."

"How can a vampire procreate? They're dead."

"Myth. Vampires are as alive as you and me. They were born of a Grigori and a woman. When a vampire mates with a human, a dhampir is born."

His face was bleak, and I had to resist the urge to reach out to him once more. As he'd said, when we touched, bad things happened. I didn't want to see again that flash of fang; I didn't want to catch a whiff of blood.

"How could I not have known this when we were kids?"

"I didn't know it. I came into my powers . . . later in life. Until then, I was like everyone else."

I gave him a long look. Jimmy had never, by any stretch of the imagination, been like anyone else.

"You tell me you're one of the good guys, but—" I broke off, uncertain. If what Jimmy was telling me was true, and after what I'd seen and heard from Ruthie, I knew it was, but how far could I trust him? By his own admission, he was tainted.

"But what?" he asked.

"How can you be trusted to help humans when you—"

"Aren't human?" he finished.

"Well, yeah, but also, you kill them."

"Do not."

The retort came so quickly, with such a childish inflection—do not! Do too!—I was struck again with the urge to laugh. I suppose the human mind, when confronted with something so vast and unexpected, had to have a stress outlet, and laughter was mine. Jimmy's was probably sex.

I contemplated him in the now dusky light of the tack room. Black hair tumbled over his forehead, shirt unbuttoned, a sheen of sweat across his collarbone, dark eyes burning in a beautiful but tense face.

"I know I'm not up on the legendary lore," I said, "but vampires still kill people, don't they?"

"I don't."

I shook my head. "I saw—"

He was across the floor faster than my eyes could register, suddenly standing so close I caught the familiar scent of soap and cinnamon with the sharp tang of something else just beneath. My gaze caught on a droplet of sweat gliding down his neck, then pooling in the hollow of his throat. I had a nearly irresistible urge to sweep it away with my tongue.

"What did you see?"

"Fangs."

Just then a stray beam of the setting sun turned the glistening moisture the shade of—

"Blood."

"Fangs and blood." His mouth quirked. "That leads you to 'murdering demon?' "

"One and one *is* two, Jimmy."

"Not always. Not anymore."

The scent of him was driving me mad. I inched away, strode toward the door. I had to get out of this room. I had to get away from him before I did something I'd regret—either used the knife I still clutched in my hand, or used my mouth in ways I'd often imagined. And the only way to get him to let me go was to piss him off so badly he couldn't stand to be near me. Pissing off Jimmy was one of my specialties.

"How many humans do they let you kill as payback for the ones you save?" I asked.

"I don't kill people!"

I turned. "I know what I saw when you touched me."

His eyes flared, and he came toward me with the speed of a striking snake. I reared back, my shoulders smacking against the still-closed door so hard I winced.

He crowded me, the heat of his body making mine tingle. "How about if I touch you again?" he whispered, his voice the one I'd heard only in dreams for so many years.

My heart skipped—excitement or dread? I wasn't sure. "Will I get another flash?"

He stepped in, his hip bumping mine. "Let's find out."

Chapter 9

For just an instant, I panicked. If I'd had anywhere to go, I would have gone. The door was at my back, Jimmy at my front. I was trapped.

"Anything?" he asked.

At first I didn't know what he meant. Then realization doused me like a pitcher of ice water—he was touching me to see if I got a psychic flash, not because he couldn't bear another second on this earth without me—and I shoved at his chest with my free hand. "Move."

He didn't; I doubted I could make him without stabbing him with his own knife, and I was tempted. The only thing that stopped me was the memory of the last time I'd used the solid silver implement. The berserker had exploded, and I'd been covered in ash. I'd discovered a bit of it in my ear this morning. I certainly didn't want to be finding pieces of Jimmy all over the place.

Of course he'd said the knife wouldn't hurt him. But he'd also said he loved me, that he'd never leave, that there was no one for him but me. So sue me if I didn't believe a word out of his lying mouth.

I stomped on his foot. "Back off!"

He didn't seem to feel it; he didn't seem to hear me, or maybe he just didn't care. His head lowered.

I opened my mouth to protest, and he was kissing me, long-fingered artist's hands cupping my hips, drawing me in. He was hard against my stomach, his chest warm against my own. I couldn't help it; I rubbed myself against him, moaning at the friction, increasing it until my nipples hardened against the soft material of my bra.

His tongue taunted mine. He tasted like heat and the night. Memories.

Air brushed my stomach as his hands swept upward, palms tracing my ribs, then cupping my breasts, thumbs sliding beneath the cotton to roll the spike of my nipples.

There was something I was supposed to remember, something I was supposed to think, to do, to wonder. I almost had it and then—

He yanked the sleeves of my shirt over my shoulders; two of the buttons popped. My arms were pinned; I struggled a little, but the movements only made another button give a dull *ping* as it lost the battle and tumbled to the floor.

His mouth left mine; tiny kisses feathered across my jaw, my neck, my collarbone. He pressed his face into the curve of my shoulder and took a deep breath. His hands, still cupping my breasts, seemed to tremble.

"Anything?" he repeated.

I closed my eyes, saw . . . nothing. Then I heard Ruthie's voice, past or present, I wasn't sure.

I'm only gonna say somethin' once; you'd best listen.

I should have known she wouldn't send me another flash. What would be the point? She'd told me what Jimmy was, and now I'd have to deal.

I opened my eyes; his face was only inches away. "Nothing."

His mouth curved as his fingers, still under my shirt, flexed. I bit back a moan as sensations I hadn't experienced in years shot through me.

"Good," he said. "I was afraid you'd be getting a news-reel on me every time I touched you. That would cramp my style."

"What style?"

Instead of answering, he yanked a few more buttons free, then lowered his head and closed his lips over my nipple.

His mouth was scalding; his tongue pressed me against the roof of his mouth, over and over, suckling. This was such a bad idea; so why did it feel so good?

"No," I whispered. His only response was to score me with his teeth. My breath hissed in. I wasn't hurt; I was even more aroused. But now was not the time; this was not the place.

"Stop," I said, but he didn't.

His fingers dug into my ribs; his mouth continued its assault on my skin. Annoyance replaced the arousal, and I brought my elbow up toward his nose. Without even lifting his head he blocked the blow with the palm of his hand. The impact vibrated all the way to my shoulder. I began to get scared.

I'd never felt physically threatened by Jimmy, probably because I'd beat the crap out of him on several occasions. I always suspected he'd let me, or at least not fought back very hard. But Jimmy was no longer the man I'd known. He was no longer just a man at all, and who was to say he wouldn't take what he wanted.

His teeth scraped me again, harder this time, and I bit back a startled cry. I wouldn't be afraid. I hated being afraid. Once I'd gotten off the streets I'd vowed never to be afraid again.

Big hopes that were too easily dashed.

My hands clenched, and the hilt of the knife I still carried bit into my palm. I brought it up without thinking, or maybe I'd been thinking it all along.

Jimmy twisted away with a slightly feral snarl. I missed sticking him by centimeters. I expected to see fangs pressing against his lips, blood trickling down my breast, but he looked the same as he always did. So did my breast.

I held the knife in front of me like a talisman. "Don't touch me again."

"I don't take orders from you."

"You took them from Ruthie, and since I'm assuming Ruthie's place . . ." My lips curved. "I always wanted to be the boss of you."

He reached out with that inhuman speed and snatched the knife from my hand. "I told you this wouldn't hurt me."

"Like I would believe anything you had to say, Sanducci."

He rolled his eyes, then stabbed himself through the palm with the blade. The damn thing went all the way through his hand and stuck out the other side. The blood I'd been dreaming of flowed, pattering onto the plank floor like a light spring rain.

"Oh, shit. Oh, hell," I muttered, taking a step forward, meaning to help, remembering what he'd done, what he was, then taking a step back.

"Give it a rest, Lizzy. I'm fine."

He hadn't burst into ashes. That was good. Maybe.

Jimmy yanked the knife out. I winced at the wet, sucking sound, and he glanced at me with a worried frown, probably wondering if I'd faint. He should have known better.

The gory wound in his palm began slowly to close. Within seconds, the blood had stopped dripping. Within minutes, his palm appeared as if it had only been cut with broken glass instead of pierced by a silver blade.

My eyes met his. "How?"

"I'm a breed. Mostly human, which is why I'm not evil, but still something more."

"I'm just supposed to believe you when you tell me you're not evil?"

"I work for the good guys. Doesn't that make me one of them?"

"Not necessarily."

"I don't kill people. I kill Nephilim."

"According to you, they're half people."

He wiped his hand on his pants, leaving a streak of blood that blended into the navy blue denim. Could be mud. Could be ketchup. Could be anything. I needed to buy darker jeans.

"The Nephilim are evil." He lifted one shoulder. "It's just the way they are."

"But you're not?"

"No. I'm not saying that some of the breeds don't fight for the other side. But given the generation or generations we've been removed, that added influx of humanity seems to have allowed us a choice."

What he was saying did make a weird kind of sense. Or as much sense as anything else did lately. Except . . .

"Why did I see fangs, Jimmy?"

"There's vampire in me; I'm not denying it. But those traits are dormant. I don't have fangs." He smiled widely; there was no joy in the expression—and no fangs in his mouth. "I don't drink blood. You saw for yourself that silver didn't hurt me."

"Does it hurt any vampire?"

"No."

I almost laughed. Trust Jimmy to bring up a defense that wasn't a defense at all. He always pushed every boundary there was, stepped over every line that he saw. That hadn't changed.

"You had to have sensed my dormant nature when

you touched me; that's the only thing that makes sense," he muttered.

He could be right. What did I know?

"I worked with Ruthie," he said softly. "She trusted me. Can't you?"

I wasn't sure. But the reasons I didn't trust him had little to do with this.

Jimmy was right. Ruthie had worked with him. She'd given me her gift. She'd told me to help him, and I'd said that I would.

"We'll work together to find out who killed Ruthie," I agreed.

"And then?"

"Then we'll see."

"You have the power now, Lizzy. You're kind of stuck."

Kind of fucked was more like it, but I kept that to myself.

"We'll *work* together," I repeated, "but that's it."

"No problem," he said, and opened the door to the tack room.

I scowled at his back. He didn't have to sound like he could care less; he could whine at least a little. Beg a little more.

"It's a bad idea for DKs to be involved with anyone." He glanced over his shoulder. "My life expectancy is pretty dim."

My gaze fell to his steadily healing hand. "But—"

"I can heal, but I can also die. Wounds inflicted by a Nephilim don't mend as fast." He flicked a finger toward his eye. "Remember this?"

In my hospital room, after I'd checked out for nearly a week, he'd still had a shiner from getting hit at Ruthie's place.

A weight seemed to settle on my chest at the idea of

Jimmy dying. I didn't want him touching me, but I didn't want him dead and incapable of it either.

I rubbed my forehead. Working with him was going to be *such* a pain in the ass.

"Besides healing"—I dropped my arm—"what else makes you special?"

"Extreme strength and speed. My eyesight is better than most. I can see a vampire behind their human disguise."

"Do all DKs have special abilities?"

"Pretty much."

"They're all breeds?"

He hesitated as if thinking, then nodded.

I let that sink in. I guess it made sense. You didn't bring a knife to a gunfight, and you didn't send just plain folks to fight demons of biblical proportions. Not if you actually wanted to save the world instead of watch it die.

Laughter tickled the back of my throat. This was all so ridiculous it had to be true.

"Wait a minute. How am I supposed to know the difference between Nephilim and breeds?" I asked. "Ruthie whispered berserker *and* she whispered dhampir."

"When something's trying to kill you, it's always a good idea to kill it back," he said.

"I'm serious."

"Me, too."

"Even if I knew the difference between breeds and Nephilim, according to you, some of your kind fight for the other side."

"It'll take time for you to get used to this. Eventually you'll learn—from books, from others, from seeing the same types of creatures over and over again—what's a Nephilim and what's a breed. But Ruthie always said that she could distinguish good and evil just from the nuances in tone and the volume of the voice in her head."

"Swell," I muttered.

"You're going to need some training and some practice, but right now we have to meet Springboard."

"They're waiting for you at City High."

"You think?"

I resisted the urge to slug him. I was getting better and better at that. "Where are we going to meet?"

Without answering my question, he slipped out of the tack room, closing the door behind him.

I reached it quickly, but with Jimmy quick just wasn't good enough. He'd not only closed the door but locked it.

I slammed my fist against the wood. "What the hell?"

"You need to stay put, Lizzy. They know where you live. You'll be safe here, and I'll be back for the meeting."

"You can't leave me behind."

"I think I just did." His voice got farther away.

"Sanducci!" I hit the door again. "Let me out!"

Silence was my only answer.

Did he think I'd never been locked up before? I'd be out of here in no time.

Then what?

Jimmy was right; I couldn't go back to my place. Not now, perhaps never. I bit my lip, worried about Megan, my job, my apartment.

"Any advice?" I asked the empty room. "Or are you only going to come to me in dreams?"

As I muttered to myself, I looked around for something to use on the lock. Flicking the light switch, I cursed when nothing happened. The electricity was either out or disconnected. Probably the latter. Who would need electricity on an old farm that was no longer used? In truth, having it would be worse than a neon sign stating: HERE I AM; COME AND GET ME!

I glanced at the single small window high up in the western wall. The sun sparkled on the dirty pane—red, pink, orange—the sky behind it was a dark but brilliant blue. What light I had wasn't going to last much longer.

I checked the doorknob, which was shiny and new, damn near unpickable, even if I'd had the tools to pick it. I should have known Sanducci would buy the best. Frustrated, I rattled the door.

And something on the other side rattled back.

Chapter 10

"Sanducci?"

That something growled. The growl didn't sound human. It sounded more—

Rrrarrrr!

"Cat," I murmured. "Damn big one."

The thing slammed against the wood, snarling now, scratching, trying to make its way to me.

I felt exposed, my hands far too empty. Where in hell was that knife?

My gaze searched the floor. The light had faded to a pale gray, shot through with streams of pink. Pretty if I'd had the time to daydream. The way my life was going, daydreams would become a fond memory. Nightmares were going to be more my style.

At first I didn't see the knife anywhere, and I had a panicked moment thinking Jimmy had taken it along. Then I caught the last flash of the dying sun off something just under the edge of the cot.

I went onto my knees and grabbed the hilt, feeling so much better with its now familiar weight in my hand, despite the remnants of Jimmy's blood on the blade. Turning, I faced the door just as the big beasty crashed into it again. The wood split down the middle like a melon.

"Wonderful."

I glanced at the knife. Silver worked on most shape-shifters. I knew that firsthand. I was pretty certain what was out there was some variation of the berserker I'd already killed, but it could be just a big cat.

I snorted. *Just?*

The thing snarled again, and I tilted my head. Sounded like a cougar, although it would be kind of odd for a cougar not only to wander so far south but to stroll into this barn and get a hard-on for me. Shape-shifter made a lot more sense, and that it did brought home to me how much my life had changed.

The door creaked alarmingly as the thing threw its body against the wood. I couldn't stay here. If the animal got in, it would kill me, despite the silver weapon. The room was too small. The beast would break through and rush me. I'd have nowhere to retreat, no way to maneuver.

I'd lucked out with the bear. I doubted I'd continue to have that kind of good fortune with everything else. My sole chance was to escape somehow, then either run and hide, or if I had to, stand and face it. My gaze scanned the small room.

Anywhere but here.

I had a cell phone, but fat lot of good it would do me. Who would I call that I could explain this to? Who could I call that was capable of killing whatever was out there and not getting killed themselves?

No one but Jimmy, and I didn't have his number.

My eyes lifted to the only other exit, that small western window about twelve feet above the ground. This wasn't going to be easy.

I stowed the knife in my fanny pack, kicked off my shoes, then tossed the mattress off the cot and leaned the metal frame against the wall. If I stood on the top, I should be able to jump and catch hold of a beam, then swing myself onto it, hop over to the ledge and shimmy out the window. Piece of cake.

But what lay outside? A sheer drop or a convenient drainpipe?

"Only one way to find out," I murmured, and scrambled up the iron frame until I was perched at the precipice.

The sound of my voice seemed to enrage the cat, which shrieked so loudly I wanted to cover my ears. However, I needed my hands for more important things.

I took a deep breath, bent at the knees, said a little prayer—if I missed there was a good chance I'd tumble off the metal contraption and sprain or strain something important—then leaped.

I caught the beam on the first try. I didn't hesitate, but arched and then swung my legs as if the thick plank were a parallel bar and I was in the middle of the state competition.

My hips rolled over the wood; a splinter sliced through my jeans. I barely felt it. As I gained my feet, another resounding crash sounded below and a huge, golden paw swept through the ever-widening hole in the door.

I needed to get a move on before the cat broke all the way in and followed me. Then things would get ugly.

After gauging the distance between the beam and the ledge, I backed up as far as I could, accelerated for all of five steps, and performed a stag-split leap over the gap. The jeans made the movement kind of awkward, but I wasn't being scored, unless I wanted to award myself a ten for making it and a zero for falling and dying by shape-shifter.

A quick glance revealed that the window opened onto the roof of the milking parlor, which ran parallel to the barn. I opened the catch, pushed the long, thin glass outward, and inched through.

Night had fallen while I'd been performing amazing feats of gymnastic excellence. The moon hovered at the edge of the world, spreading a haze of silvery light over the deserted farm. I hurried across the flat roof, thinking I could drop down, shut and lock the barn door, trapping the beast inside, then get in my car and drive away.

However, that left Jimmy with a shape-shifting . . . whatever locked in his barn instead of me. I had no way of reaching him, of warning him. He'd return to pick me up for our meeting with Springboard and the next thing I knew . . . cat food.

Maybe I'd just wait in my car until he got back. I could stop myself from running him over.

Really.

Content with the plan, at least for now, I hurried along the bank of windows. Glancing in, I could see nothing but the navy blue sky reflecting off the glass.

A sudden crash and then a thump, followed by ferocious snarling, made me jump. The animal had broken through the door. From the sounds behind me, it was kicking the crap out of the tack room. Now was my chance.

After peeking over the edge to make sure there weren't more beasts waiting for me, I hung from the roof for an instant, then fell lightly to the earth. I came around the corner and stopped. My car was gone.

"Dammit, Jimmy," I muttered. Now what?

First things first, I needed to shut the barn door with the cougar inside. I'd taken one step in that direction when the sound of a vehicle turning into the drive made me freeze.

Headlights washed over me. Something crashed inside the barn, closer now than it had been before. I gauged the distance between myself and the door. Too far.

Instead, I ran toward the approaching vehicle. Whoever

it was, I had to warn them. Just as soon as I jumped into their back seat.

The car—a huge, black Hummer—jerked to a halt, and Jimmy hopped out of the driver's side even as a tall, lanky black man unfolded himself from the passenger seat.

It was on the tip of my tongue to make a comment about the phallic nature of his ride, but before I could, Jimmy's gaze went beyond me and he cursed.

I spun, fingers groping for the knife in my pack. Should have had it out already. Stupid, stupid me.

The cat, a cougar all right, was framed in the barn doorway, the lights of the Hummer splashing over it like sunshine. I found the knife, pulled the weapon out, then stood gaping.

The animal had to be six foot three from heel to head, easy enough to determine since it stood on its hind legs. I'd never seen one do that, not that I saw a whole lot of cougars.

Something bothered me about its eyes. It took me a minute to figure out what. The headlights were so bright they made the cat's tawny fur sparkle, but not the eyes. Those were dull, as if the animal were already dead.

The cougar began to move forward on two feet, like a human. The stuttering walk broke my inertia, and I stepped toward it.

"No, Lizzy," Jimmy snapped.

Either my movement, or his words, keyed the cougar, which swung its gaze in my direction, hit the ground on all fours and headed straight for me.

I considered running for the barn, seeing if I could catch the edge of the roof and pull myself up. But I'd never make it. Even if I did, I had a bad feeling the cougar would make it too. Instead I stood frozen, knife out, hoping for another miracle.

Everything slowed. In the foreground I saw the cat speeding toward me. Behind it, Jimmy reached into the truck even as Springboard drew a gun.

Along with the slow-mo, I heard an announcer's voice.

Springboard shoots.

A puff of dirt sprang upward near the animal's feet, followed by the report of a gunshot so loud I jerked. The cat kept coming.

He misses.

Crap.

Gets his own rebound, folks, and shoots again.

This time the cougar jerked, its front legs folding even as its back legs kept churning against the ground. The momentum flipped the animal end over end, and it landed just inches from my feet.

The shot goes in from downtown.

"Three points," I murmured.

"Were those silver bullets?" Jimmy asked.

"What you think, man? I don't carry nothin' but the best."

I frowned at the dead cat. If it had been shot with a silver bullet, why wasn't it ashes?

Maybe it wasn't a shape-shifter.

Bending, I brushed my fingertips over the sheen of fur. A sudden wind fluttered what was left of my hair.

Chindi, Ruthie whispered.

For just an instant, I kept my hand on the cougar, and the wind continued to blow. I closed my eyes and let Ruthie swirl around me. She'd only been gone a week, and I missed her so badly my stomach hurt every time I thought about her.

"Lizzy?" I opened my eyes. Jimmy and Springboard stood a few feet away.

"Chindi," I said.

."Shit!" Jimmy cursed. "You shouldn't have shot it."

"Shootin' is what I do, Sanducci. You want me to stand by and let the damn thang kill the new seer?"

In Springboard's words lay a silent condemnation, as if Jimmy had stood by and let the last seer die. But that wasn't what had happened.

I didn't think. In truth, I didn't know.

"Get away from it," Jimmy ordered.

In times past I would have argued. However, those times *were* past. I might be stubborn, but I could be taught. When Jimmy said get away from the dead *chindi*—whatever that was—I got away.

"What's—" I began, but before I could finish my question, Springboard suddenly stiffened as if goosed.

The headlights of the Hummer still shone on us like spotlights, but the man's eyes were as flat as the cougar's had been both before and after it died.

Springboard lifted his gun and pointed it at my head.

Chapter 11

I didn't have time to duck. Even if I had, I doubted I was faster than a speeding bullet. Jimmy, however, was.

He tackled Springboard, knocking the weapon aside just as it went off, then driving the much larger man to the ground. Springboard's gun flew right, Jimmy's flew left as they proceeded to beat the crap out of each other.

I might be new at the seer game, but I could fit the pieces together. Springboard had tried to shoot me; therefore he was the one I was going to shoot.

I snatched up the nearest weapon. Unfortunately, Jimmy and Springboard were rolling over and over in the dirt.

Jimmy had grown up fighting; Springboard appeared to have done the same. Though Jimmy possessed superior speed and strength, Springboard wasn't exactly a tortoise, and his biceps bulged inside the silky material of his shirt. I wondered idly what kind of breed he was.

For several minutes, neither one of them had the upper hand, and I couldn't get off a shot with them so thoroughly intertwined. Then Jimmy got sick of playing around—he always did—and rammed his elbow into Springboard's nose. There was a sharp crack, a yowl, then a whole lot of blood. The two of them separated, and I cocked the gun.

"Don't, Lizzy!" Jimmy whirled. "The chindi's possessed him. If you kill the body, the demon will hop to someone else. We have to—"

Springboard grabbed Jimmy around the knees and yanked. Jimmy went down fast and hard. He caught himself with his hands but his head still bopped against the dirt, and he lay still.

Springboard, or what had once been Springboard, lifted his gaze to mine. His eyes reminded me of those in stuffed deer, teddy bears, creepy little dolls—no expression, no life, no damn reflection.

He climbed to his feet, blood still flowing down his face and darkening the once fashionable pale orange dress shirt. He walked right over Jimmy as if he weren't even there, his flat zombielike gaze on me.

My fingers tightened, but I didn't dare shoot. I didn't want that demon in me; I didn't want it in Jimmy either. But would I be able to keep myself from using the gun once he started to kill me?

I threw the weapon aside. That should help.

Springboard kept coming; I kept backing away. He reached for me with longer arms than I'd expected, nearly caught me too, then my stocking-covered heel came down on a stone. I winced, recoiled, and tripped over a much larger one, landing with a brain-jarring thud on my rear end.

I braced for his weight. Instead, he started to shriek. Light poured from his eyes, ears, and mouth, as if he were a jack-o'-lantern with a flashlight inside.

I sat up, and his arms flew out, his back bowed, and the sheen increased, flowing up and out of him like lightning. The scream no longer seemed to come from Springboard, but from the pillar of light that rose into the night.

As suddenly as it had started, the screeching stopped, and the light went out. Springboard collapsed, thankfully not on me, and lay still.

I crawled the few inches between us and checked for a pulse; he didn't have one.

Jimmy moaned, and I scrambled toward him as he rolled onto his back. The bump on his head was huge, but as I watched it seemed to get smaller, the scrape from the gravel and dirt fading.

"What happened?" he asked.

I glanced at Springboard. "I'm not sure."

He followed my gaze and cursed again. "I told you not to kill him." He grabbed my chin, tilted my face this way and that, staring into my eyes by the light of the Hummer, then frowning. "It didn't leap to you."

"No. It went—" I pointed skyward with one finger.

"How?"

"You tell me."

He lifted a hand to his forehead, encountered the bump, winced, and lowered it again. "A chindi is a demon that possesses animals. It's often sent for purposes of vengeance."

"On me?"

"Hard to say. I'm not sure how much control the sender has over the demon. Usually a chindi just kills everything in the vicinity."

"How did whoever sent that . . ."—I waved my hand at the bodies of Springboard and the cougar—"know where we were?"

He shook his head, then groaned and rested his cheek on his knees. "No one knew about this place but me and you."

"You're forgetting Springboard."

"He didn't know until I brought him here."

"Well, I certainly didn't tell anyone." I couldn't have.

I'd been locked in the freaking tack room, but we'd get to that later. "Why don't you tell me what you know about chindis?"

I half expected him to blow off my question. But he answered in a voice that reminded me of my sophomore biology teacher, Mr. Desre, who'd spent the year reading to us from the textbook instead of making learning fun.

"A chindi can't be killed with the usual weapons. The body it's inhabiting will die, and the demon will jump to another."

"You seem to know a lot about them."

"I've seen one before."

"And how did you kill it?"

"I didn't. I returned the chindi to the one who sent it by reciting a prayer of protection inside a charmed circle." His lips tightened as he stared at Springboard. "You'd better tell me exactly what happened."

"He tried to grab me; I fell and he started screaming, then light shot out of his eyeholes and—" I waved a hand at the body.

"No chant of protection?"

"As if I'd know one."

"Any prayer will do."

"Thanks for the tip. It would have been helpful *before* I accidentally killed him."

"Did he touch you?"

"No."

He leaned his head on his knees again. "There was something about killing a chindi. It's been so long since I saw one. Let me think a minute."

Whenever I tried to remember something, silence was best. So I sat in the dirt next to a dead man and a dead cougar and waited for Jimmy to—

His head came up; his eyes had sharpened to dark

pools of onyx. He reached across the space separating us with that queer flash of speed and yanked my blouse open. The few buttons I hadn't already lost popped, striking the ground with dull thuds.

"Hey!" I smacked his hands away; my fingers curled into fists. "You are so asking for an ass-kicking."

He ignored me, his gaze focused on my chest.

"To kill a chindi," he said, "all you have to do is lay turquoise in its path."

The stone, which lay above my heart, seemed to burn into my skin.

Jimmy reached out and lifted it, his fingertips brushing my breasts, lingering longer than they needed to. "Turquoise in the path. Coincidence?" His eyes met mine. "I don't think so."

"I don't know anything about chindis, and I've been wearing this since—" I broke off.

"He gave this to you."

Not a question, so I didn't answer. Jimmy knew damn well *he* had given it to me. He had to have seen it when he'd been touching and kissing and suckling me not very long ago. Maybe he hadn't really registered it being there because he was as used to seeing the turquoise nestled between my breasts as I was.

"What difference does it make where I got it, we're just lucky I had it."

"Luck is overrated." He let the stone fall back where it belonged.

The tiny blue-green pebble brushed against my skin like a chill wind, and I shivered. For just an instant I could have sworn I'd felt . . . him.

There'd been other times in my life when it had seemed like I was being watched. Times I'd woken up sweating and frightened and sensed I wasn't alone. But I always was.

Jimmy got to his feet and offered me a hand. I took it, but as soon as I was vertical, I let him go.

"What exactly are you saying?" I asked.

He stared at the sparkling sky. Out here, away from the city, the stars were so bright they twinkled. The moon spilled down, spreading a milky sheen over the abandoned farm, intensifying every color—the bright red barn against the May-green grass, surrounded by the blue-black sky. The picture it made would look great on a postcard. We could start a whole new tourism campaign: DISCOVER THE DEMONS OF DAIRYLAND.

I rubbed between my eyes. Maybe I *had* left the hospital too early.

"What I'm saying," Jimmy answered, "is that I find it a little far-fetched that someone sent a chindi. A creature that is virtually indestructible, unless a hunk of turquoise, which you conveniently wear around your neck, is cast in its path."

"Only you and I know about this." I frowned, fingering the necklace. "Well, Ruthie, too, but I don't think she's chatting with anyone else these days."

"You're forgetting someone."

"No I'm not," I said mulishly.

Jimmy sighed and switched his gaze from the stars to me. "There's one more thing you should know about the chindi."

"What's that?"

"It's a Navajo spirit."

"Shit."

Jimmy lifted his face to the sky again as he stuck his hands into his pockets and rocked back on his heels. "Yep."

Chapter 12

"Why would he—" I stopped. Why did Sawyer do anything?

"Relax," Jimmy said. "He didn't mean to kill you."

"How you figure?"

His gaze lowered to the turquoise, which lay like the stone it was against my chest. "How many people have turquoise on them? Especially around here."

"Huh?"

My mind still wasn't functioning as well as it should. I blamed the walking cougar and the possessed dead man.

"Sawyer knew the demon couldn't hurt you while you wore his gift," Jimmy said.

"Sure would have been nice if I'd known it." I rubbed my arms, chilled despite the warm-for-the-month-of-May evening breeze.

Sometimes I wondered why I still wore the stone. In the beginning, the turquoise was the only jewelry I owned, and it was beautiful, a stark statement of brilliant color in a world where there was so much gray. There was also the added incentive that it drove Jimmy bonkers, which was always fun. In the end I didn't feel dressed without it. If I were honest, I didn't feel safe.

I glanced at the cougar. Had this been why?

"He couldn't have known I'd still be wearing it," I murmured.

"I bet he did know just that."

"But—"

"He wouldn't kill you, Lizzy." Jimmy's lips twisted. "Me? That's another story." He strode toward the barn.

"Wait!" I hurried after him, grabbing his arm.

"Let's clean this place up and get on the road."

"To where?"

"You know where."

"No." He shook me off and continued on his way. "I'm not going, Sanducci, and you can't make me."

He spun around so fast I took a step back. "I *can* make you, Lizzy, and I will. We've got no choice."

"There's always a choice."

"Not in this."

I stood in the barnyard as he disappeared inside, considered hopping into his Hummer and leaving him here. But then what?

I'd have to hide. Forever. I wasn't up to that.

Instead, I followed, determined to convince Jimmy that his plan sucked.

The tack room was trashed—the mattress shredded by razor-sharp cat claws, stuffing trailed everywhere. The bedframe lay cockeyed, one corner still against the wall, another against the floor, the third and fourth waving back and forth like an overgrown, rusted teeter-totter.

As I came through the door, Jimmy snapped his cell phone shut, tossed it into a bag with one hand and removed a T-shirt with the other. "Put this on." He flipped the garment in my direction. "Your blouse is toast."

"Whose fault is that?" I retorted.

"I just gave you a new one. Quit bitching."

I lifted the T-shirt. "Van Halen?"

He shrugged as if to say, *You know how it goes.*

I did.

Jimmy had been gifted with all sorts of T-shirts. He wore them with jeans and a sport coat, had been photographed himself wearing them in London, Paris, Rome. What began as a joke became a trademark. If Sanducci wore your T-shirt, he'd deigned to take your picture. You had arrived.

I thought back to the photo he'd taken of Van Halen—Eddie and Alex, Michael, Sammy and David Lee. How he'd gotten them all in the same room was anyone's guess. How he'd gotten them to pose and not kill one another was a downright miracle. The portrait had graced their latest *All-Time Hits* CD. The thing had sold three million copies. I had one myself.

Jimmy headed back outside. I hurriedly shoved my dusty stocking-covered feet into my shoes, then lost the buttonless blouse and drew the T-shirt over my head. It smelled like him, and I was struck by a wave of nostalgia so deep I staggered. Would I ever get past loving Jimmy Sanducci? God, I hoped so.

When I stepped from the barn, Jimmy was kneeling next to Springboard and shoving something into the dead man's pocket.

"What are you doing?"

"Wrapping things up neatly for your cop friends."

"Huh?"

He sighed and withdrew the item from Springboard's pocket.

"Ruthie's crucifix? How did you get that? She never—" I paused.

She'd never taken it off while she was alive.

"You came back?" I asked.

He bent once more to plant the necklace on Springboard. "I was too late for her, but I knew she'd want you to have this—" He straightened, his eyes meeting mine, the grief there an echo of my own. "I took it, then I tried to wake you up, but the sirens . . ."

"You ran."

"Like a rabbit."

"How could the Nephilim have hurt her if she was wearing a crucifix?"

Sadness spread over his face, settling in his eyes. "Only a few beings will be stopped by a crucifix."

"How can you touch it?"

"I'm not one of them."

"But—"

"I'm dhampir, not vampire. There's a difference."

"So you say."

"I didn't burst into flames, did I?"

He was so cavalier I had to ask. "Does a crucifix really destroy a vampire?"

Jimmy gave me a look that made something in my chest shift—like I was a prize student and he was a lifetime teacher. "Very good. We'll make a seer out of you yet." I half expected him to pat me on the head. "Always doubt the so-called legends. Not doing so will get people killed."

"You didn't answer the question."

"Any blessed item will *repel* a vampire. But . . ." He shook his head. "It takes a lot more than that to kill a demon of such power."

"What about sunlight?"

"That will kill some. Depends on the type."

I blinked. "There are types?"

"Of course. The bruxa, from Portugal, can only be killed by use of a magical amulet. The liderc, from Hungary, must eat garlic—and good luck getting them to do that. The vjesci, from Poland, must be buried in sand."

"This is too complicated."

"You'll get used to it."

I doubted that.

"As soon as the case is closed," Jimmy continued, "and I bet it won't be long now, the police will give you Ruthie's necklace back."

"They didn't tell me her necklace was missing." They had to have known. Everyone knew Ruthie wore that crucifix every minute, every day.

The light dawned. "They withheld the information. Only the killer would—"

"Let's go." Jimmy walked away from Springboard without a backward glance.

He climbed into the driver's seat and started the engine. I had no choice but to get in.

"You're setting him up."

"I need to be out from under the cops." Jimmy put the car in drive. "If they think Springboard killed Ruthie, I will be."

"You think that just finding her crucifix in his pocket will convict him?"

"Since he's not around to argue, I hope so."

I glanced over my shoulder as Springboard's body and that of the cougar's became smaller and smaller in the rear window, then faded into the shadows altogether.

The crucifix might be enough to close the case, though I didn't think it would be enough to get Hammond and Landsdown completely off Jimmy's back. Still, I doubted they'd track him to New Mexico if they had another suspect tied up neatly with a bow. Their superiors wouldn't let them.

We reached the end of the long dirt drive and turned onto the two-lane highway that would return us to the freeway. From there we could go just about anywhere. Unfortunately we were going to New Mexico. I was still trying to figure out how to avoid that.

"You said the DKs are breeds." Jimmy nodded. "What was Springboard?"

"The way this is supposed to work is that you tell me what kind of beast lies behind the human face, not the other way around."

"Well, excuse me for screwing up the way things are *supposed* to be. But I'm a little seer come lately, so why don't you just tell me what Springboard was?"

"Hyena," he snapped. "About an eighth."

"He was one-eighth hyena." Laughter bubbled, and I swallowed hard to make it go away.

Jimmy cast a quick glance in my direction, then returned it to the road and continued to speak. "Bouda was once a country in Africa—maybe it still is, I don't know—which was governed by a matriarchal society of witches who could shift into hyenas."

"Nephilim."

"Yes. Eventually the shifters themselves became known as the bouda."

"So Springboard could become a hyena under the light of the silvery moon?"

"Boudas can shift any time they want to; they aren't bound by the moon. And Springboard wasn't a full-fledged bouda, but a breed, several times removed."

"What does that *mean*?"

"He could shift, but it wasn't easy for him. Took too long, so it wasn't exactly something he wanted to do in the heat of battle. Springboard was better on two feet, with a gun or a sword. In human form he was stronger and quicker, we all are. As a hyena he was a predator. They have some of the most powerful jaw muscles in the animal kingdom."

I frowned, wondering what, exactly, that particular gift had done for him.

"Adult hyenas fear only the big cats as predators," Jimmy finished.

Pretty strange that a big cat had been the death of him. Or maybe not so strange after all.

"Because he was part hyena, the chindi jumped to him?" I asked.

Jimmy's eyebrows lifted, as if he hadn't thought of that. "Maybe so. Although humans are animals too, I've never heard of a chindi possessing anything but the furry. That doesn't mean it couldn't happen."

"Could it have been sent for him?"

"Doubtful. No one knew he'd be at the farm."

"No one was supposed to know we'd be at the farm either, but someone did."

"And I plan to find out who."

Silence fell between us for a minute, then I had another thought. "Springboard's autopsy—won't they find traces of hyena fur, blood, something?"

"He wasn't in hyena form. But even if they did . . ." Jimmy let his voice trail off, and I understood.

"That would make the case more open and shut, because they probably found traces of animal fur at the murder scene."

"Considering the number of shifters there, I can't imagine they wouldn't have."

"Did you see a hyena?"

Jimmy shook his head. "But that doesn't mean one wasn't there."

We were looking for a traitor. Was it possible that we'd found him already, and that he'd been killed by accident?

No.

"There won't be any explanation for hyena fur," I mussed. Or any other type of fur for that matter. Ruthie hadn't even owned a dog.

"Won't be our problem. We'll be long gone."

Jimmy hit the on ramp and accelerated, heading west past Madison instead of south toward home. I'd known he would, yet I still tensed at the proof of it.

"I don't want to go there, Jimmy," I said quietly.

"I know."

"Then don't make me."

At first he didn't speak, though his fingers tightened on the steering wheel. "In a different world, I wouldn't. But I need to talk to him, and you need to stay with him."

"Stay?" My voice squeaked. "No. You can't— I can't—"

"You have to learn how to control your new ability. Ruthie would have taught you, but she's gone."

"She's not gone," I said desperately. "She could teach me—" I spread my hands. "In my dreams."

He was already shaking his head. "We don't have time to wait around on the off chance that might happen. You know he's the best at training, otherwise Ruthie would never have sent you there in the first place."

No matter how much I argued, there would always be that truth.

"Correct me if I'm wrong," Jimmy said, "but as of right now only by touching something do you get any communication from the Great Beyond."

"I had a dream."

"You and Dr. King," he muttered. "Bet they weren't the same."

I crossed my arms over my chest and stared out the window.

Jimmy sighed. "You have to learn to access your power without touching the Nephilim. It's too dangerous. The only chance I see of making that happen is to take you to Sawyer."

I made one last attempt to thwart the inevitable. "He frightens me."

At first, I didn't think Jimmy was going to acknowledge my words; then he spoke softly into the darkness. "He frightens me too."

Chapter 13

After that, there wasn't much left to say. Jimmy was going to deliver me to New Mexico. It wasn't as if I hadn't been dumped there before.

The summer I was fifteen, Ruthie had handed me a plane ticket and driven me to Mitchell Field. She'd walked me to the gate—pre-9/11 people could still do that—and sent me on my way with a hug and the admonition to "learn all you can. This man knows what he's about." But her frown and the way she'd clung just a little had made me uneasy before I even boarded the plane.

One of Ruthie's friends picked me up and drove me the rest of the way. The woman appeared as old as Ruthie—probably sixty back then, but in my youth I'd figured she had one foot in the grave. She was Navajo— her face sun-bronzed and lined, her hair black and long with only a few silver threads. Her hands, clutched tightly on the wheel of her dusty tan station wagon, looked like monkey's paws—shriveled, bony, and dark.

Her name was Lucinda, but I only knew that because Ruthie had told me, then Lucinda had nodded when I asked. She never spoke a word between Albuquerque and the reservation.

I wondered how they knew each other, when they'd

met, but I didn't ask. I was too worried about where I was going and this man I was about to meet. But now, looking back and knowing what I know, I think Lucinda was a seer too.

She'd pulled up in front of a house and outbuildings at the base of the mountains, motioned for me to get out, and when I did, she'd left in a big hurry, spraying dust and gravel behind her. I'd been too young and clueless to be disturbed by her behavior. I'd figured Lucinda was late for . . . something. It hadn't occurred to me that she might be running before she caught sight of Sawyer—or perhaps before he caught sight of her.

I discovered quickly that while Sawyer might know what he was about, he was also withdrawn, bleak, secretive. Though it was a relief to meet someone who was actually "weirder" than I was, it was also a bit frightening. He had powers beyond anything I'd ever encountered. I'd been fascinated by him.

At first.

The memories of New Mexico faded as Jimmy and I left Wisconsin, crossing over the Mississippi and into Iowa. On both sides of the river, the terrain was hilly, with high bluffs and lots of craggy rock formations. Within the hour it would flatten into corn fields as far as the eye could see, dotted here by a farm and there with a tiny town.

"You want me to drive?" I asked.

Jimmy snorted. "If I let you behind the wheel, we'd end up in Canada instead of New Mexico."

"I wouldn't—" His dark eyes pinned me, and I didn't bother to argue any longer. He was right. I probably would sabotage this little road trip if given half the chance. I wouldn't be able to stop myself.

"What happened to my car?" I asked.

"Switched it with this one. Don't worry, it'll be there when you get back."

If I got back.

"Shouldn't we ditch such a monstrosity?" I eyed the huge console in front of me. I felt like I was flying in the *Millennium Falcon*, the Hummer was so large and high off the ground. "We're kind of conspicuous."

"Don't worry. There are DKs in every sector of life. This car's untraceable."

"Too bad it isn't unseeable," I muttered.

Jimmy's hand covered my knee, and I jumped. "I won't let anything happen to you. I definitely won't let the cops drag us back to Milwaukee."

"You won't have much to say about it."

He sighed and withdrew. "Soon they'll be busy dealing with Springboard."

"How soon? Who's going to know he's there?"

"I had another DK call in an anonymous tip. The cops should be at the farm by now. The uproar that's going to cause will keep them occupied for a few days. By then we'll be at—" He broke off.

I knew where we'd be, and he was right. No one would find us there.

"You're going to be a suspect again," I said. "You were supposed to photograph Springboard, then he turns up dead."

"Except he'll be dead by natural causes."

I cast him a quick glance. "Really?"

"He most likely died of a stroke or a heart attack when the chindi left his body. They'll find the cougar and believe that caused his death. There isn't a mark on him, Lizzy."

"Discovering Springboard at your farm isn't going to help your cause."

"It should take them a few days to figure out who owns that place. Longer if we're lucky." He shrugged. "Maybe Springboard came looking for me when I didn't show up for the shoot. Got to the farm and ran into the cougar. I didn't touch him, and no one can prove that I did. Besides, it won't take long before they decide that Springboard's their man for the Kane murder and stop searching for anyone else."

Silence fell between us. My eyes were heavy. It had been a long day.

"Are we there yet?" I murmured.

Jimmy gave me a small smile. "Twenty hours to go. You might as well sleep. Everything will be all right."

It wouldn't be, not everything; we both knew that. But I went to sleep anyway. Sooner or later I'd have to drive. I preferred that to stopping so Jimmy could sleep.

Him. Me. A hotel room. Nothing good could come of that.

Besides, in dreams, I saw Ruthie.

I had barely closed my eyes when I heard her voice. "You hate me now?"

I stood next to the picket fence; Ruthie waited in the doorway. "I could never hate you."

She shook her head, turned and went inside. I had no choice but to follow.

I found Ruthie in the backyard this time, staring at the empty swing set. The place was quiet. Too quiet.

"Where are the children?" I asked.

"Gone on." Her sigh was the wind in my hair. "But there'll be more."

Since the children who came to Ruthie's version of heaven had experienced hell on earth, her sadness was understandable. It bothered me that she would still be bearing such a burden when she should be enjoying paradise.

"I'm helping Jimmy like you asked," I said, hoping to lift her spirits. So to speak.

She didn't answer, instead watching the brilliant blue

horizon as if waiting for someone. Was it always daytime here? Why shouldn't it be?

"Could you give me a crash course on managing your gift so I don't have to—"

Her gaze shot to mine. "You have to."

Damn.

"He's the only one who can help you," Ruthie said. "Even if I weren't . . . here, I wouldn't be able to teach you what you need to know. You're so much more powerful than I ever was, Lizbeth. You were destined to lead this army, not me."

"Lead?" I suddenly had a hard time breathing. "An army?"

"What did you think you were going to do, child?"

"Your job."

"My job was to keep the world from self-destructing until you were ready to take over."

"I'm not ready."

"So get your behind to Sawyer and get ready."

"I don't want to go anywhere near Sawyer."

The feelings I had for him were complicated. He both attracted and repelled. He'd made things clearer, and he'd muddied them up. When I'd left him after a summer of training, I'd been stronger, but I'd never been able to learn everything he wanted to teach me. I suspected that some of the lessons were about things I really shouldn't know. Sawyer walked a fine line between good and evil, and there were times he wallowed in the darkness, times I felt he wanted to drag me there with him.

"I don't recall askin' what you wanted." Ruthie tilted her head as if someone were calling her. "Springboard's here." Her gaze met mine, and her eyes were moist. "There are more arriving every day. Make sure you're not one of them."

"I'll do my best."

Her eyes sharpened, and I waited for her to tell me she "didn't appreciate" my sass. Instead, she returned her attention to the impossibly beautiful horizon.

"They're coming," she whispered, and the tears that had threatened spilled down her cheeks like rain.

The last time Ruthie had said "they're coming," I awakened to a berserker in my room. The thought of meeting whatever was making her cry had me trying to wake myself from my dream so I could face the newest nightmare. But I couldn't move, couldn't break free of the glaringly empty backyard where children used to play.

"Jimmy," I said. "He's alone."

"He's been handlin' things for years without you."

"I thought I was supposed to help him."

"There's helpin' and there's helpin'. You're a seer, not a DK." She frowned, listening again, then spat out a word I'd never thought to hear Ruthie Kane use, especially in paradise. "Times are hard. We're gonna be a little short on help. You'll be the first demon-killing seer in history. Congratulations."

"What? I'm not a breed. I don't have any superpowers."

"You will."

Aw, hell.

"Go on back now. Save whoever you can, and know"—Ruthie touched my arm, and I saw a sign, a road, a town—"the rest will be here with me."

Lightning flashed from a sunny sky, followed by a crack of thunder that made me flinch and close my eyes. I woke up in the car. The only light on the highway was the garish golden beam of our headlights splashing across black asphalt.

I peered out the window. Acres upon acres of flat, flat land. Very few trees.

"Iowa?" I guessed.

"Kansas."

From the look of things, same difference.

In the glow of the dashboard, Jimmy's skin had a pasty hue, but his eyes were alert. He held himself as if he were ready for anything.

"Why'd we get off the freeway?" I asked.

"You mumbled 'Hardeyville' in your sleep. When I saw the exit, I figured it was a sign."

Just then a billboard flashed past on our right. ENTERING HARDEYVILLE — POPULATION 1256.

"Guess so," I murmured.

The place appeared exactly as it had in my dream vision. Why wouldn't it?

The highway ran through the center of town, becoming Main Street at the first intersection. Not a stoplight in sight. I doubted there were too many traffic jams in Hardeyville.

The buildings were old, mostly brick, occupied by the types of businesses necessary to keep a small town alive— grocer, hardware, barber, physician. Residential roofs spiked on each side road that shot off from the main drag.

The place was eerily silent. Sure, dawn hadn't even begun to lighten the horizon, but as I lowered my window, I didn't hear anything—not a dog, not a bird, not the distant hum of a plane, train, or automobile.

"What are we dealing with here?" Jimmy asked.

"Not a clue."

"I hate going in blind."

"I hate going in at all."

"You're staying in the car."

I snorted. "Not."

"Lizzy, you're a seer."

"According to Ruthie, I'm both."

He glanced at me, then away. "You talked to her?"

"How do you think I knew about Hardeyville?"

"Dumb luck?"

"Yeah, that always works."

"If she told you to come here, why didn't she tell you what *was* here?"

"I'm getting the impression that 'easy' isn't in my job description. So far I've had to touch the Nephilim to find out what they are."

"That's going to get old fast," Jimmy muttered.

"It already is."

Sooner or later, more than likely sooner, I was going to touch one monster too many.

Jimmy cursed, low and vicious, and I glanced at him with a start. He stared out the passenger window. I turned my head and froze.

Something furry, actually several somethings, more like a pack, with long, spindly legs and massive heads, slunk down a side street in the opposite direction.

"I didn't think there were any wolves left around here," I murmured.

Jimmy slid the Hummer over to the curb. "There never are."

Chapter 14

Jimmy reached beneath his seat to retrieve his gun. I felt beneath my own but wasn't so lucky.

"Stay here," he repeated, and got out of the car.

I might not have had any DK training, but I had been a cop. I could shoot things. Hit them too.

I opened the door and followed him to the rear of the Hummer. The back end was a traveling armory. Guns, ammo, knives, forks—what would he do with those?— swords, syringes.

"I can see why you didn't want to ditch it," I said.

"Get. In. The. Car."

I reached for a box of bullets clearly marked *silver* and a rifle while I was at it. I grabbed a pistol, too, and the appropriate ammo. Never could tell when you might need both short- and long-range firearms.

"So," I said as I began to load my weapons, "we just start shooting?"

"Dammit, Lizzy." He grabbed my elbow, whipped me around, fury and fear at war on his face.

"I won't let you go alone," I said quietly. "I can't. So don't ask it of me."

"I'm telling you." His voice was low and desperate.

"I'm not listening." I jerked free of his grasp, finished

loading the silver bullets, and strode toward the last place I'd seen the slinking shadows.

"Wait."

I paused, tensed to fight if I had to. But, short of winning that fight, then tying me up, Jimmy wasn't going to stop me, and he knew it.

He joined me on the sidewalk, gaze darting from building to building, then to the roofs and the alleyways. "One shot should turn them to ashes."

"And if it doesn't?"

His mouth thinned. "Then they aren't shifters."

I remembered the chindi. That would be bad. I'd have to touch them to discover what they were; then we'd have to figure out how to kill that particular type of Nephilim. What if Jimmy didn't have the necessary tools in his handy-dandy Hummer?

"One thing at a time," he murmured. "First, shoot a few and see how much dust we raise."

"Sounds like a plan." I moved forward, but he shouldered me back.

"Stay behind me."

I didn't bother to argue; I just marched a larger circle around him and continued to walk at his side. "If I'm behind you, I might shoot you instead of them."

"You're not that lame."

"Who said it would be an accident?"

He choked on a laugh as I began to smile. At least we were happy when the werewolves found us.

The alley was dark, but the horizon behind the rangy beasts had gone gray with approaching dawn, throwing them into stark silhouette. There was something off about those silhouettes. They almost looked human, as if men, and a few women too, crept on all fours, backs hunched, heads swaying to and fro as they caught the scent of prey. The wolves also seemed much bigger than the average wolf. Not that I'd ever seen any outside the Milwaukee County Zoo.

Other than their size and strangely humanoid shadows, they resembled wolves. I couldn't determine the shade of their coats in this light, but their eyes glowed yellow.

"Don't stop shooting until they're all dead," Jimmy said.

"What if—?" I began but never finished.

Didn't need to, because my question *What if they don't die?* was answered as the first silver bullet plowed into the nearest wolf, and it exploded outward, coating the animals on either side of it with ashes. Their snarls ended mid-chorus as we sprayed the pack with ammo.

Surrounded as we were on both sides with concrete and stone, the sound of gunfire was deafening. Above us the sky continued to lighten as we finished the job.

Sudden silence descended. In front of us lay only ash, which stirred and lifted onto the morning breeze.

"Cleanups are a cinch," I said in my best fifties-house-wife voice.

Jimmy ignored me, moving down the alley, skirting the tiny piles of disintegrated werewolves to peek around the corner. I tensed, expecting him to start shooting again, but he glanced back, shook his head.

The eerie stillness I'd marked upon entering Hard-eyville continued. Shouldn't the townspeople have been alerted by the gunfire? Shouldn't they be spilling into the streets? At the least, calling out to one another or us?

"The werewolves will return to human form at sun-rise," Jimmy said, staring out at the empty town.

I lifted my gaze to the slice of sky between the two buildings. It had turned blue-gray.

"Let's get going," he continued. "It's much easier to determine a werewolf in wolf form than human."

Crossing the short distance between us, I neatly side-stepped the quickly dissipating piles of ash. "What gives it away?"

"You saw their shadows?" I nodded. "If it's a moonless night, that makes things harder. Werewolves are bigger than the average wolf, reflecting the weight of their human counterparts. Real wolves, even Alaskan timber, rarely go above a hundred and twenty pounds."

"A lot of people don't either."

"True."

I frowned. "Then how do you know?"

He shrugged. "If I see a wolf, I shoot it."

My mouth dropped open. "Aren't wolves endangered or protected or something?"

"You gonna arrest me?"

I remained silent for a minute. I didn't like the thought of blasting any wolf that I saw, but what was the alternative?

Allowing werewolves to roam free. I didn't like that any better.

Jimmy noticed my hesitation and made an exasperated sound. "Real wolves don't venture into populated areas. They're afraid of humans. If you see a wolf where there are people you can bet your sweet ass it's either a werewolf or rabid."

I nodded, understanding. "In either case, shooting them is a good idea."

"Now you're catching on," he said, and slid out of the alley.

I hurried after. "What about when they shape-shift back into a human?"

"What about it?"

"How can you tell if they're a werewolf?"

His eyes met mine. "You can't. Or I can't, which is why I have you."

"I shouldn't go around touching everyone in the universe. And if I touch them and get the werewolf vibe, you can't just shoot them on the street."

"I can't?"

We were hurrying down a road parallel to Main, where we'd left the Hummer. More shops lined the sidewalk—a Laundromat, a drugstore. At every window, Jimmy paused and peered through the glass. They were all empty.

"You're going to wind up in prison for murder if you don't watch yourself," I muttered.

"They aren't human, Lizzy, so it isn't murder."

"How you gonna explain that when they come for you?"

"I'm not." He stopped and faced me. "You're right, shooting them in the open is bad business. But it's an easy enough thing to lure them somewhere isolated and do the deed."

I began to ask how he enticed them to shape-shift just so he could shoot them, then paused. What if he said he didn't bother? And I had a sneaking suspicion that's exactly what he would say. Would I ever be able to look at him again without seeing him shoot a person, then walk away as if it were nothing?

According to Jimmy, the Nephilim weren't human.

Except they were. At least half.

I rubbed my forehead. This was a moral dilemma I wasn't up to dealing with.

I lowered my hand, lifted my chin and met his gaze. "We're a little short on villagers. What next?"

His wary stance relaxed at the proof I wasn't going to push for difficult answers. At the moment.

"We keep searching," he said. "Eventually someone, or something, has to turn up."

We did the best we could, hurrying from shop to shop, then house to house, ringing bells, tapping on doors. We found no one, and I began to get twitchy. There had obviously been people here once; now they were gone as if they'd disappeared into thin air. As far as I knew, that wasn't possible. Unless . . .

"Could this have been a town of werewolves?" I asked.

Jimmy snorted. "Yeah, right."

We'd reached the outskirts of Hardeyville. A short distance away loomed what appeared to be the school—brick like everything else, but squat, with a flat roof and a whole lot of concrete parking lot rimmed with playground equipment. Jimmy stood where the sidewalk ended and the dirt began, scowling at a brand-new field house.

"Why not?" I asked. "Maybe a few came for a visit, then turned everyone in the place."

"Turned?" As if he were having a hard time tearing his gaze from the gymnasium, Jimmy faced me. "What the hell are you talking about?"

"A few werewolves decided they wanted a place for themselves; they wanted a pack." The more I thought about it the better I liked the idea. "So they scouted out a nice town in the middle of nowhere, and they bit everyone in it."

He was shaking his head before I finished. "We aren't living in a B movie. Werewolves can't make other werewolves by biting them."

"Then how do they make more werewolves?"

"They don't really need to. There are enough to keep us busy for a very long time."

"Where are the pets?" I asked. We hadn't found one dog, cat, or parakeet, though we had seen evidence of all three.

"There's something about shifters that makes domestic animals go bananas. Either they took off and they aren't coming back, or they were—"

Appetizers. My mind helpfully filled in the blank.

"If dogs go nuts at the sight"—or maybe it was the scent—"of shifters, why don't we have a few on the payroll?"

"Not a bad idea, and some DKs do, but since most of us travel a lot and have our cover jobs, dragging a dog along with us is more of a pain than it's worth. We aren't all Paris Hilton."

My lips twitched at the image of Jimmy carrying a Chihuahua everywhere he went.

As we approached the school, a strange hum filled the air. I glanced at the sky, but the sound was too soft to be a plane or a helicopter, too loud to be nothing. Jimmy either didn't hear it, or he didn't care. Maybe he already knew what we'd find.

Thousands of flies swarmed at the entrance, butting their heads into the glass in an attempt to enter, bouncing back, swarming together and buzzing, buzzing, buzzing.

"Fuck," Jimmy said, his tone conversational. Then, ignoring the flies, he yanked open the door.

The smell hit me right away. Not as bad as I expected, really, but not good either. They hadn't been here very long.

The brand-new basketball court was ruined. I didn't think blood came out of wood very well, especially not that much of it.

Jimmy stood in the doorway and surveyed what appeared to be a mass murder. I got a pretty good idea what Jonestown had looked like. Except there were no remnants of poison Flavor-Aid, just blood on blood and then, hey, more blood.

"They lured the whole town in here." Jimmy's voice was quiet, even though no one in the building was alive to hear. "Then they shut the doors and had some fun."

"Why?" I whispered, voice hoarse, eyes burning.

"Because they could."

"You said the Nephilim want humans for food, for slaves."

"Or amusement." His eyes remained on the carnage. "They must have loved this."

I gagged. Sure I'd been a cop, and I'd seen bad things, but I'd never seen anything like Hardeyville.

"Lizzy!" Jimmy snapped. "Pull yourself together. We're gonna have to check them all."

"What?"

He turned his head. "Someone could still be alive."

He was right. I followed him, splitting off when we reached the first row, moving in the opposite direction, feeling each body for a pulse.

It wasn't that simple. As I'd already learned with Ruthie, shape-shifters went for the throat. Defensive wounds on the hands and wrists screwed up those pulse points too. In truth, most of the bodies were so mangled, there was no way they were alive. But I checked them anyway.

Blood crept past my knuckles, washed across my wrists, and started up my forearms. The flies began to dribble inside; I'm not sure how. We had to have only let in a few when we arrived, but somehow they always found their way into a party.

No one had been spared. Men and women. Young and old. By the time Jimmy and I met again at the entrance, I was shivering and shocky.

Jimmy took one glance at my face and his hardened. He grabbed me by the shoulders, and I tensed, expecting him to shake me until my brain rattled. Instead, he turned me around and pointed at something that made me flinch. "See it?"

A baseball cap, the shade of the material unrecognizable as the blood fast turned black in the rising heat, the insignia obscured, but the size revealing it as a Little League cap even before I took in the small, white hand reaching out for it and falling short.

"The only way to live with this is to suck it up and kill them all." Now he did shake me. Just once but hard. "Can you do that?"

I swallowed, tasting things I never wanted to taste again but knowing that I would, and nodded. "I'm okay."

He leaned down, peering into my eyes for several seconds, brow creased. He didn't seem to believe me, but he did let me go. "Good. Now—"

"Hey! Help! Someone help me!"

I whirled toward the roomful of villagers. No one moved among the dead. How could they? So I spun back, just as a man stumbled from the hallway into the gymnasium.

Tall and thick at the arms and the neck, he had wild eyes. He had blood on him, but then so did we. His salt-and-pepper hair was matted with sweat. His skin was winter pale, his clothes torn and dark in patches. He took one look at the room and stopped, staring, gaping, mouth moving as no sound came out.

"Touch him," Jimmy murmured.

"Wh-what?"

He jerked his head toward the windows, set high in the walls above the bleachers. Golden light filtered through.

The sun was up.

I lowered my gaze. "Hey, mister," I said softly, and the guy stopped staring at the dead and stared at me.

His eyes full of fear and grief, he hurried forward. "Thank God you came. I hid and they—" His voice broke.

I offered my hand, and he went for it gladly, almost desperately. I understood the need to connect with someone, to share horror, to lean and be supported.

I'd already begun thinking of how we'd find clean clothes, load the guy into the Hummer, take him to a safer place. Then our hands met, and my hair stirred in a sudden, impossible breeze.

Werewolf, Ruthie whispered.

I turned to Jimmy and said, "Shoot him."

Chapter 15

The guy disintegrated into ashes at the same time the report of the gun exploded so close I heard nothing but that for several minutes. As I was covered in sweat and blood, the residue stuck to me. I understood how being tarred and feathered had once been a horrible punishment.

"Lizzy?" Jimmy's voice came from far away, but it actually sounded concerned. What had happened to the tough love? I must have looked even worse than I felt.

I met Jimmy's eyes, and he frowned at whatever he saw in them. "You okay?"

I blinked. Ash cascaded off my eyelashes like snow falling from the trees. "Dandy." I sneezed. "What now?"

"We had to—" he began, and I held up my hand, startled in spite of myself at how bloody it was.

Lowering the gory appendage, I said, "You won't get any argument from me, Sanducci. Let's move on."

I was starting to catch the nuances in Ruthie's whispers, the subtle differences between a warning for a Nephilim and a breed or even a hell-sent vengeance demon.

Just now there'd been an increase in volume and intensity that created a hum at the edges of my brain, a hum that hadn't been there when she'd told me about Jimmy.

Of course the word *werewolf* was probably a good clue. They kind of had a reputation for being bad-ass, one I'd been aware of even before I'd known they were real.

Jimmy stared at me for a few seconds, then gave one sharp nod. "We have to torch this place."

"It's brand-new."

"A terrible accident while the entire town is at a community event is a lot more palatable than mass murder by shape-shifters."

He stepped out of the gymnasium and I followed. "The building is brick, how you gonna burn it?"

"Don't worry; I've done it before."

A quick trip to the Hummer produced gasoline and a few sticks of dynamite.

"Isn't that going to seem suspicious?"

"People see what they want to see. No one left in town to say otherwise, it'll look like an accident. I'll make it look like one."

Ten minutes later, flames shot toward the neon-blue sky. Jimmy turned, but instead of heading toward the car, he went toward town. "We need to make sure there isn't anyone left."

"You think there might be?"

"No. Werewolves are pretty thorough. But we'll look."

He didn't have to say we were searching for both human and non. When we'd returned to the Hummer for the gas, we'd also restocked our supply of silver bullets.

Noon had come and gone before we'd searched every house and business. We didn't find anyone else, dead, alive, or anything in between. I wasn't sure if that was good or bad. I decided not to think about it at all. Yep. I was definitely starting to catch on to this job.

"We'll clean up, grab some fresh clothes and food, then get on the road," Jimmy said.

I didn't like the idea of using dead people's things,

but what choice did we have? We couldn't ride around Kansas, or any other state for that matter, covered in blood and ashes. That was bound to raise some eyebrows.

"This one." Jimmy flicked a finger at a three-story clapboard, painted a soothing robin's-egg blue. The shutters were white; spring flowers sprouted all over the yard, mocking the scent of death and smoke that hung over Hardeyville.

He climbed the porch steps and walked right in. No one locked their doors here. I'd discovered that for myself as we'd meandered through the town searching for survivors and werewolves.

The house was shadowed and cool, all the shades still drawn. The inhabitants hadn't woken up this morning. They'd been a little dead.

I rubbed my forehead, wishing my mind would stop talking.

"Why this one?" I asked.

"Young couple, near our age and size," he answered shortly. "I'm gonna shower first." He started upstairs.

I opened my mouth to argue, then snapped it shut as a picture in the living room caught my gaze. I forgot all about Jimmy and his selfish, rude, typical behavior, drawn inexorably toward the photograph.

They could have been us. Or the us Jimmy and I might have become if we were different people. Hell—

"If one of us *was* people," I muttered.

In a different world.

The husband was dark-haired, but the wife was blond. From the photo, they'd been married in springtime, perhaps only the last one, perhaps this one. Hard to say.

He was tall and rangy, his dark tux a perfect accent for his coloring. She shone with joy in an ivory sheath. No veil, her hair tumbling in curls around her bare shoulders. They'd had their whole lives ahead of them.

And now they didn't.

I wandered around the room, peering at other pictures. The happy couple skiing. Dancing. The wife and her parents. The husband and his. They'd both had siblings. I thought I recognized a few from the gymnasium. By the time I'd made the circuit, I was shivering again.

The water still ran upstairs. I hunted around for a second bathroom, found one on the first floor that only housed a sink and toilet, then stomped upward, intent on kicking Jimmy out before all the hot water disappeared.

Not that I couldn't just stroll to the next house on the block and use their hot water, but right now I wanted to argue. I needed to. I was mad. I was scared. I wanted to punch someone. Jimmy would let me punch him.

On the second floor, I took inventory—master bedroom, guest room, office—

"Son of a—" I muttered, staring at the pastel green walls with a border of giraffes and elephants. There wasn't any furniture. Yet.

Had she been pregnant, or just hoping?

I didn't know, would probably never know. Right now, I couldn't bear to know.

I crossed the hall to the bathroom, planning to rattle the door, shout for Jimmy to hurry up. But when my hand touched the knob, the door swung open. Steam flowed out. The water still ran, but other than that the room was eerily silent.

The chill came back. I shoved the door wider with my foot, drawing my gun, bracing for a wash of red across the white shower curtain, another body, the end of a life with Jimmy in it.

I tried to breathe. Couldn't. No blood. No body either.

Not a shadow beyond that white curtain. His gun lay on the toilet seat, but where was he?

"Jimmy?"

No response. I inched inside; my own gun lifted, finger on the trigger.

The room was small. I could see all of it in my peripheral vision. I reached for the shower curtain and yanked it back; the rungs thundered across the steel rod. I flinched; Jimmy didn't.

He sat in the tub fully clothed. But that wasn't what worried me the most. He didn't look up. Didn't move. Didn't react. Just sat there as the water pounded on his head, cascading down his face like rain.

Or tears.

"Jimmy?" I tried again, got no response. Again. I was going to have to do something.

I laid my gun next to his and locked the door. If anyone showed up, at least we'd have advance warning. Then I lost my shoes, considered my clothes and decided I didn't have the time before stepping right in with them on, just as he had. Then I pulled the curtain around us, cranked the hot water hotter and sank down next to him in the tub.

I wasn't a nurturer, hadn't even known what nurturing was until Ruthie. She'd been good at touching, cuddling. Only problem was most of the kids she took in weren't good at being touched or cuddled, me included. Eventually I'd settled down, trusted her enough to let her hug me once in a while. But hold me? Rock me? Pet me? I'd never settled down that much.

Because the things I heard, felt, knew were true, touching people was something I tried to avoid. Most often what I saw wasn't something that I wanted to.

As a result, my movements were stiff. We bumped heads, shoulders, I think I smacked him in the nose

when I tried to put my arm around him. But I got Jimmy
to lean on me for a second, before he slid lower and laid
his head in my lap.

I waited for a jolt, some knowledge I didn't want, but
nothing came and I relaxed. Sometimes I got something,
sometimes I didn't, and I'd learned to shield myself more
and more as the years had passed. I couldn't have survived otherwise.

The water pounded on Jimmy's head. He didn't react.
I shifted my shoulders to block it, ran my fingertips over
his face. His eyelids fluttered closed. At least it was
movement.

The tub was large, one of those old-time ceramic deals
with legs. We were still packed pretty tight. I wondered
how long the hot water would last. I wondered what in hell
I was supposed to do with a catatonic DK.

I continued to stroke Jimmy's face; he seemed to be
relaxing against me, not so rigid anymore. I let my fingers drift to his hair, tangled the tips in the lightly curling
strands, kneading his scalp.

Talk to him.

That hadn't been Ruthie's voice. I'm not sure whose
it was, maybe my own. Hopefully. I didn't need any
more voices than I already had telling me what to do.

What should I talk to him about?

Memories. Good ones.

Did we have any? I let my mind drift back.

I thought of the time Ruthie had let us have a dog,
a stray that had wandered up the road and refused to
leave, then reconsidered. Dog stories, or near enough,
were what had gotten us into this mess in the first place.

"Remember when we were invited to that house on
Big Cedar Lake for the day? Half of us had never seen
a lake beyond Michigan, and you certainly don't swim
in that."

Any time before August the big lake was icy, not to mention all the dead fish and floating gypsum.

"So Ruthie stuffed us all in the van and off we went."

The day had been perfect. Eighty-four degrees and not a cloud in the sky. The air had been filled with the laughter of children, the scent of hot dogs on the grill, lemonade, cookies.

"We were fourteen," I continued.

I'd worn a hand-me-down—what wasn't a hand-me-down at Ruthie's?—Green Bay Packers T-shirt over my swimming suit. There was no way I was going to let anyone, especially Sanducci, see my chest. But, oh, how I'd wanted to dive into that smooth clear water.

"Ruthie coaxed me to do it." I leaned against the side of the tub, ignoring the heavy weight of my soaked clothes, concentrating on the memory, the joy of it, and the rhythmic movement of my fingers through Jimmy's hair.

"She put on a swimming suit." My lips curved. "And dived right in."

Ruthie's suit had bagged off her bony behind. Her skinny arms had appeared chickenlike framed by the straps of the tank. But no one had dared laugh. Maybe no one had noticed. To every single one of us, Ruthie was the most beautiful being on this earth, and that had nothing to do with her appearance.

Since Ruthie had done it, I did too. The water, not icy but cool enough to shock at first, had become welcoming, refreshing, revitalizing.

I hadn't been the best swimmer. No lessons. I'd learned because I'd had to or drown. But the water hadn't been deep. We'd played games. Gotten sunburned. Eaten too much.

"You made s'mores."

My gaze flicked to Jimmy's face. His eyes were open and someone was home.

I let my thumb stroke his cheek. "You ate five and got a gut ache."

"It was the best day." Our voices sounded in unison.

I smiled into his face. He reached up and cupped my cheek. For an instant our shared past was right there with us, something that made us stronger, better, saner.

"Jimmy, I—"

He sat up, pulling away from my stroking fingers, from me. "I'm okay."

"You don't seem okay."

"You don't know what I seem."

Standing, he didn't waver; his face had gone hard again.

I tried not to feel rejected and failed. The sweet memory we'd shared soured, crowded out by other memories of unhappier times.

He'd taken me and discarded me. He'd told me he loved me, then fucked someone else. He'd disappeared without a trace and he hadn't come back. Those were the things I needed to remember about Jimmy Sanducci.

He stuck his head under the shower stream, scrubbed the blood from his hair and hands, then stepped out, dripping water all over the floor. Pig.

"Finish up," he ordered without even looking at me. "We're back on the road in fifteen."

The door closed seconds later.

"Asswipe," I muttered.

It didn't help.

Chapter 16

We were back on the road in thirty. I doubted the extra fifteen made much difference.

By the time I'd finished in the shower, Jimmy was downstairs dressed in dark jeans, a black T-shirt, and he'd even managed to find black shoes. I found it a bit creepy that he could fit into the dead man's clothes so well, right down to the footwear.

He'd made eggs, toast, coffee. I slurped mine without comment. What was there to say?

We'd done what we had to. We'd do it again, of that I had no doubt. Jimmy had lost it for a minute, but he'd gotten it back without too much trouble, then he'd pushed me away, both physically and emotionally. Nothing new there.

I'd also chosen jeans, but my shirt was hot pink with tiny green and white flowers; my shoes were also pink and at least half a size too large.

The outfit had been the least of all the evils stored in the closet and drawers. The dead woman had had a thing for pastels, which were definitely not *my* thing. Despite my light eyes, I was too dark everywhere else to pull off pink.

We each left the house with a carry-on bag stuffed with more clothes. When I'd gone searching for our bloody discards, I hadn't found them. When I'd asked where they were, Jimmy had pointed to the still burning school. I took that to mean he'd tossed them into the inferno, which solved the problem nicely. If we wanted this to look like a tragic accident, leaving blood-splattered clothing any-where in the vicinity would be a bad idea.

Taking it along in the car would be a worse one. Can you imagine a deputy finding that on a routine traffic stop? We'd be locked up until the next millennium and any explanations of a werewolf attack would only add to our chances of incarceration. We'd look and sound like lunatics.

Jimmy continued to drive. He still didn't trust me not to make a U-turn while he was sleeping and race as far away from Sawyer as I could get. Being an ass hadn't decreased his intelligence one iota.

The day was half over. We'd lost time by stopping in Hardeyville, but since no one was expecting us, it didn't matter. Besides, I wasn't in any hurry to arrive.

"Shouldn't we be meeting with Ruthie's DKs?" I asked.

"It'll have to wait." Jimmy kept his eyes on the road.

"I really think I should meet them."

"Not yet."

"But—"

"No, Lizzy. You need to be trained. Now. Every day we aren't on the job makes them another day stronger. We can't afford that."

I stared out over the flat Kansas landscape, and I knew that he was right, but that didn't mean I was happy about it.

"So we're going to Sawyer's, and you're going to learn whatever you have to, and fast, or we're going to see a lot more towns like Hardeyville."

Since I never wanted to see another town like Hard-

eyville again, I silently gave in to the inevitable. A visit
with Sawyer. More training. I'd have to be near him, listen to him, touch him.

Around Sawyer there was always an air of barely sup-
pressed violence. He was a wild, unpredictable animal.
I'd never known what he would do. It had taken me
weeks to stop flinching whenever he moved fast. Since I
hadn't seen him, in person, for nearly ten years, I had no
doubt I'd be flinching again soon. I hated it.

"You okay?" Jimmy asked.

"No." I turned my face to the window and took in the
scenery. Wisely, he left me alone.

The rest of the trip was uneventful. Jimmy drove. I
didn't. I slept; he didn't. I expected a visit from Ruthie;
none came. Instead, I dreamed of Hardeyville, and I
feared that we would lose every battle to come, because
I wasn't ready for this, and I wasn't sure I ever could be.

We approached the outskirts of the Navajo Reserva-
tion near dusk. The reservation spread across three states:
Utah, Arizona, and New Mexico, with the largest portion
in Arizona. The area occupied by the Dineh, what the
Navajo call themselves, was larger than ten of the fifty
United States.

The terrain was so different from home. Flat, arid
plains of salmon and copper gave way to mountain
foothills dotted with towering Ponderosa Pines. Canyons
surrounded by high, spiked, sandy shaded rock existed
not far from red mesas immortalized in at least a dozen
John Wayne movies.

Sawyer lived at the very edge of the reservation
near Mount Taylor, one of the four sacred mountains
that marked the boundaries of Navajo land, known as
the Dinetah, or the Glittering World.

As we got closer to our destination, my shoulders

tightened. My neck ached. I found myself leaning forward, fighting the opposing pull of the seat belt as I strained to see the house and outbuildings.

I was so focused on what was coming that I almost missed what was already there. But a dark flash to the right drew my reluctant attention.

A wolf loped at our side. Hard to say if it was real or—

Well, it was real, as in *there*. But was it an actual wolf, or was it another were?

I opened my mouth to tell Jimmy, then shut it again. His policy was to shoot any wolf that he saw, and it wasn't a bad policy if a wolf was found near humans. But this one wasn't. The animal was running along minding its own business.

And it was so beautiful. Sleek and black. Wild and free. I'd always liked wolves, or at least the idea of them. Until yesterday.

The beast wasn't huge, as most of those in Hardeyville had been, but it could be a woman, a small man, hell, it could even be a teenager. What did I know? But if it was a Nephilim, we needed to kill it before it killed someone else. I gave in to the inevitable.

"Jimmy," I murmured.

His gaze went immediately past me, narrowed, and he jerked the Hummer to the right as if he meant to run the wolf over. Between one blink and the next, the animal was gone.

Jimmy wrestled the Hummer back on the road as I pressed my nose to the glass and squinted.

"Where did it go?"

He didn't answer, just continued to stare at the road, fingers tight on the steering wheel, jaw working as he ground his teeth loud enough to make me wince. He seemed angry, not scared, and I wasn't sure why.

"It disappeared," I murmured. "That wasn't a were-wolf."

Or at least not the kind we'd seen in Hardeyville.

The more I thought about it the more certain I became that this wolf had not been an actual wolf. I didn't know much about them, but I doubted they could keep pace with a car on the highway. We had to be going seventy. And that vanishing act. Too damn strange.

The car lurched to the right again, and my gaze flicked to the side of the road, expecting to see the black beast, if not running, then attacking. But outside the window, the empty desert loomed.

I had bigger problems than a speedy, disappearing wolf. I had Sawyer. His place materialized out of the desert like a mirage.

Darkness had fallen in the last few minutes as it always did here—fast and hard. The colors at dusk were some of the most beautiful in the world—vivid fuchsia, muted gold, and hunter's orange swirling through the brilliant blue of an endless ocean. In the evening they faded like a watercolor painting brushed by a cool black rain.

The Hummer's headlights washed over the homestead. Someone waited in the yard. I didn't have to get any closer to know who that someone was.

The house—a small ranch with two bedrooms, a kitchen, bath, and living area—sat right next to the traditional Navajo hogan, a round dwelling made of logs and dirt.

Fashioned after the sky, which was in turn considered the hogan of the earth, the building contained no windows and only one door, facing east toward the sun, so the inhabitant could greet each new day.

Behind it, dug into a short rise, was a smaller hogan, which was used as a sweat lodge. Between the two, a ramada, or open porch, had been built. This was used in the summer months for both eating and sleeping.

Jimmy stopped the car and I got out, moving jerkily as if I were in a trance. Maybe I was. What I wanted to do was run, hide, burrow in somewhere and be forgotten, but the first sight of Sawyer pulled me like a magnet. I couldn't stay away.

I'd never understood what he was. Psychic? Perhaps. Magic? Probably. He was a mystic, a medicine man, but even that didn't explain all the things he'd done, the power that rolled off him like the heat that wavered above the pavement on a scalding summer day.

"Phoenix," he murmured, his voice deep, the cadence slow and even, as if he had all the time in the world to do anything that he wanted.

He'd always called me by my last name. I'd figured that was to keep a certain distance between us. Understandable, all things considered. However, the way he said it always sounded as if he were whispering secret nothings in front of the world.

Behind me I heard Jimmy scrambling out of the car. I didn't spare him a glance. He'd brought me here. He'd soon learn why I hadn't wanted to come.

In a normal world, it would be considered beyond inappropriate to send a fifteen-year-old girl to stay in an isolated cabin with a single man. In a normal world it would probably be grounds for jail time. But, as already established, mine was not a normal world.

Though I'd seen things in his eyes then that had frightened me, things I didn't understand, things I wasn't old enough, wise enough, foolish enough to put a name to, Sawyer had never once touched me with anything other than respect. Maybe he'd been afraid of Ruthie.

But Ruthie was gone.

I continued forward. Sawyer waited. The headlights were still on, the car still running. Even without the light I'd have been able to describe the man who'd walked often enough through my dreams.

He wasn't much taller than me—perhaps five ten—but he'd seemed huge, imposing from his aura alone. His hair was long, though he always tied it back with whatever he found handy—string, ribbon, the dried intestines of his victims. I'm exaggerating. He rarely used anything as mundane as string.

His face wasn't handsome. The angles were too sharp for that. But his smooth bronzed skin and his cover-model cheekbones, which only emphasized the ridiculously long and thick eyelashes that surrounded his strangely light gray eyes, were mesmerizing. Those eyes softened the face if you didn't stare into them too long and realize that behind their gaze was one of the scariest men alive.

He wore nothing but a breechclout, his typical attire. I'd always wanted to ask him why he walked around dressed like an escapee from a historical romance novel, but I'd never had the courage. Instead I'd done a little research and discovered that what he wore was common to the Navajo.

About three centuries ago.

Most breechclouts were worn with leggings and a loose shirt. Sawyer's wasn't. I could see every ripple and curve of his incredible body. As a teen I'd known he was hot; I just hadn't known then what to do with it.

I'd come here when I was fifteen. I was now twenty-five. Ten years added to however the hell old he'd been then, yet he hadn't aged at all. There wasn't a line on his face; there'd never been so much as a hitch in his step no matter how long we'd trained, no matter how hard we'd worked.

I stopped over an arm's length away, feeling the pull

to go nearer, gritting my teeth against it. I didn't want him to touch me. I never had.

This close I could see his tattoos. They wound up his arms, down his back, across his chest. Nearly every inch of skin I could see and most likely every inch I could not had been etched with the likeness of an animal.

My gaze shifted to his right bicep where there'd once been a howling black wolf. There still was—along with a mountain lion across his chest; a tarantula crept down his forearm, a hawk took flight from the small of his back. There were others too, all as predatory as the man whose skin they marked.

Frowning, I lifted my gaze from the wolf tattoo to Sawyer's face. He was watching me.

Jimmy came up behind me, and I turned. I'm not sure what I meant to ask, but as I moved, Sawyer suddenly reached out, his long, strong fingers wrapping around my elbow. I gasped, both at the scalding heat of his skin and at the touch itself. I'd made certain I wasn't close enough for him to grab. So how had he?

The wind came up from nowhere, its whisper a single word. *"Skinwalker."*

Yanking my arm from Sawyer's took no small amount of effort, but I did it. Unfortunately, I stumbled into Jimmy, got my too big shoes tangled with his, and fell hard on my ass.

"Dammit," I muttered. "Isn't *anyone* human any-more?"

Chapter 17

Jimmy growled, an unearthly sound that made the skin on the back of my neck and all the way down my arms prickle, as he put himself between Sawyer and me. Sawyer just smiled a smile that made the gooseflesh intensify until I was shivering with it.

"I'm okay. Stop. Shit." I struggled to my feet, trying to shove myself between the two of them, who were circling and snarling like wild dogs. Jimmy shoved me back.

"Hey!" My hands balled into fists. He didn't even look at me.

"Don't touch her," Jimmy said.

Sawyer's eyes flattened along with his mouth. "I'll do whatever I have to. As she will."

Jimmy took a swing. Sawyer ducked it easily. I threw up my hands and got out of the way. I'd lived among men like this all my life.

Well, maybe not men exactly like this, since I'd lived among actual *men,* but the principle was similar. Street kids. System boys. Cops. Tough guys were all the same. Once they decided to beat the shit out of one another, you might as well grab a cup of coffee and watch because you weren't going to stop them.

The battle was like none I'd ever seen—probably

because it was a battle and not just a fight. Sawyer and Jimmy had powers beyond the realm of mere mortals. As Jimmy had said, superior speed and strength were his. Sawyer's speed and strength—though lesser than Jimmy's—weren't too shabby either.

When one man landed a blow, the other flew several feet. They flitted around the yard, here, there, onto the roof of the house and then tumbling off, landing hard, getting up and slamming at each other again.

"This isn't getting anywhere," I shouted.

Jimmy glanced my way. Blood trickled from a cut in his lip, though not as freely as it would have on a human.

Sawyer took advantage of his distraction and his fist shot out, headed for Jimmy's chin, but Jimmy saw it coming and dropped to the ground, rolling quickly out of Sawyer's reach.

"I'm not the kid I once was," Jimmy said. "You can't take me anymore, old man. Those days are done."

Old man?

Sawyer appeared to be thirty, but then he always had. Good genes? Or perhaps no genes? I had no idea what constituted a skinwalker. Was he Nephilim, breed, or something else entirely? Ruthie's whisper had been vague.

Sawyer's face shimmered. I saw wolf-man-wolf, as if a battle were being raged beneath the skin, behind those freakishly light eyes. Then he was man again, and he stayed that way. For now.

He turned away, dismissing Jimmy like a servant. Jimmy rolled onto his feet and sprang. Right before he would have plowed into Sawyer's back, the other man ducked and Jimmy sailed over gracefully, landing in front of me as if he'd just completed a violent game of leapfrog.

"That's enough," I said softly, firmly.

Jimmy glanced over his shoulder. I didn't think he was going to listen, but he slowly lowered his head, breathing in a measured pace—in through the nose, out through the mouth, calming himself.

Sawyer walked toward me, and I had to force myself not to back up as he came near.

"That was you on the road," I said. "The wolf."

He lifted his brows but didn't answer.

I turned to Jimmy. "Right?"

He straightened; dust sprinkled off his clothes, swirling through the garish beams of the Hummer's headlights. "Why do you think I tried to hit him?"

I contemplated Sawyer, who'd stopped several feet away from us and stood watching with an eerie stillness that had always given me the willies.

"You brought me here to be trained," I continued, "so why would you try and kill him before that happened?"

"He wouldn't have died. He's a damn skinwalker."

"You two obviously know each other a lot better than I thought."

"He trains some of us." Jimmy's lip curled. "For a price."

"You think I should do it for free?" Sawyer asked.

"You're a breed, just like me."

"No." Sawyer walked toward his house. "I'm not anything like you."

He disappeared inside.

Jimmy joined me and together we contemplated the open doorway.

"What is he?" I asked.

"You know."

"*Skinwalker* doesn't mean jack to me. You say he's a breed. He says he isn't."

"He is." Jimmy tilted his head. "Maybe."

I smacked myself in the forehead. "Maybe?"

"He's not Nephilim."

"Because?"

"They're evil."

"He's not exactly what I'd call a good guy."

"No." Jimmy sighed. "He's different. He's right about that. But he is like me. Kind of."

"Dammit, Jimmy, you're giving me a headache." I rubbed my forehead where I'd just smacked it. Maybe I was giving myself one. "Why don't you start by telling me just what in hell *skinwalker* means?"

Instead of answering, Jimmy went to the Hummer. I glanced at the open door, then at Jimmy. It wasn't much of a choice; I followed. If he thought he was jumping in the car and taking off without me, he'd find out differently when I landed on the hood.

But all he did was reach in and switch off the engine, withdraw the keys and shove them into the pocket of his borrowed jeans.

Seconds later the headlights went off with a tinny *thunk* and shadows descended over us both. Sawyer's house remained dark and silent. Was he even inside?

"A skinwalker is a Navajo—" He stopped abruptly and I moved closer, trying to see the expression on his face. The moon had just sprung over the horizon, spreading a milky glow across the earth. I wasn't certain, but I thought he looked confused.

"A Navajo what?" I prompted.

"Witch."

"Sawyer's a witch." I had a sudden flash of him buzzing by on his broomstick, and I choked on a laugh. "Right."

Jimmy cast me a disgusted glance. "He's a medicine man. That you knew. You had to."

"Yes." I managed to control my mirth. Now wasn't the time. I wasn't sure there would ever be a time for laughter again.

"In Navajo tradition certain medicine men are *yee naaldlooshii,* those who walk about with it."

"Walk about with what?"

"The skin of an animal."

I considered his words, which had two meanings. Those who walked about in the skin of an animal—as in wearing one atop their own. Many Native American tribes had costumes made from animals, headdresses that were the actual heads of beasts.

The other option, and the one I believed we were talking about, was for human skin to transform into the skin of an animal.

"Shape-shifter." I shrugged. "Obviously, after what we saw in Hardeyville, that doesn't make him all that special."

Jimmy's smile was rueful. "As much as I hate to admit it, he is. Skinwalkers transform through magic. They wear a robe fashioned with the likeness of their spirit animal. They perform a ceremony beneath the moon and—" He spread his hands.

"They become the animals they want to be."

"No."

"But you just said—"

"I said *animal.* Singular. One per person and one only. Their totem or spirit animal."

"But not Sawyer."

"His power comes from within. The magic is in his blood, from his Nephilim mother. His skin is his robe."

I thought of all the animals tattooed on Sawyer's flesh. Jimmy was saying Sawyer could become every one of them. That actually explained quite a bit.

When I'd stayed here that summer, there'd been nights

I came awake to the calls of animals that could not walk these hills. Usually, when I went to my window, nothing was there.

Usually.

I'd ended up doubting my sanity more often than not. At fifteen, that isn't a good doubt to have.

Jimmy lowered his voice, as if he feared the wind could eavesdrop and carry his words to far-off, listening ears. "They say his mother was a Dreadful One and his father a medicine man who followed the Blessing Way and helped his people."

"I don't understand."

"The Dreadful Ones are monsters." He spread his hands. "I'm not exactly sure what kind."

And I doubt anyone had ever had the balls to ask Sawyer. I certainly didn't.

"The Blessing Way is the basis of the Navajo religion. Chants and songs that keep life on an even keel."

"So Sawyer's father was a holy man?"

"Yes. Which no doubt made his corruption all the more fun for her. Medicine men who dabble in black magic are considered witches, brujas. They're renegades, and they're hunted down by the Navajo and executed."

"Still?"

"There are always stories."

"And him?" I jerked my head toward the house.

"He's too powerful to kill. Many have tried, none have succeeded."

"Is that why he lives way out here?" I asked.

Jimmy shrugged. "Maybe. He's an outcast from his people. Always has been."

"So Sawyer's father was a medicine man, one of the good guys, yet he slept with a Nephilim?"

"He didn't mean to. She took the shape of his wife. Night after night she seduced him until she became pregnant and then—" He glanced at the house again, then back. "She killed him."

I winced. "Black widow much?"

"I can see why he is how he is. He probably can't help himself. The Navajo are matriarchal. Inheritance passed through the mother's side. They believe, and I'm inclined to agree, that the mother's blood is stronger, but—"

"But what?" I asked when he remained silent.

"Yes," said Sawyer. "But what?"

I nearly jumped out of *my* skin. Jimmy and I both spun toward the sound. I don't know if I expected to see Sawyer or not. One part of me thought that maybe he could hear us from afar with his super-duper batlike hearing; or perhaps he was actually a bat, swooping down low and eavesdropping, then speaking in his human voice. Though I hadn't observed a bat tattooed anywhere the eye could see, that didn't mean he couldn't have one engraved on his ass.

But there was nothing supernatural about his presence. Except that he stood right behind us, and neither one of us had seen or heard him approach.

"How do you do that?"

I reached out to shove him back. He was too close. Then I remembered how his skin had been so hot, scalding almost, downright unnerving to touch, and I didn't want to touch him again.

I let my hand fall to my side, rubbing it surreptitiously on my jeans, my palm itching, stinging despite never going near him at all.

"Do what?" he asked mildly.

When I'd been here the last time, the first time, he'd often appeared where I didn't expect him, scared the hell out of me every time. Then I'd put it down to his being silent as a stalking tiger.

My gaze went to the tiger carved on his thigh. Hell. Maybe he had been.

"Skinwalkers can move faster than the eye can track," Jimmy answered when Sawyer did not. "In their animal forms they appear and disappear like magic when it's merely speed."

I remembered seeing the wolf on the road, then in a blink it had been gone.

"Wouldn't you consider that kind of speed a certain type of magic?" Sawyer murmured.

Chapter 18

Into the silence that followed Sawyer's question, the trill of my cell phone sounded horrifically loud. I jumped, my heart jerking so hard my chest ached, then fumbled the thing from my pocket, nearly dropping it before I managed to check the caller ID.

Murphy's. I had to answer.

"Did you get the autopsy report?" I asked.

"Well, hello to you too."

"Sorry. Hello. Did you?"

"Where in hell are you, Liz?" Megan lowered her voice to a near whisper. "The cops are flipping out."

"I'm not a suspect. They didn't tell me I couldn't leave town."

"Why would you? Now of all times."

"I can't tell you that, Meg."

"Fine," she said, then paused a few beats as if she didn't want to tell me what she'd heard. Or maybe she just didn't know how.

I turned away from Sawyer and Jimmy. I couldn't concentrate with them in sight. If they wanted to kill each other while I dealt with my phone call, they could go right ahead.

"Let me make this easier for you," I said. "They found traces of animal fur."

"How did you—" She stopped. Megan understood better than most that I knew things I should not, and there was no explaining just how.

"The homicide twins told me the cause of death was a knife wound," I continued.

"Not."

My shoulders relaxed. I hadn't really believed that Jimmy might have been responsible, but a different cause of death certainly helped his case with the cops.

"Wounds, yes," Meg continued. "Torn, jagged, vicious, but not from a knife."

I knew what they'd been from—tooth and claw—but I waited for her to say so.

"The wounds were consistent with an animal attack, but the actual cause of death was blood loss."

I winced. "Too many wounds."

Her hesitation had my neck prickling. "Meg?"

"The ME said the blood loss wasn't consistent with the number and depth of the wounds. She thought they—"

The unpleasant sensation had left my neck, traveling all over my body. "She thought they what?"

"Drank her blood."

I dropped the cell phone.

Someone handed it to me. I stared at the thing and wasn't sure what to do with it.

"Lizzy?" My eyes met Jimmy's. "Finish this."

Slowly I reached out, took the phone, and turned away again. "What does that mean?"

"You tell me. The ME believes Ruthie was attacked by animals, yet the police report says there was nothing but ashes and you at the site."

"I didn't do it."

Her voice gentled. "I never thought you did, even before the revelation of the bizarre forensic evidence. But you know something."

"I can't—"

She sighed. "Tell me. Right. Why did I even ask?"

"Sorry."

"When will you be back?"

"I'm not sure." I still wasn't sure I'd *be* back, and I was saddened. Ruthie was gone, but Meg was there. She was the only one I had left now. I faced the two men.

Except for them.

"Take as long as you need, Liz. Your job will be waiting for you."

"Thanks. For everything."

Megan hesitated, as if she might say good-bye, but then she didn't. "You need to stop blaming yourself."

She'd told me this before. I still wasn't able to follow her advice.

"Max trusted you."

"One time too many."

"He told me everything, Liz. About your hunches. About how you could touch stuff and know where people were. You saved lives over and over. You saved him."

"Not enough."

"When is it ever enough? I don't blame you. He wouldn't blame you. *You* need to stop blaming yourself. You have a gift and you should be using it."

"I am," I whispered.

"Good. You've been drifting since Max died. You lost your purpose and that's no way to live."

Silence fell between us. I wasn't sure what to say. I'd known that Megan didn't blame me for Max's death. I'd thought she was delusional. I'd hung around waiting for her to lash out, to give me the beating—mental, physical, didn't matter—that I deserved, but she never had.

"I'll be in touch," I said, and disconnected.

I did feel, for the first time in a long time, that I was moving forward instead of standing still. Though I'd been repeatedly tested and terrified, I'd also been exhilarated. I felt alive again, thanks to the constant threat of violent and bloody death.

"How much of that did you get?" I asked.

"All of it," Jimmy said. At my lifted brows, he glanced at Sawyer, then shrugged. "We can both hear pretty well."

"Swell."

Jimmy cast Sawyer a glare. "What do you know about Ruthie's death?" he demanded.

"Me?" Sawyer put his hand to his bare chest with an exaggerated show of surprise. "I was here."

"So you say, but we all know you lie. You can move faster than light. Who's to say you weren't there, and a few hours later right here again. You wouldn't even need a damn plane."

I frowned. "You can transform into animals."

Slowly Sawyer lowered his hand, trailing his fingers along his sternum, his rib cage, his belly. The stark lines of the tattoos seemed to undulate in the half-light from the windows. For an instant it seemed that the animals traced into his skin were dancing.

I jerked my gaze to his. I could see nothing in their gray depths but myself. I felt a strange tug, one I'd never felt before. Not with him, not with anyone.

"You know what I am and what I can do," he said.

"There were all kinds of animals at Ruthie's."

His lips curved. "You think one of them was me?"

I didn't know what I thought anymore. Who could I trust? Who should I kill?

"Touch him."

I started at the voice so near to my ear. Jimmy's voice.

I pulled my gaze from Sawyer's with difficulty. "Are you crazy?"

"You had a gift even before Ruthie gave you hers. You could see things. What will you see if you touch him?"

I might not see anything. Then again—

I returned my attention to Sawyer, who smirked.

Leaning over, Jimmy whispered, "I'm not sure why. Sawyer could hear every damn thing that we said. Touch him and see where he was. Isn't that what you do? Find people?"

Our eyes met and I remembered. Touching him, kissing him, loving him, and seeing that he'd been touching and kissing and loving someone else.

I stepped back. "I don't want to."

Jimmy cursed and slapped something cool and hard and heavy into my hand.

His gun.

"Do it for her," he ground out through his teeth. "If he was there, shoot him in the head."

"Will that kill him?"

"I have no idea," Jimmy said. "But it'll certainly slow him down."

Then he stalked into the house, leaving the door open behind him. I stared at the gun for several seconds.

"Are you going to touch me, Phoenix?"

Sawyer's whisper caressed my skin like the wind, but there was no wind, there was only him and me and the gun. I stared at the doorway through which Jimmy had passed and felt betrayed, lost, alone.

What else was new?

I turned and Sawyer was so close, I stumbled back. "Don't *do* that!"

"What have I done?" He followed, one step, two. "Gotten close enough to touch. Isn't that what you wanted?"

I wanted nothing less, but when had what I wanted ever been what I could have?

Desperate to put off the inevitable, I asked, "Wh-why would the beasts drink her blood?"

His head tilted, an odd birdlike movement. My eyes flicked to the eagle emblazoned on his neck.

"Power." He leaned in until his cheek nearly brushed my hair, inhaling deeply. "Seers reek of it."

I gritted my teeth, tightened my grip on the gun, and tried to lift my free hand, but I couldn't make it move.

"How do you want to touch me?"

His voice was the night swirling all around me, a voice I'd heard in my dreams far too often and too well. That voice was both familiar and frightening.

Years had passed. Sawyer hadn't aged, but I had. That seemed to have changed everything.

Slowly I leaned back so that I could meet his gaze, and then I couldn't look away. In his eyes swirled the images of all the animals that graced his body.

"Touch me," he ordered. "Any way, anywhere. I won't mind."

I shivered, but I touched him. I saw centuries, aeons, all rushing toward me, then past me. My hair blew back; the wind felt so cool.

He'd been everywhere, in every form. He'd lived as an animal; mated as one too. He'd loved; he'd lost. He'd hated and killed. He was like all of us and yet like none of us.

The gun fell to the ground with a thump as I lifted my hand to place my right palm against his chest in tandem with my left. I wanted to trace every tattoo, see where every part of him had been and what it had done.

My fingers smoothed flesh that was already smooth. I couldn't feel any indentation where the tattoos began and

he left off. Shouldn't I? I had no idea. I'd never touched a
tattoo before. However, these seemed as if they were a
part of him, as if he'd been born with them rather than
having them added one by one.

I had a sudden and inexplicable urge to trace every
line, every curve and color with my tongue. To taste
him, to drink in his scent as he had drunk in mine. There
was power here, more than I'd ever imagined. He could
do many things, but had he done what I feared? Had he
killed Ruthie?

I lifted my gaze. His face was so close our noses
brushed. The essence of the beasts no longer lurked in his
eyes. Now I saw only Sawyer. I wasn't sure if that was
better or worse.

I wasn't a mind reader. I couldn't go in and wallow
around in a brain, then pick and choose the memories
and thoughts I wished to see. When I touched someone,
I saw things—where they'd been, what they'd done—
but not everything.

Situations that packed strong emotions—love, hate,
joy, terror—were what came through. Which is how I became so good at finding the missing. People most often
disappeared after emotional scenes—fights with family,
kidnappings, assault, murder.

Because of what this man had taught me, I'd learned to
control the seeing or the not seeing—for the most part.
Without that switch, I might brush against someone on
the street and know things I didn't want to. With Sawyer,
what I wanted to know, he wouldn't let me see.

"You're jamming me," I said.

"Of course."

"You have something to hide?"

"Doesn't everyone?"

"Let me in."

His hands were suddenly on my forearms, holding me to him, keeping me from running, something I suddenly, make that always, wanted to do. "No," he murmured.

"Then let me go."

His lips skimmed my forehead, so hot when I was so cold. "Never."

Our hips bumped, and I felt something I'd felt a dozen times before, but never from him. I wrenched myself free and turned around.

Jimmy stood in the doorway.

Chapter 19

"What did you see?" Jimmy asked.

Fury flowed through me. How long had he been standing there? Would he have continued to watch if I'd given in to the strange temptation to touch Sawyer in ways I still wanted to touch Jimmy?

Jimmy's eyes, his face, gave away nothing. He just leaned against the door and contemplated first me, then Sawyer, waiting for an answer.

"Bite me," I muttered, then wished I hadn't. Both of these men—and I used the term loosely—might be capable of just that, in ways I didn't want to imagine.

"Was he there?" Jimmy pressed. "Did he kill Ruthie?"

"I don't know," I admitted. "He's—"

I wasn't sure how to explain what I'd felt in Sawyer's mind. He'd let me see so many things, but he'd also closed himself off as no one else I'd ever touched had been able to do.

"He's what?" Jimmy asked.

"He can block me."

Jimmy scowled. "Then he's hiding something."

"Maybe I just don't want my mind picked like an apple tree," Sawyer said reasonably.

"That's not what she does."

"Has she touched you and seen what you've been up to, Sanducci?"

I winced; Sawyer noticed and smirked. "I wondered what had happened to make you leave, little boy. Should have known it was your dick that got you into trouble."

Jimmy turned and walked away. He was good at that.

"Phoenix," Sawyer said softly.

Though I didn't want to, I faced him. The sight of him brought back the feel of his skin, the rolling sweep of his mind, and the ancient aeons of his life.

"How old are you?"

"I've lost count."

No wonder he was impossible to kill. The longer a person lived, the wiser they became, and wisdom was power. In Sawyer's case that was a literal interpretation.

"Were you there?" I asked, though I have no idea why. He wouldn't tell the truth. I wasn't sure he knew how. "At Ruthie's?"

"No."

Yep. Definite waste of time. I didn't believe him.

But I also didn't believe he'd come to Milwaukee, joined up with a group of shape-shifters, and attacked Ruthie. If he'd wanted her dead, he could have done it on his own, in ways much less obvious and a whole lot less bloody.

"Even if I was there"—his gaze shifted past me to the house where Jimmy had retreated—"I wasn't alone."

"I know he was there. He tried to save her."

"So he says." Sawyer's lips curved. "Did you know, Phoenix, that certain vampires have the ability to control animals? They can make them do anything that they wish."

"He isn't a vampire."

"I suppose he told you that too."

I blinked. I only had Jimmy's word that he wasn't a

bloodsucking fiend. Crap. I'd only had his word that he loved me, and look how that had turned out.

I shook my head. I couldn't condemn him based on his shitty relationship skills, no matter how much I might want to. If Sawyer believed Jimmy'd had anything to do with Ruthie's death, he'd kill him. Jimmy had the same plan, only in reverse, and it would be ugly—long, drawn-out, painful, and bloody.

Of course, if Jimmy *had* killed her, I'd be right there for the kill-Jimmy party. It wouldn't matter if I loved him or not, right was right and justice was inevitable.

"He's descended from a vampire," Sawyer said. "He's drawn to evil, fascinated by it. He can't help himself."

"He kills them." I hesitated. I wasn't sure of anything anymore. "Doesn't he?"

"So far." He lifted his shoulder—the one that sported a shark—in a lithe, graceful movement that had the dark skin rippling like water. "That fascination, that connection, is what makes him so very good at what he does. But you can never trust a breed, Phoenix. They're only one step away from the darkness. Anything could push them over."

"What about you?"

His mouth curved. "Oh, you can't trust me either. You know better."

I did, but that hadn't been what I was asking, and he knew it.

How close was Sawyer to the darkness? For that matter, how close was he to the light?

Suddenly he sobered, his gaze turning toward the desert. "Seers are dying." I stiffened, and he glanced back, eyes stark. "DKs too. Not a lot. Or at least not yet. But enough to be worrisome."

"How? I thought only the DKs knew the identity of their seer."

"Exactly."

"Isn't there someone in the—" I suddenly realized I had no idea what this group of seers and demon killers was named. "Whatever the hell you call yourselves."

"The federation." Sawyer spread his hands. "It's a word. We needed one."

"Isn't there someone who knows all the identities?"

"Ruthie."

She wouldn't have told; I was certain of that.

"Someone else?" I insisted. "An office administrator? The accountant?"

Sawyer didn't dignify that with an answer.

"This shouldn't be happening," I murmured.

"But it is."

His gaze remained on me, as if he were waiting for me to ask something, do something. I wanted to run, but I wouldn't, couldn't. I was stuck with Ruthie's power; I had no choice but to learn how to use it, and this man was the only one who could help me.

"Ruthie was the leader of the light," I said. "What does that mean? What did she do?"

"Ruthie never really led, per se." Sawyer snapped his fingers and a match appeared. He lit the hand-rolled cigarette he'd produced out of nowhere as well. My gaze swept down his nearly bare body.

Literally.

He took a deep drag, blew the smoke through his nose. The cloud surrounded the dancing flame and as it died, darkness descended once again.

"How did you do that?"

"How do you think?

There'd been other times, other places, when things had appeared from nowhere. I'd rationalized them all away, but those days were done. Sawyer was a shape-shifting witch; he could probably do anything.

"The seers get their orders from . . ." The glowing scarlet tip of Sawyer's cigarette slashed back and forth with the movement of his hand. "God. Ghosts. Unfallen angels. Who knows? Each runs his or her own little universe. There's no need for interaction. It's not like we have a convention or anything."

"No," I agreed. "But you could probably use a secret handshake."

His dark gaze flicked to mine. I shrugged. Sometimes I just couldn't help myself.

I stared into the suddenly chilly evening common to the desert. Keeping the identities of the seers confidential was a good idea. The less people who knew about them, the less chance an un-people might kill them. But that plan seemed to have gone out the window.

The federation's security had been breached, and we didn't know by whom or how. But I did know who was going to be responsible for finding out.

"The seer's identity is known to no one but his or her DKs?"

"Yes. And the DKs are only known to their particular seer and other DKs they might have worked with."

I stared at the ground, trying to work out what might have happened, but I was tired and the problem was complicated.

"We won't solve this tonight," Sawyer murmured. "We'll be lucky to solve it at all."

My head came up. Sawyer was gone. The glow of his cigarette had disappeared too, though I still smelled it.

His voice was disembodied, swirling all around me. "We'll get started tomorrow."

"I don't want to start anything," I muttered.

"Every hour, every day we delay could mean another death. The more seers and DKs we lose, the more innocents will die."

I closed my eyes, thinking of Hardeyville.

"Go to bed, Phoenix."

I opened my eyes. My gaze went first to the hogan, then to the house. I didn't really want to sleep in either one.

I could sleep in the car, the sweat lodge, the ramada. Uncomfortable, true, but they all had a big advantage.

There was only room enough for me.

In the end, I slept in the house. I'd had to use the bathroom, and there was no way I was turning up my nose at indoor plumbing. Who knew what lurked in the darkness just out of sight. Even if it were only the commonplace beasties and bugs, I didn't want to meet them in the desert with my pants down.

The last time I was here I'd learned quickly that when night fell I needed to stay in my room or risk seeing things I couldn't explain.

Like Sawyer coming in from the desert, naked and covered in blood, his eyes wild, unfocused, inhuman. That made a lot more sense now than it had then.

We'd never spoken of it, of course. His expression had made me believe that if I did, he'd have killed me. I still believed it.

Once inside, I found no trace of Jimmy beyond the closed door of the first bedroom. I assumed he was asleep or at least pretending to be, but I didn't check. Right now any contact with Jimmy would lead to an argument— when didn't it?—and an argument could lead to—

My mind filled with the images of all that might transpire in a bedroom with Jimmy Sanducci. But doing those things in Sawyer's bed, in Sawyer's house, with Sawyer right next door . . .

Wasn't going to happen.

I fell asleep easily. That should have been my first

clue. It usually took me a good half hour, sometimes more, to drift off. But that night my head was so full of information, problems, men, I shouldn't have slept at all. The instant I closed my eyes, I found myself in Ruthie's world.

The house was full again. Though the sounds of children at play should have lifted my spirits, the knowledge that they were here because they were dead put a damper on things.

I skirted the front yard and headed for the back. The first kid I saw wore a Little League cap. Why did it look both familiar and different?

"Because it's clean," I murmured. The last time I'd seen that hat it had been black with blood.

Now the insignia could be read as a huge red *C* on a bright blue background. THE CUBS. Another team that annoyed the hell out of me.

I stood outside the gate and watched the children play. I recognized something about each and every one of them. It didn't take long to understand that these children had once lived in Hardeyville.

Ruthie's sadness the last time I'd dreamed of her made sense. She'd known they were coming. She'd known I would be too late to save them.

Guilt washed over me once more, but there was nothing I could do except try my best to make certain the same thing didn't happen again.

The distant cry of a baby had me glancing at the house. Ruthie came through the back door with a squirming bundle. I didn't remember a baby in that field house—thank God. That might have sent me into gibber-jabberville along with Jimmy.

I tilted my head at the thought. Maybe Jimmy had seen the baby. Or—

I had a sudden flash of a pastel green room with giraffes and elephants cavorting across the brand-new wallpaper. Ah, hell.

Ruthie bent and placed the bundle in a carriage, murmuring softly. The child quieted.

"You gonna come in?" she asked without turning around. "Or you gonna keep standin' out there starin' like a fool?"

I came in.

Several of the children stopped what they were doing. A few of them waved. The little boy in the Cubs hat kicked me in the shin. I guess I deserved it.

"David!" Ruthie said sharply. "It wasn't her fault."

He scrunched up his face, mutiny on the way, but when Ruthie started across the grass in our direction he caved, running off to join a game of tag already in progress.

"Why?" I asked when she reached me. "Why send me there when it was already too late to help?"

"Some things are meant to be. No matter what we do, we can't change them."

"How could *that* be meant? What kind of God does that?"

Ruthie smacked me in the mouth. I guess I had it coming too.

"You won't stand on sacred ground and blaspheme, Lizbeth. You won't blaspheme at all."

"Yes, ma'am." She shot me a glare. "I mean, no, ma'am."

"Everyone has their time. There's nothing that can be done if God is calling them home."

I *did* believe that. You couldn't be a cop for very long and not. Stray bullets missing one woman just because she'd ducked to pick up her child. Not her time. Another equally stray round killing a second woman for exactly the same reason. Must have been her time.

I'd seen a hundred examples just like that, both on

the job and off it. Terminal cancer disappearing without a trace. Perfectly healthy thirty-year-olds dropping dead on the street. Was the universe that random? I'd had to say no, even before I'd seen this place.

"How do you know it was their time?" I asked. "How do you know that it wasn't my fault, that I wasn't good enough?"

"They were dead before I showed you the location. They were already dead when it was shown to me. How could you have done anything more than what you did?"

Some of my sadness eased, though not all. I couldn't look at this playground full of children gone to heaven too soon and not feel guilty for every birthday I'd ever had.

"You did what you were supposed to do," Ruthie continued. "You killed the Nephilim in Hardeyville. You saved the next town on their list, the next person who might have innocently crossed their path."

There was that.

"Jimmy had—" I paused, uncertain if I should tell her about the momentary meltdown. What happened to DKs who lost their edge? Were they sent into a town very much like Hardeyville without any silver bullets?

"I know," Ruthie murmured.

Of course she did.

"He seems all right now." Except for his annoying tendency to poke Sawyer with the proverbial stick.

"He is."

"Does he do that a lot?"

"Never."

"Never?" I frowned. "Well, I guess it was pretty bad. All those kids. The—" I glanced at the carriage.

Ruthie's salt-and-pepper eyebrows lifted toward her salt-and-pepper hair. "You think what he saw in Hardeyville sent Jimmy over?" She made a tsking sound.

"Lizbeth, he's seen worse than that a hundred and one times before."

"Worse?" I echoed. I did not *ever* want to see worse.

"Jimmy's been doing this since he was eighteen, but he's been doing it alone."

"Then you'd think—" I stopped. You'd think it would have been easier for him with a partner, but then again—

"He's never had to see the carnage through your eyes, never had to live with the possibility of losing you to one of them."

"He lost me a long time ago." Or maybe *lost* wasn't the right word. He'd thrown me away. "Why would he care?"

"You don't think it would kill him to watch you die? Wouldn't it kill you to watch him?"

Considering I'd imagined his painful and torturous death many times, I decided not to answer that. In truth, the idea of Jimmy dying before my eyes did make me a little uneasy.

"Springboard tried to shoot me," I pointed out. "Jimmy didn't start gibbering then."

"That was unexpected. He only had time to react, as did you. Hardeyville was different."

"That's for sure."

"Jimmy always knew you'd become a seer. It was your destiny, just as it was his to become a DK. But seers are protected. They don't walk the front lines. Until you."

"Desperate times," I murmured.

"Desperate measures," she agreed.

I wasn't sure what to think about this information. If I believed Ruthie, and why wouldn't I, that meant Jimmy still had feelings for me. I'd learned to live with the knowledge that we were over, that he didn't love me, had probably never loved me. But what did I do with the concept that he cared at least enough to worry I might die by werewolf?

I shook my head. I couldn't deal with this now. There were too many other pressing issues.

"Sawyer says seers and DKs are dying."

Ruthie's face went stark. "I know."

"Is there anyone else who has the list of federation members?"

"There isn't a list. It was all up here." She tapped her head. "They would have come to you one by one when it was safe, sent by the voice that guides them to swear allegiance, letting you touch them and gauge their strengths, their weaknesses, their loyalty."

"If there isn't a list and you're dead, then how—"

"Whoever's controlling the Nephilim has powers well beyond mine. I've tried to see who it is, or how our secrets are being discovered, but I can't."

I wanted to curse, but my mouth still stung from when she'd smacked me the last time.

"Why am I here?" I asked. "Is there another town that needs saving?" Although after Hardeyville, *saving* probably wasn't the right word.

"I'm sure there is, but you won't be going."

"I can." My voice was too eager. "No problem. You need me, I'm there."

Her lips curved. "Nice try. You're in New Mexico to learn how to hear me without touching them."

"Can he teach me?"

"Yes." Ruthie looked away, her eyes troubled. "But you aren't going to like it."

Chapter 20

I woke with a gasp, as if breaking past the surface of the water after a dangerously long dip. I sat up, heart pounding, I wasn't sure why, until I saw the long tall shadow of a man in the doorway.

At first I didn't know who it was. Jimmy? Sawyer? Someone I hadn't met yet? Then I caught the drift of smoke, saw the tiny pinprick of red at the end of a cigarette.

"What is it?" I asked.

"Does it have to be something? Can't I walk through my own house in the middle of the night?"

I suppose he could, but if he was watching me sleep, that was kind of creepy. Of course he'd always *been* kind of creepy. I didn't think he could help himself.

There'd been so many times at the age of fifteen when I'd wanted to leave this place, that man; I'd been desperate to run away and never come back. But running off into the desert was a death sentence. I'd often felt like staying here was one too. But I'd made it out alive.

Last time.

There'd been occasions I'd woken in the darkest part of the night and felt his presence, as if he were sitting at the foot of my bed. My skin would tingle, perhaps

I should say crawl, as if he'd touched me when I was unaware. But always, when I turned on the light, he wasn't
there.

The feeling of being watched, sometimes followed,
had continued even after I'd escaped. In truth, I still felt
him sometimes in the darkness, would catch the lingering
scent of cigarette smoke or hear his voice in the whisper
of the wind.

"Come here." Sawyer didn't wait for me to get out of
bed; he just turned and walked away.

I didn't want to go anywhere with him. But I also
wanted this to be over as quickly as possible. According
to both Ruthie and Jimmy, the only way to do that was
to listen to the man.

"Hell," I muttered, and swung my bare legs over the
edge of the bed.

When I'd packed clothes in Hardeyville, I hadn't
packed any pajamas. The dead woman had only owned
sexy lingerie, and I wasn't in the mood. So I was sleeping in a T-shirt.

I found a pair of shorts in the duffel and slipped
them over my legs before I left the deceptive safety of
the bedroom and trailed after the shadow that was
Sawyer.

I didn't have far to go. He paused at the next bedroom, the one where I'd assumed Jimmy lay. The door
was open. The bed was empty.

Sawyer quirked a brow in my direction. My gaze
went to the front door, and I ran.

He was climbing into the Hummer. He was leaving me.
Again.

"Jimmy?"

He froze, one leg in the vehicle, one leg out. For an
instant I thought he meant to keep going. What would I

have done if he had? Run after him? Pounded on the window? Begged him not to go?

In hell.

But he stopped, sighed, turned. "You weren't supposed to wake up."

I glanced into the house. Sawyer still stood in the hall. The cigarette was gone. I couldn't see his face. Right now I didn't want to.

I shut the door and crossed the dry, harsh grass of the lawn, ignoring the pain against the soles of my bare feet.

"Where are you going?"

"I told you I'd question every one of Ruthie's DKs and find out who betrayed her."

"You have to do that now?"

"Why not? You'll be busy."

There was something in his voice I didn't like, but I wasn't sure what it meant. "Stay."

"No."

"Just like that? What if—" I paused. I'd been going to say, "what if I need you to?" but I still had enough pride to keep that to myself.

"This has to be done, Lizzy, and I'm the one who has to do it."

"I thought I was supposed to meet all my DKs. I could go with you—"

"No."

He said that a lot. I liked it less every time.

"But—"

"You have to stay here. With him. You have to learn what he knows, become what you were meant to be. And I have to go and do what I know how to do, because I'm already exactly what I've always been meant to be."

"Which is?"

"A killer."

I flinched. "You aren't—"

"Don't lie. Not to me and not to yourself. The whole white-picket-fence dream you built around the two of us, that wasn't ever going to be, even without the Nephilim."

White picket fence. How did he know? I hadn't even realized how appealing they were until one had shown up in Ruthie's heaven.

But then he'd always understood me so well. Which was why it hurt so much when he betrayed me. He'd known exactly how to do it so the pain was almost, but not quite, unbearable.

I could have borne dealing with Sawyer as long as Jimmy was with me. Now what was I going to do?

Whatever you have to, Lizbeth.

Was that actually Ruthie, or just my own thoughts speaking in her voice? Didn't matter. The voice was right. I'd do whatever I had to do. I'd lived without Sanducci before, and I could do it again.

"When will you be back?"

His quick glance revealed the truth. He wasn't coming back.

"I'm your seer," I said. "How am I supposed to give you your assignments?"

Providing I managed to receive them without getting myself killed in the process.

"Same way as Ruthie did." He lifted his hand, thumb to his ear, pinky to his mouth. Sign of the cell phone.

I looked at the ground. My feet were dirty. I shouldn't have run outside without shoes.

Why was I thinking such mundane thoughts at a time like this? To avoid thinking the nonmundane ones.

Jimmy's shoes appeared in my vision, then his hand, holding a business card. Talk about mundane. What would it say? GOT A PROBLEM? CALL 1-800-KIL-LERS.

I accepted it without glancing up. I tried to brush my

fingers against his, who knew what I'd see, but he was too quick, too smart, and he was gone before I could manage it, moving toward the Hummer with a long, sure stride.

He opened the door and paused. "Don't forget about the chindi."

"What about it?" The thing was dead. Wasn't it?

"You can never trust him. Never."

Yet he was leaving me here. Alone. With him.

As if he'd read my mind, Jimmy continued, "I don't think he'll hurt you. You wore the turquoise. You were protected from it."

I fingered the necklace Sawyer had given me, which lay beneath the black T-shirt.

"Learn what you have to and get gone." He glanced over his shoulder and our eyes met. "Promise?"

I was tempted to tell him he had no business asking anything of me, but I couldn't. Because what he was asking was what I wanted too. So I kept my mouth shut and nodded.

Jimmy got into the car and drove away.

I stood in the yard and watched the headlights get smaller and smaller, then disappear altogether. The night was cool. I rubbed my arms, stomped my feet. I'm not sure what I was waiting for. Sawyer wasn't going away.

I turned, and he spoke from the open doorway of his hogan. "You'll never be number one with him."

I didn't bother to wonder how he'd gotten from the house to the hogan without a sound. I just went inside and crawled back into bed, where I lay in the darkness, stared at the ceiling, and knew that Sawyer was right.

Morning came far too soon. When didn't it?

I awoke to bright desert sunshine and the scent of coffee. Thank God Sawyer wasn't one of those annoying health nuts who refused to have a coffee pot in their house. Considering his love affair with nicotine, good health didn't appear to be on his top ten list of concerns. I suspected eternal life, or something near enough, was the reason.

The pot was half full; Sawyer wasn't in the house. I found myself reluctantly charmed that he'd made coffee for me. He couldn't be all bad if he did that.

Then again, lack of electricity in his hogan could be the cause. If he wanted coffee he'd have to make it here. There was nothing charming about it.

I showered quickly and got dressed in the dead woman's clothes. That was really starting to bother me. You'd think after a few days they'd start to feel like mine, but it wasn't happening.

I poured a second cup of coffee, having downed the first one like water before I'd stepped into the shower, and headed outside. Sawyer crouched in the yard, cooking bacon and eggs over an open fire.

"Got anything against a stove?" I asked.

"Doesn't taste the same."

"You like hickory-smoked eggs?"

He didn't answer.

I looked around for a lawn chair. No such luck. So I shifted awkwardly, waiting for him to finish or speak. After several minutes, I couldn't stand the silence.

"I need to go to the store for some clothes, better shoes."

Though the reservation was desolate in certain areas, like this one, it wasn't without its share of retail establishments.

"No," he said.

What was it with that word lately? Everyone seemed to be enthralled with it but me.

"I had to borrow—" Or was it steal?

"We don't have time." Sawyer slid half the bacon and two eggs onto a plate and held it out.

"I'll pass," I said. "Got any wheat toast?"

"Eat." He set my plate on the ground and filled one of his own. "You're going to need it."

I hadn't eaten since yesterday. Today was not going to be easy. While training, Sawyer not only forgot meals but such niceties as bathroom breaks and sleep. The man could go for days without food or water or rest. He often did.

When we were finished, we picked up our plates and went into the house. Sawyer loaded the dishwasher. For an instant I paused at the incongruity of him cooking breakfast in the yard over an open fire, then loading a dishwasher as if it were the most natural thing in the world.

"It's time," he said, and pushed the start button.

I jumped as the machine sprang to life with a dull roar. Sawyer walked past me without a glance. By the time I got outside, he'd tossed something funky onto the fire, which then leaped higher than his head.

He sat in the dirt cross-legged and stared into the dancing flames. He seemed fascinated by them, so I plopped down and stared too, but all I saw was fire.

"Open yourself," he murmured.

I tensed so fast and so hard, my back screamed in protest. "You know I—"

He turned his head; his eyes were pools of black, the pupils dilated so large, they'd overtaken the gray of the irises. The sun blazed down. How could he keep his eyes open without agony shooting into his brain from the abundance of light?

"To know the truth, you must open yourself."

"I don't know how." I never had.

All those years ago Sawyer had tried everything to get

me to open myself to the heavens, the earth, the father, the mother, all manner of beings and places and New Age—or was that hippie?—claptrap. I couldn't do it.

"Open your mind." He placed his palm against my forehead.

My eyes crossed. I should have closed them, except that would be like turning my back on a wild animal, and I knew better.

"Open your heart." His palm lowered to my chest. Fingers spread, his pinky brushed the swell of one breast, his thumb paused just short of the nipple on the other.

My borrowed shirt was cotton, thin from repeated washings. The heat of his skin seemed to burn through the fabric, scalding what lay beneath. Awareness sprang to life, and for just an instant another world shimmered at the edge of my vision before winking out as if it had never been.

Our gazes met. Mine narrowed; his stayed wide and eerily black.

"Open yourself," he intoned.

I lifted my hand and removed his from my chest. He blinked. His eyes went back the way they were supposed to be—human, not . . . whatever they'd been—and the dancing flames fell back to the earth with an audible whoosh.

"Don't touch me," I said.

When he touched me I didn't feel like myself. When he touched me I wanted something I had no business wanting.

Him.

Chapter 21

The crunch of tires on gravel had us glancing toward the road. I hadn't realized I'd been hoping to see a Hummer until my stomach dropped at the sight of a pickup truck.

It dropped even farther at the sight of the woman who climbed out of it.

Short and slim, with naturally blond hair and dewy pink skin, she had blue eyes, of course. Her Levi's fit like a second skin; her denim shirt was unbuttoned halfway down, bestowing enticing peaks at her perky breasts; her cowboy hat framed a beautiful oval face, and her boots were just dusty enough to make her human. She looked strange in these clothes, probably because the last time I'd seen her she hadn't been wearing any.

"What in hell are you doing here?" I demanded.

"Have we met?"

Not really. She'd never seen me, and I'd only seen her once, all those years ago when I'd touched Jimmy and discovered he'd been touching someone else.

My hands curled into fists as I got to my feet. Sawyer was already standing, contemplating me with both amusement and concern.

"Elizabeth Phoenix, this is Summer Bartholomew."

I'd taken an aggressive step forward, as if I wanted to

beat her face in. I did, but I wasn't going to. It wasn't her fault Jimmy couldn't keep it in his pants.

Then Sawyer finished, "One of your DKs."

"My DKs. What about Lucinda?" It would seem that a DK in New Mexico should have a seer in New Mexico, but what did I know.

Sawyer cut me a quick glance. "Lucinda's been gone for years."

I was amazed at the wave of sadness that washed over me. I hadn't even known the woman. But she'd been Ruthie's friend, her colleague. Lucinda's loss seemed to emphasize Ruthie's, which was just foolish considering how often Ruthie dropped into my dreams. As long as she continued to do that, Ruthie wasn't really gone.

"*She's* a DK?" I looked Summer up and down; I couldn't help it, I laughed. "She's a pixie."

Her chin lifted. "Fairy actually."

"You're a fairy," I repeated, the words sounding vaguely homophobic, even though I was certain she wasn't a gay male masquerading as a petite blond female. She was a real live fairy. How's that for a sentence you don't hear every day?

"Where are your wings?" I asked.

"Kind of a myth."

"But fairies aren't?"

"You're standing next to a skinwalker, and you're balking at fairies?"

I glanced at Sawyer. "Am I supposed to kill her? I'm confused."

He shook his head but kept silent, visibly delighted at the encounter. I wanted to smack him, but that would involve touching him, and I wasn't going to go there.

"I'm not a Nephilim," Summer said, her voice a little higher, her face a bit more tense. "Tell her, Sawyer."

"Obviously not, if you're a DK."

"A breed then?" I asked.

"No." Summer came closer. "I'm a *fairy*."

I really wished I had a weapon, though what killed a fairy? The enormity of what I didn't know washed over me in a wave of exhaustion so strong I nearly staggered.

"Supernatural creature means Nephilim." I took a few steps backward, thinking if I could get into the house, I could grab the gun I'd taken from Jimmy's arsenal, or maybe my knife.

I didn't like the way Sawyer watched us, as if waiting to see what we might do. Was Summer a test? Maybe I should touch her.

Duh.

Striding forward, I wrapped my hand around her forearm. She was startled at the sudden shift, and her bright blue eyes went wide as her pretty pink mouth shaped into an O.

The instant I touched her I saw Jimmy, wearing what he'd worn last night—make that early this morning. I let her go as if she were a snake.

"He went to see you."

Her gaze met mine. "Yes."

"Why?"

She glanced away, her cheeks turning pink. Stupid question.

"He sent me here to tell you—"

"He couldn't call?"

Did he think I wouldn't recognize her? Sometimes Jimmy was so damn dense, he worried me. Then again, most men were.

"Your cell phone isn't working." She waved at the mountains. "Might be those."

I reached into my pocket and withdrew the phone. I'd

spoken with Megan; the thing had worked just fine then. But mountains were tricky. One minute you had service and the next—

I glanced at the display. Blank. I shook it. Not that shaking had ever helped.

"You don't need that here," Sawyer said.

I had a sudden, sneaking suspicion and opened the battery case. It was empty.

I scowled in Sawyer's direction. "Give that back."

He lifted a brow and didn't answer.

"I *do* need it. Jimmy couldn't call. He had to send—" I waved my hand furiously in Summer's direction.

"Yes, well, that was poor form, wasn't it?"

Poor form? Had he learned English from the English?

I narrowed my eyes. How much did Sawyer know about Jimmy and Summer? More than I wanted him to, obviously.

My cheeks burned, but there wasn't anything I could do about it short of finding the memory sector of Sawyer's brain and destroying it.

"You're here to learn," he continued. "You don't need any interruptions."

"A phone call would have been much less of an interruption than this."

"What did you see when you touched her?" Sawyer murmured. "Sanducci banging the natives again?"

I lifted my chin. "I have no idea." I'd let her go before I'd seen too much.

"He came to question me," Summer said. "He's questioning all of Ruthie's DKs."

"You must have passed the test," Sawyer drawled. "You're still breathing."

She cast him a quick, suspicious glance. "Jimmy wouldn't—"

"Oh, he would," Sawyer interrupted. "I don't like much about him, but I do like that."

"Why are you in New Mexico?" I asked.

It seemed a bit too coincidental that we were here and so was she.

"She's supposed to keep an eye on me," Sawyer murmured.

In Summer's face I saw a shred of fear. Maybe she wasn't as blond as she looked.

"You think I didn't know?" he continued, his voice so deceptively soft and conversational, I got a chill. Summer appeared as if she might puke.

"It isn't—"

"It is. You're a spy for Sanducci."

She had the good sense not to deny it. I wondered what he would have done if she had.

"It doesn't matter now. We have much bigger problems than a lack of trust between him and me. What happened?"

For an instant she stood there blinking her baby blues as if she had no idea why she'd come. Sawyer gave an impatient growl that had us both jumping as if goosed. "Why are you here, Summer?"

"Oh—yes. Jimmy, he—" She swallowed and glanced at me apologetically. "There's been another death."

My heart caught. *Jimmy.*

I must have made a soft sound of distress because Sawyer blew a derisive breath out his nose. "Worry about yourself, Phoenix, Sanducci is nearly as hard to kill as I am."

"He's fine," Summer said quickly. "He left—"

"Focus," Sawyer snapped. "Who is dead?"

She spread her hands. Her nails were manicured and painted the same pink as her lips. I wanted to snap them off, one by one. Her nails, not her fingers. At least not yet.

"A seer. In New York City."

"How?"

"I don't know. Jimmy wouldn't tell me. As soon as he got the call, he went to check things out."

Sawyer's gaze shifted to Mount Taylor. "Run along," he murmured.

She ran.

When the rumble of her engine had faded to nothing but a purr, I murmured, "Fairies? Seriously?"

"I'm afraid so."

"But they're not Nephilim."

"No. They're not human either."

"Let's cut to the chase." I rubbed my forehead. "Just tell me what she is. How she got here. What she does."

"Besides Sanducci?"

I let my hand fall back to my side and met his eyes. "Yes, besides that."

He hesitated, glancing north with a worried frown, before turning back. "You know the story of the angels' fall?"

He didn't wait for my nod, but continued as if he were in a hurry. "When the angels were cast out, God closed heaven. The good ones were on one side of the gate with him, the rebellious ones were on the other. Those who disobeyed his command and interbred with the humans were confined in a hell dimension."

"Tartarus," I murmured.

"Yes. Their offspring, the Nephilim, remained on earth."

"Why didn't God send them all to hell?"

"He will, once we win this war. But earth isn't Eden. There has to be evil. The Nephilim are our test."

"If the Grigori are locked up in a fiery pit, they can't

create more Nephilim. We keep killing them off and eventually we'll win."

"Theoretically. However, Nephilim can breed with Nephilim and then you get some really strange things."

I rubbed my forehead. "Stranger than what we've got?"

"Nephilim are evil, but put two of them together and what do you think you'll get?"

"Double the evil, double the fun."

"Exactly."

"Then why aren't we overrun?"

"Nephilim are beings of incredible selfishness. They certainly don't want to give birth to something that will need their care and attention for the next decade and more. Be glad they're that way or we'd be outnumbered to the point of extinction."

I guess every cloud did have a silver lining, or was that every silver lining came with its own personal cloud?

"Explain why the fairies aren't Nephilim."

"When God closed the gates, some of the angels trapped outside had not given in to temptation. They weren't bad enough for hell, but they weren't good enough for heaven, so they became fairies."

"Okeydokey." Pretty much anything made a certain sort of sense these days.

"Fairies are unable to use their supernatural powers on anyone who is on an errand of mercy, which means all the DKs and seers. They're fairly trustworthy."

I scowled at the idea of trusting Summer, although really it was Jimmy who needed a good swift kick in the ass. He usually did.

"What kind of supernatural powers are we talking about?"

"They can fly."

"Without wings."

"Handy, yes?"

"Then why in hell did she bother with a car?"

"Flying people tend to get noticed, especially during the daytime. That skill is used sparingly."

"What else?"

"Casting spells. Altering their appearance." He paused, his gaze intent on my face. "Seeing the future."

So Summer the fairy was psychic. Was that supposed to make us BFFs?

Not happening.

"Are all of the fairies on our side?"

He didn't answer right away, perhaps waiting for me to break down and quiz him about the nature of the fairy's psychic abilities. He'd wait a helluva long time. Unless the fairies knew how to get rid of their abilities, I didn't have any interest in sharing info.

"Sawyer," I pressed. "Are they all on the side of good?"

"Unfortunately, no. Some have been won to the Nephilim."

"How do you kill a fairy?"

Surprise spread over his face, followed quickly by a smirk. "Bloodthirsty today?"

"I thought that was what I was supposed to learn—how to kill these things."

"Fairies aren't Nephilim."

"But some of them are on the side of the Nephilim, which means they're open season. So how do I kill them?"

"According to legend, fairies can be killed with cold steel or rowan."

"In other words, I freeze a knife or shove a bush down her throat."

"Whatever works."

"While we're on the subject of killing legendary beings, what takes out a skinwalker?"

He looked down and didn't answer. I hadn't expected him to.

"What about a dhampir?"

That question brought his head up. "You plan on killing Sanducci?"

"You never know."

Sawyer laughed—one short, sharp burst that sounded rusty. I couldn't recall him ever laughing before.

"Perhaps I'll tell you one day, but not this day."

"Why the hell not? You don't like him either."

"I like this world as it is, and as much as I dislike Sanducci, for now he's necessary."

"And when he isn't?"

Sawyer just smiled.

I turned and watched the last wisp of dust die in the wake of Summer's truck. "You know who she was talking about? The latest seer who died?"

Sawyer nodded, his gaze turning north once more.

He'd told me all those years ago that north was the direction of evil to the Navajo. Terrific. I followed his gaze, but there was still nothing there. Or at least nothing that I could see.

Then a sneaking suspicion entered my mind. Sawyer had trained certain seers and DKs. Were those the ones who'd been dying?

His gaze flicked to mine. "Sanducci wouldn't have left you here with me if he truly believed I was killing members of the federation."

"You read minds?" I'd always wondered.

"Faces," he corrected. "You need to do a better job with yours."

"I'll get right on that, as soon as we figure out who the traitor is and put a knife through his or her treacherous heart."

His lips curved. "I bet you wish it *was* me."

It would certainly solve half of my problems. If, by chance, sticking a knife into Sawyer's heart would actually kill him. I didn't think that it would.

"Obviously I couldn't have killed a seer in New York while I was here with you," he pointed out.

I had no idea what he could do, but I thought it was a lot more than he let on.

Sawyer turned suddenly and headed for the hogan. Before I could register the movement, he'd already ducked inside. The woven mat, which was all he had for a door, fell back into place. I stood outside, uncertain if I should knock or barge right in. I barged in.

A fire pit had been dug in the center of the earthen floor, directly beneath the smoke hole. On the west side lay his sheepskin bedroll and neat stacks of clothing. Mats woven of grass, some of bark, were strewn about near the walls like chairs.

Sawyer was already plucking dried herbs from tiny bags, which hung from the logs near the north side of the hogan.

"Where are you going?"

"You don't want to do this the easy way." He pulled two backpacks—incongruous in the middle of this traditional Navajo dwelling—from behind his bedroll. "There's always the hard way."

"Do what? And when has anything ever been easy with you?"

"You will learn to open yourself. I'd hoped the urgency of the situation would help, but it hasn't, and we no longer have time to wait. You need the power now."

"And just how do you propose we accomplish that?"

"Vision quest," he said shortly, and tossed one of the backpacks in my direction. "Get your things."

Chapter 22

Sawyer donned suitable clothing for a mountain death march. Since the temperatures would be lower at the higher altitude, where there could still be pockets of snow despite the calendar's insistence it was spring, he covered his white T-shirt with long-sleeved flannel and shoved his slim feet into heavy socks and hiking boots. A lightweight ski jacket disappeared into his backpack.

He produced the same outfit for me, right down to the hiking boots. Every size was correct.

I lifted my gaze to the man who lounged in the doorway of my room as if he meant to stay right there for all eternity.

"How'd you know?" I asked.

His oddly light eyes swept from my head to my toes. Wherever his gaze touched, I burned. "I'm good with sizes."

I bet he was good with a lot of things.

I shook my head. I did not want to go there. Not now. Not ever.

Sawyer's lips curved, and once again I got the impression he could read my mind. Or maybe it *was* just my face. I hadn't tried to keep what I was thinking a secret.

"I meant . . ." I was gritting my teeth. The words came

out tight and angry, which only made his mouth curve more. "Did someone tell you we were coming?"

That someone would have had to be Jimmy—who else would have known?—but I couldn't see Jimmy dialing Sawyer for any reason.

Sawyer's eyebrows lifted, and he spread his big, hard hands. "I have no phone."

"You've got something," I muttered, then tilted my head. "Have you been talking to Ruthie too?"

His smile faded. "No. I have my own connections."

I had no doubt that he did. I just wondered if his connections were in heaven or hell.

Once, back then, I'd woken in the night. A flicker of firelight had illuminated my window, drawing me across the room.

He wasn't alone.

I should have gone back to bed, pulled the covers over my head, and stayed there. But I was curious what the goat was for.

I was an old fifteen. I had several ideas, most of them pornographic. I couldn't have been more wrong.

The goat bleated. Sawyer slit its throat. I slapped both hands over my mouth to keep from screaming.

The blood poured onto the ground. Wherever it struck, smoke billowed, a column that grew taller and taller as the blood continued to flow. He bathed his hands in the red river, then laid the broken animal down with something resembling tenderness.

The contrast between the violent sacrifice of the life and the gentle laying to rest gave me goose bumps on top of my goose bumps. We always fear what we can't understand.

He spoke, his deep voice ringing through the oddly silent night, in a language I didn't know. His glistening hands rose, and behind him the fire seemed to leap higher than the mountains, shifting from red flame to a silvery molten glow.

The fire and the smoke twined together, then shot around the edge of the clearing, a living thing, whirling and whirling as if trying to break free.

Sawyer barked one word, an order, and the dancing flame paused, lengthened, and became a woman of smoke. No colors, only black, white, and gray, yet I could see her very clearly standing in the puddle of blood he'd made.

She was Native American—perhaps his age, hard to say, with hair streaming to her ankles and a nose and two cheekbones that fought for prominence in a face that should have been etched in stone—ancient and new, both beautiful and deadly.

They stood together, neither speaking nor touching, though the air seemed ripe with the promise of both. He'd conjured her; for what purpose, who could say?

The Navajo are superstitious about their ghosts, their legends and magic. Yet I knew, even before she glanced up, that what I was watching I was not meant to see.

I never moved; I did not—could not—make a sound, but suddenly her glistening black eyes left his and instead bored into mine. The spell over me broke, and I dove beneath the covers, shivering, whimpering the night away. In those eyes I'd seen all that was dreadful in the world— hatred, murder, evil for the sake of evil alone and an underlying joy of it.

With the light of day, the fear should have left me, but it didn't. I felt that being seen by the woman of smoke was a very bad thing; she would come for me. Not that day or the next, but someday. Her coming was inevitable.

Sawyer still stood in the hall watching me. I could

ask him about that night, but I knew with a certainty I had about very few things that he wouldn't answer me. Most likely he'd deny ever having conjured her at all.

I slammed the door in his face, then changed my clothes. Moments later I followed him across the long expanse of land toward the sacred mountain of the south, *Tso dzilh,* better known as Mount Taylor.

"You aren't going to lock the house?" I asked.

"Why?"

"Anyone could come by and take things."

"Do you know why I live out here, Phoenix?"

I had a pretty good idea.

"My people have very little tolerance for witches. In order to avoid the constant assassination attempts, I live as far away from the rest of them as possible. But I can't leave. I need to be within the circle of the sacred mountains. To leave here is to die."

"Seriously?"

He cast an impatient look over his shoulder, then paused. "Do you really think killing me would be as simple as tossing me across the imaginary line that separates the Glittering World from the land of the *Bilagaana*?"

"Bilagaana," I repeated.

"Whites."

When he talked like this it made me believe that we were not only from different generations, but, most likely, different centuries.

"So you *could* go; there's nothing stopping you?"

"Not exactly."

"What exactly?"

"I can only depart the Dinetah as an animal, never a man."

"Seriously?" I repeated.

"Do you think I make this up?"

"Sometimes. So, if you step over the invisible line, bam, you shape-shift?"

He shrugged, which I took as a yes.

"Bummer."

"There's nothing I need that isn't here with me now."

My gaze went to his face, but as always it was inscrutable.

"All right," I said slowly. "Let's get back to the no-lock policy."

His eyes glittered for just an instant—animal, man, animal—before he turned away. "While they might try to kill me, they're a little too scared of me to steal from me."

I could understand that.

We walked for an hour at high speed. Luckily I'd stayed in shape since leaving the force. Still, keeping up with Sawyer left me breathless.

"What's the rush?" I managed.

"You heard Summer. A seer in New York is dead."

"Yes, and I'm sorry about that. But why is this one different from Ruthie or any of the others who've died?"

"The seer in New York was very old, very powerful."

"And Ruthie wasn't?"

"Ruthie appears to be a lot more powerful dead than she ever was alive," he said softly, as if the thought had just occurred to him. He paused in his headlong rush, then zoned off as if several other interesting thoughts had come on the heels of the first.

I cleared my throat, and he glanced up, eyebrows lifted. "New York?" I reminded him. "You were going to elaborate on why this seer's death is more catastrophic than any of the others?"

"Yes." He still sounded distracted, but he went on. "New York has always been a place where the Nephilim throng. Without that seer in place, chaos is coming."

"I thought it was already here."

"Things are taking more of a downward turn than I ever thought they could." His distraction fled, and his gaze bored into mine. "You *will* come into your full powers immediately. I don't care what we have to do to make that happen."

I didn't care for all this talk of making something happen, especially when that something involved me.

"So the answer to everything is to hightail it into the mountains for a vision?" I asked. "I couldn't have one on level ground?"

In his face I suddenly saw something I'd never seen before. Not fear exactly. I doubted I'd ever see that. But grave concern. For me.

"You think they're coming here," I said.

He looked north again. "I know they are."

The sun shone with a fury, yet suddenly I was so damn cold.

"I can take care of myself."

"You can't. Not yet." He started to walk again. "I won't let anyone hurt you while you're with me." He said the words as if he were telling me what we'd have for dinner. "But you can't stay with me. We both know that."

There was something in his voice that made me twitchy, something I didn't want to examine too closely, so I went back to walking and talking.

"Jimmy thinks you sent a chindi after us."

"I didn't. Not that he'll believe me."

"Make *me* believe you."

"Why?"

"Dammit, Sawyer!" My shout startled a few birds from the nearby scrub. "You want me to trust you, let me trust you. For once, just answer a question."

He continued inexorably on. I had to follow or be left behind. I considered the latter, but in the end I hurried to catch up. I wasn't a complete idiot. I was safer with him.

"Do you think I mean you harm, Phoenix?"

I considered the question. If he'd wanted me dead, he'd have killed me years ago. Why wait until I was stronger? Unless he hadn't known what I'd become.

I snorted. He'd known. Probably before anyone else.

"All right," I allowed. "You didn't send the chindi after me."

"Obviously, since I gave you the turquoise."

I touched the stone where it rested beneath two layers of clothing. Funny, that only made me suspicious again.

"You think I sent it for Sanducci?" he asked.

"Did you?"

"No."

"Someone did."

"That goes without saying." He sounded bored. I suspect being accused of sending evil Navajo spirits to kill people did get old fast.

"I wish I knew who," I murmured.

"I'm sure you'll find out."

He had that much faith in me? Despite myself, I was warmed by the praise.

"Anyone who has the power to send a chindi has the power to send a whole lot more. Something new should show up to kill you any day now."

The warmth died. Constant references to my imminent death were getting old fast, as well.

"Jimmy said a chindi is a vengeance demon."

"That's one interpretation."

"It isn't true?"

"A chindi is a malevolent spirit released with the dying breath of a Dineh."

"A ghost?"

"Perhaps."

I loved it when he was so specific.

"Chindis wander the night. Never whistle after dark or you will call one to you."

I frowned. Had the chindi been summoned because someone whistled after dark?

"I doubt there were any wandering Navajo ghosts in Wisconsin," Sawyer murmured.

My gaze flicked to his back. I hadn't said that out loud.

"A witch is the only one capable of sending a chindi on a mission of vengeance."

"Like you."

"We've already established that I'm the most likely suspect. Yet still I deny it."

This wasn't getting us anywhere. I couldn't prove he'd sent the chindi. Even if I could, what good would proving it do me? I had to stay; I had to learn. If Sawyer had tried to kill Jimmy by possessed cougar, that didn't change one damn thing.

Conversation became too difficult as we continued up the mountain. I had no idea where we were going, but Sawyer seemed to. Our path was direct; our pace rapid.

I was thankful I'd eaten the eggs that morning, because there was no stopping for lunch, even if we'd had any; all water was consumed on the trail with barely a pause to tilt our heads, swallow, and move on.

Eventually, night hovered just above the horizon, pressing down on the last orange remnants of day like great black clouds. Stars winked against a curtain the shade of midnight. The moon burst free of bondage, spreading a glorious wash of silver over the scrubby bushes and crooked trees surrounding us.

"That's it." I sat on the nearest smooth, large rock. There were quite a few. "I'm done."

Sawyer kept walking, disappearing quickly into the darkness. The night closed in around me, chill ebony air. I shut my eyes, tilted back my head, and tried to open my mind, my heart, myself. I still couldn't.

In the distance something howled. Wolf? Coyote? Dog? I couldn't tell. Did it matter? Tiny animals scuffled through the underbrush. Insects buzzed around my head. I could have sworn a snake slithered around the rock upon which I sat. As long as the reptile didn't start to rattle, I'd ignore it.

Sawyer had refused to allow a weapon of any kind on this trip. According to him, a vision quest must be completed without them. I'd taken his word for it, but right now I wished desperately for a gun.

I caught the scent of wood smoke and my eyes flew open. Either a forest fire was cruising down the mountain, and I was dead, or Sawyer had made camp.

My gaze swept the tree line. Flames did not dance merrily in my direction like escapees from *Fantasia*. I didn't hear the telltale *whoosh* that would signal impending, agonizing death.

Must be suppertime.

Though I'd sworn not to move, the prospect of food, however bad, changed my mind. I strode into the stand of pine and fir exactly where Sawyer had disappeared.

The ground tilted downward; the foliage thickened. I could smell water along with the smoke. Cool, clear water.

My pace picked up. The sharply canted path spilled me out of the trees so fast I nearly fell into the lake.

A fire burned in front of the hogan built on the bank. The night had turned chilly, and I hurried closer, reaching out to the flames.

"Sawyer?" I called. No one answered.

I stepped to the door of the hogan, rapped on the wood,

stuck my head inside. Empty. However, his backpack leaned against the wall.

I set mine down, then snatched a sheepskin bedroll from the ground and placed the bedding next to the fire.

Without anything to do, I stared into the flames. My head would nod, and the jerky movement would startle me awake. Each time it did, I caught the drift of shadows at the edge of my vision. But when I glanced at the trees, the lake, the mountain, nothing was there.

I dragged my eyes open one last time before I lost consciousness. The flames had turned every shade of the rainbow, and they smelled just like sun-warmed grass.

Chapter 23

Sawyer walked out of the trees wearing nothing but his tattoos. If I hadn't known this was a dream, I might have run for my life. But since it was, I got to look my fill.

The firelight played across his skin, etching the curve of his hip, the ripple of his abdomen, the spike of his rib cage in sharp relief. As he stalked toward me, the shadows came alive, swirling around him, taking on the shapes of his beasts. The air seemed to whisper in an ancient language, and the flames leaped higher than before.

He didn't speak; his eyes shone pale against the bronze of his face. They seemed lit from within, the way a small animal's eyes glow when caught by the headlights of a car.

I'd come to my feet; I don't know when. He stopped so close I could feel his heat, along with his erection. I made an involuntary movement, rubbing the delicious hardness against my belly. Too bad I still wore all my clothes.

He smelled like grass. Had he been rolling in it? Perhaps the scent was merely invading my senses from the blazing fire, which now illuminated the clearing like a spotlight spewing a rainbow. Colors sparkled all around us like rain.

Reaching out, he brushed a fingertip across my cheekbone, and when he pulled it back, a dewdrop twinkled, silver on bronze.

His spooky gray eyes holding mine, he lifted his finger to his mouth, and the moisture dissolved on his lips. He suckled the tip. I felt the pull in my stomach, then lower still, as a moan threatened to break free.

The flames leaped and danced. I was suddenly so hot. I shrugged out of the flannel shirt, lost the jeans, boots, underwear, and socks. The air stirred like springtime against my skin.

I wanted to feel every inch of him with my hands and my mouth. I wanted to lick the wolf, scrape my teeth against the shark, suckle the skin where the tiger paced.

Since this was a dream, I could touch him and more. So I did.

He didn't make a sound. His hand cupped my head gently, fingers tightening as I roamed ever lower.

I licked the long, hard length of him, my tongue twining along the same skin as the image of a rattlesnake.

Was that supposed to be a joke? I didn't bother to ask.

He sank to his knees, bringing us hip to hip, heart to heart, face to face. I took his hand and saw the centuries. They were long; they were lonely. No one had ever been like him until me.

I jerked, and our hands separated. I wasn't like him. I never could be.

"Shh," he murmured. As he leaned closer, his hair brushed my face; then his lips took mine.

I no longer saw anything; I could only feel. His tongue in my mouth, his hand on my back, his palm cupping my breast.

Energy surged between us. If I didn't know the night was clear, I'd have thought lightning had struck nearby. But the breeze was gentle, warmed by the fire, not a hint of rain anywhere. Yet that sensation of electricity, the faint scent of ozone, lingered. The more I touched him, the more I wanted to. What should be weird, if not down-right frightening, I understood now to be inevitable.

He pulled me closer, held me tighter. I caught at his shoulders, unbalanced, then found myself captivated by the amazing smoothness of his skin. My fingertips traced the places where his tattoos roamed. I felt nothing, as if they weren't even there.

His thumb flicked my nipple, and I gasped as the sensation shot through me, arching into his palm, begging for more, wanting everything. He replaced his hand with his mouth, his hair shrouding his face, cascading over my skin. I hung on as he suckled me and behind my closed eyelids beasts of prey flickered.

Like an X-ray—white against black—wolf, eagle, tiger, rattlesnake; everything I touched I could see. While his scalding mouth did such remarkable things I nearly came from that touch alone—hey, it had been a *long* time since I'd had sex of any kind, even imaginary—I dreamed what it would be like to become those animals, and I wanted it almost as much as I wanted him.

I lost any semblance of control, hands groping, nails scraping, teeth too. I had a sudden desire to mark him, as any animal would. My mouth learned his shape, his size and scent. My lips wandered through boundless tropical waters where predatory sharks roamed, across deserts in-habited by venomous snakes, then traversed continents—American eagle to Siberian tiger—where my teeth drew on the tender skin of his thigh until I'd left my mark.

He growled, the sound untamed, when I closed my hand around him, ran my thumb over his damp tip. The sky seemed to fill with the hiss of a rattler, and I froze. Maybe this wasn't the best idea I'd had in years.

"Lie back," Sawyer murmured, his hand on my breast no longer caressing, but urging me to recline. "Close your eyes. Breathe."

I inhaled—wood smoke and grass, a soothing, familiar scent—and forgot everything but him, me, us, and what we could do right now.

His body slid along mine as he joined me in repose. He traced a finger across my belly, the skin rippling in its wake. The finger took the path down my hipbone, across the soft skin at the juncture of my thigh, then tangled in the black curls for an instant before unerringly finding the part of me that awaited it.

One stroke and he stopped. Before I could complain his mouth replaced his finger. My legs fell apart to give him access. His tongue flickered over me, quick and clever, teasing me to a gasping, arching peak. Then he blew on the dampness left behind, his breath an August breeze, cool and soothing after a scorching hot day.

Suddenly he licked me, a long, thorough lap, like a cat. His tongue even felt rough, and I cried out, my hands flying up, finding nothing, no one.

When I opened my eyes, I was alone, my body glistening in the firelight.

"Shh." The word was the wind. Smoke billowed all around me, creating a curtain between this clearing and the world. I breathed it in, any panic eased, and my eyes slid closed once more.

I drifted, both awake and asleep, aroused, unsatisfied, waiting for—

A hand on my belly.

Lips against my neck.

Legs entangling with mine.

One sharp thrust and the dissatisfaction fled. Still damp and engorged, I nearly sobbed at the friction—so good, so right, so there.

I needed, I wanted. Oh, how I wanted. More. Harder. Deeper. Every thought that I had, he obeyed.

The connection went on and on; the orgasm seemingly just out of reach, nearly there, almost and then suddenly farther away. That strange sense of lightning, ozone and smoke, of flowing energy, continued. Where before I'd been limp, almost drugged, the longer he thrust, the more aware, the more alive I became.

There was something I needed to do, something I needed to know, and that something was just on the other side of orgasm.

"Open," he said, the word like thunder crashing all around us.

I opened—my eyes, my legs—and I saw him above me, too solid to be a shadow, too ethereal to be real. His eyes sparkled—the moon, the lightning, just him—who knew? He shifted my hips so he could reach into the very center of me, and at the first driving thrust, he came, heat like fire inside, bursting me open just as he'd wanted.

I connected to the universe; I saw what he'd meant; I understood all that had been denied me before. As my hands smoothed over his back, his shoulders, his neck, I felt the power of every beast shimmering at the edge of my world.

The knowledge, the sensations, the damn orgasm was too much. My mind, my heart, my body seemed to implode and everything went as dark as Sawyer's soul.

I awoke inside the hogan. I had the faint memory of stumbling in here alone as the fire died.

I glanced through the smoke hole in the ceiling. Dawn threatened. Had Sawyer ever come back last night?

Images flickered. Him. Me. Doing things that had to be illegal in many Middle Eastern countries. In my dreams he'd been here for hours. I'd come several times, once screaming as he plunged into me from behind. His lips, his teeth at my neck, his chest to my back, hips to my flanks, a rhythmic slap that resounded in the quietest part of the night.

Despite the submissive position, I hadn't felt dominated. I'd been the one in control; the things in my mind had been the things that we'd done, at my unspoken request. And with every orgasm, I'd seen what he'd meant by opening myself, connecting to the power within. In those fantasies I'd believed I could run my fingertips along the edge of the stars, plunge my fist into the moon, walk across the sun and never be burned.

I snorted. If I didn't know better I'd think I'd been drugged.

But I hadn't eaten since we'd left Sawyer's. The only thing I'd drunk had been water from the same canteen as him. Sawyer hadn't been loopy. I didn't think. I hadn't seen him since he'd disappeared into the trees last night. Maybe he'd gone into the mountains for his own acid trip.

I sat up, and the sheepskin fell down. I was naked. I didn't remember removing my clothes. Except in that vivid sex dream.

I was starting to have a very bad feeling.

I dressed and stepped out of the hogan. A wolf stood at the edge of the clearing. At the sight of me, his snout opened in a welcoming, doglike grin, and the dead rabbit tumbled free, making a dull boneless thud as it hit the ground.

"I'm not cleaning that," I said.

The wolf cocked its head.

"Seriously. Eat it yourself."

He shook his body as if he'd just come out of the lake, but no water flew free. Instead he shimmered, caught in a moonbeam. His fur twinkled with a hundred thousand sequins, and his outline twisted, re-formed, grew and grew, pushing against the moonbeam, appearing to be caught inside a silvery balloon, until he burst free a man.

My eyes ached. Probably because I hadn't blinked from the instant Sawyer had begun to change. I hadn't wanted to miss anything.

Sawyer's shifting of shape was different from any I'd seen before. The berserker had shaken, out came the fur, then bam, he was a bear. Sawyer's transformation was more elaborate. There'd been something almost magical about it.

My gaze wandered over the tattoos. I thought of the legends of the skinwalker. The robe they wore to make magic happen.

"Why don't you just wear a robe?" I asked.

He reached down and grabbed the rabbit by the ears, stalking toward the ashes of last night's fire, uncaring that he was naked. I didn't mind. My own clothes felt too tight, itchy, wrong somehow.

"Do I look like a man who'd own a robe?" Dropping the rabbit near the cold fire, he ducked into the hogan and returned with a knife, then hunkered down next to breakfast.

"I meant the robe of the skinwalker. Why did you—" I broke off as he glanced up, making a vague motion to indicate his naked body.

"Why did I what?" His voice was soft, but the tone was harsh. I had a feeling I'd stepped over a line, but I wasn't sure when or how.

"Wouldn't a robe be easier?" I murmured. And less painful.

"I wasn't after ease but power. As much of it as I could get."

His eyes glittered, and the wind came up, howling down the mountain like a lone wolf, making me suddenly glad for the clothes I'd been wishing away only moments before. This man wasn't a pet; he wasn't a friend. He was dangerous.

"The robe is for amateurs," he continued. "Men of medicine who rely on a spell to attain their single spirit animal. I don't need a spell, no ceremony, no chant. I wish to be, and then I am."

Slowly he stood, his hand trailing up his stomach, his chest, over his arm and shoulder. I was unable to keep myself from following that trail, from remembering how he'd tasted.

I shook my head. That wasn't a memory but a dream.

"My animals are a part of me," he said. "As she is."

My gaze jerked from his biceps to his face. "What are you saying?"

"There's more evil than good in here." His palm skated over the left side of his chest.

"That's not true. You're the same as the others. Nephilim and human."

"I told you before I'm not like them. My mother was a Nephilim, true, but my father was more than a man."

That shiver came back, stronger than before. "Jimmy said—"

Sawyer's hand slashed through the air, through my words. "Sanducci's version leaves quite a bit out. My father was seduced, yes, but once he knew the truth he embraced the darkness. He became a skinwalker who wore the robe."

"An amateur," I whispered.

"Compared to me." He dipped his head. "She was *Naye'i*."

"A Dreadful One," I guessed.

"A monster. Yes. She was beautiful but evil. She thrived on chaos, breathed it in like a drug. She could make anyone do anything that she wished."

I didn't know what to say. What had his life been like

being raised by a monster and the man she controlled? I probably didn't want to know.

"She convinced him to welcome his bear spirit; he lived as an animal all of the time. He killed at her bidding. He died with the blood of thousands on his soul, and because of her, he didn't care."

I thought of all the animals tattooed on Sawyer's flesh. Not one of them was a bear.

"You care," I said.

"Do I?"

I opened my mouth to say that I knew he did. That he wouldn't be working with the federation, training seers and DKs, if he truly enjoyed killing just for the sake of killing, if he wasn't trying to atone somehow for all that his parents had done.

Then I thought of another question. "In the story your mother killed your father."

"Yes."

"Why? Seems like she had a good thing going." In murdering psycho bitch hell.

"Have you ever heard, Phoenix, how witches gain their power?"

"Aren't they born with it?"

"Some. Others take it."

"How?"

"By killing someone they love."

My gaze flew to his, but I could read nothing there, as always. "Your mother wasn't a witch, she was a—" I stopped, frowning. I wasn't certain what she'd been.

Sawyer lifted his brows at my unvoiced question, but he didn't enlighten me.

"She wasn't at first," he agreed, "but after . . ." He spread his hands. "She became more powerful than any Dreadful One or any witch ever known before."

"And you?"

He lifted his brows. "Me?"

"How did you gain your power?"

"Didn't Sanducci say that a mother's blood is stronger?"

"Sanducci says a lot. I try not to listen."

His lips twitched. He looked away, and I knew that he wasn't going to tell me how he'd acquired his magic. I opened my mouth to insist, but he spoke first.

"Do you know where I was all night?" he murmured.

"What? No."

Slowly he stood, the hand he'd been rubbing over his heart skimming past his stomach, over his limp but rather large rattlesnake until he rested his palm on his thigh.

I frowned, uncertain what he wanted, why he was asking me this question, and then I saw the mark.

At the tip of his index finger, as if he were pointing to it, a crimson circle marred his skin. I had a flash of my mouth on his cock, his thigh, the need to taste, to draw him in, to mark him, to make him mine.

"You know where I've been, Phoenix."

My hands clenched into fists so tightly they ached. My palms stung as my nails dug in.

I knew where he'd been, all right.

He'd been in me.

Chapter 24

I don't know how the rock got into my hand. I had to have bent and picked it up off the ground. But I don't remember anything until I threw it at his head.

I expected him to dodge, to duck or maybe to put up a hand with his preternatural speed and catch the thing. Instead, he just stood there and let it hit him in the face.

A gash opened on his cheekbone. Blood trickled down. He made no move to staunch the flow but continued to stand next to the cold, dead fire and stare.

He'd done something to make me think that last night had been a dream, to lower my inhibitions, to erase my unease and fear. A spell, a potion, who knew with him. Just because I was attracted to the man's body didn't mean that I wanted to be coerced into an act so intimate.

When I'd been on the force, date-rape drugs were rampant, and every time I'd had to deal with some poor kid who'd woken up and not known where she'd been or who she'd done, I'd only gotten angrier about it.

I stalked toward Sawyer. "What did you do to me?"

He lifted a brow.

"Oh, shut up." He didn't point out that he hadn't said a word.

Blood dripped into the dirt, turning black on contact.

"Here." I tore off an end of my flannel shirt and shoved it into his hand. He lifted the cloth and pressed it to the nick I'd made.

My gaze caught on the fire, or what was left of it—ashes, charred wood, and stalks of something I didn't recognize.

"What is this?" I pointed.

"What do you think it is?"

"Peyote? LSD? Something funky." I squatted and took a deep drag. Sun-warmed, fresh-cut grass. A pleasant enough scent; then my eyes crossed and colors swirled sickeningly. "You drugged me. Bastard."

My voice sounded far way, the anger of my words, the anger that tightened my chest, not reflected in my lethargic tone.

I stood, walked to the lake, threw water on my face, then gave up and doused my whole head until the misty rainbow went away. When I opened my eyes, bare feet had appeared at the edge of my vision. I glanced up, abruptly straightening when my nose nearly brushed his dick.

"No wonder you wouldn't let me take a gun. You knew I'd kill you."

The cut on his face had stopped bleeding. It appeared to be healing right in front of my eyes. I remembered what Jimmy had said about killing him. The gun wouldn't have done me any damn good.

"You didn't seem too angry last night," Sawyer said. "Last night you liked it."

I swung at his head. This time he ducked, grabbed me before I fell in the water, and hauled my elbow behind my back until it ached. I bit my lip and refused to let out a single squeak.

"Do you see now why I say I'm different?" he whispered in my ear, his lips so close I felt them move against my lobe, causing me to remember things I shouldn't and want them again with a desperation that frightened me. He might be a skinwalker like his father, but I was starting to agree that he had a lot of his mother in him too.

Why had he drugged me? Was he that desperate for sex? I found it hard to believe. Maybe he was an outcast from his people, but he was gorgeous—at least on the outside. Most sweet, young things could care less about the inside. If all he wanted was sex, he could have gotten it anywhere.

Which meant he'd wanted sex with me. Why? He didn't love me. You couldn't love someone and do what he'd done. Although considering his life so far, I doubted Sawyer knew very much about love at all.

Not that I was an expert.

He tugged a little harder on my arm, bringing my thoughts back to the problems at hand. There were a lot of them.

"All right," I agreed, desperate for him to let me go so I could stop feeling his body aligned to mine, remembering how it moved, how I'd felt when he was inside of me. "You're evil. Happy?"

He stiffened, but not in a way that made me think he was aroused, or even angry; it was as if he'd seen something, maybe heard something.

"Not really," he murmured, and let me go.

I stumbled away, spun around. Sure enough, he wasn't looking at me, but at the wash of trees on the north side of the clearing.

Out there something howled, then something answered. No, that wasn't right. A whole helluva lot of somethings answered.

He muttered several words in Navajo that didn't sound like *hello*.

"What is it?"

"I'd hoped we would have more time."

My eyes narrowed. "For what? If you think I'm going to let you drug me and do me—"

"Coyotes only howl at night," he said.

"Well." I paused, uncertain. "That was random."

The trees shifted in a sudden breeze; the foliage danced as several animals with scraggly, gray-brown fur slunk into the clearing. The sunlight sparked off their eyes, making them shine like polished ebony.

Or maybe not so random after all.

"If coyotes only howl at night," I murmured, "what are those?"

"More than coyotes."

I was afraid of that.

Sawyer faced what now appeared to be a pack of coyotes larger than any coyotes I'd ever seen. Probably because these were the "more than" variety. I was going to assume that meant shape-shifter.

From prior experience I knew that some shifters were on our side—like Springboard. But some—like the berserker—wanted us dead. Or at least they wanted *me* dead.

I didn't have to wonder for long whose side these were on since they'd formed a half-circle between me, Sawyer, and any chance of escape. The lake was at my back; I guess we could swim for it, but they'd only follow. I wasn't very good at fighting for my life while swimming for it at the same time.

One of the coyotes charged. Sawyer did a graceful ball change and kicked the animal right in the nose. That must have hurt like hell in bare feet, but Sawyer didn't even flinch at the impact.

The shape-shifter wasn't so lucky. The sickening crunch of flesh and bone was followed by a yelp as its head snapped back. He went down, pawing frantically at his bruised, maybe broken, snout.

Instead of running, like real coyotes should, the pack growled and stalked closer, their half-circle of doom tightening.

Sawyer laughed, the sound so out of place I jumped. The coyotes even paused, tilting their heads, staring at him with their shiny black eyes before lifting their lips in silent snarls.

"Have you lost your mind?" I asked softly, furiously.

"They have."

"The coyotes?" I watched them warily. I wasn't sure what to do with ten coyote shifters; I certainly didn't need ten *crazy* coyote shifters.

"Whoever sent them."

"Why's that? From my angle, we're inches away from getting our butts handed to us in several bloody pieces."

"Wait a few minutes, our angle will change."

"Is the cavalry coming?"

"In a manner of speaking." He trailed one finger over his bicep, where the black wolf howled, then glanced at me. His eyes had shifted to yellow lupine orbs. "A lone coyote will run from a wolf."

I frowned. "They had to have known what you could do."

"Which is why they sent so many." His outline shimmered. The coyotes howled, not in fear, more like a battle cry.

"One wolf and ten coyotes," Sawyer continued, his voice rumbling as the change rolled closer, "outnumbered."

"Terrific," I muttered.

"And there lies their mistake."

"What mistake?"

Sawyer reached for my hand, drawing it toward his bicep. As my palm met the wolf, the earth seemed to move; the world around me flared electric silver.

"There isn't just one wolf anymore."

Chapter 25

I didn't know what was happening.

That's not true. I did know what, I just didn't know why. How could I possibly be shifting into a wolf along with Sawyer?

The light was so bright, I had to close my eyes. My body went first cold and then burning hot. Beneath my palm, Sawyer's bones shifted, crackling, seeming to break and then reknit in a different direction. His skin rippled as fur sprang free. When I opened my eyes, my hand was already a paw.

I toppled downward—bipedal to quadrupedal cuts the height by half. By the time my hands, knees, paws, claws—whatever—hit the dirt, I was a wolf.

I could still think; I knew who I was. Liz. I knew the enemy. Coyotes. Sawyer? Friend? Foe? Not sure. My wolf nature knew him as pack. The person deep within me wanted to tear out his throat.

Several of the coyotes took one glance at us standing shoulder to shoulder and ran. Cowards.

Sawyer snarled, his wolf voice as deep as his human voice and twice as threatening. Two more coyotes disappeared into the trees. Unfortunately the four largest snarled back.

The fight was dirty, bloody, to the death. Nothing I hadn't done before, just not as a wolf. I have to say, it wasn't bad. I was faster, stronger, with the built-in weapons of tooth and claw. No more worrying about where I'd left my knife or if I had silver bullets in the gun.

The coyotes split up. Three went for Sawyer, the other for me. I would have been insulted if I hadn't been so glad. My attacker didn't waste time but went right for my throat. I ducked and rolled, just as I would have as a human.

But I had two extra legs that didn't bend quite as well as real legs did, or maybe I just didn't know how to work them yet. The extra strength gave me speed, but that only made me crash into the earth harder. The roll wasn't really a roll, but a goofy-looking collapse and slide.

The coyote recovered and jumped on my back; his teeth sank into my shoulder. Yelping, I tried to throw him off, couldn't, so I rolled again, smashing him into the ground, and he let go. I scrambled free and, before he could right himself, I did to him what he'd planned to do to me.

The arterial spray blinded me. I wasn't used to fighting with my face. I backed away sneezing and pawing at my snout. I was tempted to jump in the lake, but as soon as my vision cleared I saw Sawyer.

He'd already killed one coyote and was chewing his way through another. But the third was huge, and he wasn't going to fight in the way of every movie villain, politely allowing Sawyer to finish what he was doing before he tried to kill him. The big coyote preferred the tag-team method.

But then so did I.

I charged across the space separating us and plowed

into him just as he sank his teeth into Sawyer's back. The coyote grunted and let go, though not without taking a bit of Sawyer with him. I had to give Sawyer credit. Despite the pain, he didn't stop what he was doing, which was holding the other shifter down, teeth buried in his throat, until he quit moving. There had to be a quicker way.

A way I needed to find because the third coyote recovered from my broadside blow with such ease I knew he could wear me down. If I tired, I was done, because my only weapon against this one was my speed and determination.

He charged me as I'd charged him, but I saw it coming and got out of the way. He stopped, turned, and launched himself before I had time to recover. Maybe speed wasn't going to save me after all.

I cast a quick glance at Sawyer. He was still screwing around. I gave a sharp yip as the big coyote knocked me over. The yip turned into a yowl when he bit into my leg; I scrambled to protect my soft underbelly.

Kicking and clawing, I managed to hit him in the face, near enough to the eyes that he released me, but my leg wouldn't hold when I tried to get up. My right flank sank to the ground.

The big coyote's mouth opened in a lolling, victory grin. He hovered over my prone form, letting me think about what he meant to do. From the expression in his eyes, I had a bad feeling I was going to wish I were dead long before I was.

He turned in Sawyer's direction; I'm sure he meant to lope over there and kill him; I wasn't going anywhere. I used the last of my strength to yank on his hind leg as he'd yanked on mine.

The bones crunched between my teeth; he went down with a thud and I twisted, forcing him onto his back. He scrabbled frantically, trying to defend his underbelly, but it was too late. Sawyer was there, and he finished him off, much quicker than he'd finished off any of the others.

I lay for a minute, panting. The clearing was awash with blood and fur and bodies. Groaning, I tried to get up. Sawyer used his head to nudge me back down.

He shimmered, body lengthening, fur shortening, face melding back into that of a man as he rose from four legs to two. If I didn't know better I'd think he'd been performing some strange, Navajo mountain ritual, complete with red war paint.

I whined. I wanted to change back too, but I didn't know how. Panic made my heart thunder. What if I stayed this way?

"Relax, Phoenix."

I understood him. How strange. If I was a wolf, how could I understand words? But I was a woman too. I had all my memories. I knew who he was, who I was.

"Imagine yourself as yourself and yourself you will be."

Amazingly, that gibberish made sense. I closed my eyes and focused on my own image. Heat flooded through me, followed by icy cold. I saw a bright flash beyond my closed eyelids, as if lightning had flared from the clear blue sky. A breeze blew, ruffling hair, not fur. I opened my eyes and lifted my hand, tilting it this way and that, fascinated with each one of my five fingers.

I couldn't stop shivering. I wasn't sure if that was because of the sudden loss of fur, or the dampness of the blood on my skin. I was naked, like Sawyer; the clothes I'd been wearing lay in shreds across the ground.

I touched my face and my palm came away coated in red. My mouth tasted of hot copper pennies; my nose filled with the scent of them. Leaning over, I retched.

"You'll get used to it."

My head came up so fast, the world rocked. "What was in that fire?"

"You think—" Sawyer broke off.

"It *wasn't* in the fire?"

He strode to the lake, stepping neatly over the prone forms of the coyotes. Were they really dead? I couldn't detect any breathing, but that didn't mean they wouldn't start. However, Sawyer didn't appear concerned that they might suddenly heal all their wounds and try to kill us again, so I decided not to borrow trouble. I had enough without it.

Sawyer dived in. The splash and trickle lured me. I began to crawl in that direction.

"What are you doing?" Sawyer stood hip deep, lifting water and splashing his chest, rubbing his arms, loosening the dried blood and dirt.

"I need to wash."

"Walk."

"But my—" I paused, frowned, then glanced at the leg the coyote had mauled. It appeared to be healing at warp speed.

I scrambled backward, as if to distance myself from the bizarrely knitting thing, but it was part of me and followed. I twisted, trying to see the wound on my shoulder where the first coyote had bitten me. I was too covered in blood to tell for certain, but I thought that one was completely gone.

"What the hell?" I whispered.

"Shape-shifters aren't easy to kill." His voice was matter-of-fact. He wasn't telling me anything I hadn't heard before, except—

"When did I become a shape-shifter?"

"Last night," he said simply, and ducked beneath the surface of the lake.

First things first; I joined him. My mind wasn't working quite right. I kept catching scents that distracted me. Blood, death, coyotes. How long was that going to last?

I had a lot of questions. I just couldn't seem to keep one of them in my head for more than an instant. So I dived into the chilly lake, keeping my distance from Sawyer. I had no doubt he was the source of this change in me. I wasn't going to let him get close enough to change me again.

By the time I'd washed all evidence of the battle from my body, Sawyer had dragged the coyotes into the trees. I wondered momentarily why, then decided I didn't care as long as they were gone.

I climbed out of the water and used the towel he'd discarded; the dampness on the cloth that he'd rubbed all over his naked body made me tingle. I couldn't stop remembering the things I'd done with him, things I'd believed to be a dream but knew now to be real.

I felt less scattered, more myself. Although yesterday I never would have walked around camp stark naked, today it didn't matter. Sawyer had seen all of me, touched all of me too. What did I have to hide? Nevertheless, I went into the hogan and donned my last set of mountain attire.

When I came out, he'd started a fire; this time the flames burned yellow, red, and orange, no rainbow connection. I didn't smell anything but wood and meat. He'd donned his breechclout again, then skinned the rabbit and now roasted it on a spit.

"Are they dead?" I asked. Not the most important question, but one I could handle.

Sawyer nodded, staring into the flames, turning the rabbit spit slowly.

"They can't heal? Like . . . us?"

He shook his head.

"But they're shifters."

"One of the ways to kill a shifter is a fight to the death with another shifter. The wounds don't heal."

"Ours did."

"Because we shifted shape, which accelerates the healing process; when you're dead, you can't shift."

My gaze wandered over him. "How is it that your tattoos don't heal?" I asked.

"They weren't made by a human wielding a needle, but by a sorcerer who wielded lightning."

"They're magic tattoos," I clarified.

He glanced up; the hair casting over his face did nothing to hide his wry expression. "Obviously."

Since his explanation of magic tattoos actually made sense, I moved on.

"I still don't understand why we couldn't just blast the coyote shifters with silver like Jimmy and I did with the werewolves in Hardeyville." Besides the fact that we'd left all our weapons at home. That decision looked stupider by the minute. But it hadn't been *my* decision.

Sawyer's lips tightened when I said Jimmy's name, but for once he answered my question. "These weren't werewolves. They were coyote shifters."

I threw up my hands. "So?"

"Werewolves are people who can turn into wolves. Coyote shifters are coyotes that can take human form."

That made me pause. I hadn't considered the shifting might work both ways.

"They were born animals and learned to walk as humans?"

"Cursed to walk."

"Cursed," I repeated.

"By a witch."

"You?"

He sent me a disgusted glance before returning his attention to the rabbit. "I'm not the only witch in the world, Phoenix."

"Why would walking as a human be a curse?"

"Why wouldn't it?" he muttered.

I frowned. "Explain the powers of a coyote shifter."

At first I thought he'd refuse, but despite what had happened last night and today, he was still supposed to be my teacher, preparing me to lead a battle I had no business leading.

"They're coyotes most of the time," he said. "But one night a month they walk as humans, and they howl in despair for their coyote form."

"Isn't being human an advantage? Power of speech. Indoor plumbing. Fingers."

"Humans who've never had the joy of being a beast don't understand."

I'd had the joy. It hadn't been so great.

He must have read my expression because he continued to explain. "Being an animal means freedom. No job. Few worries. As a wolf, you belong to a pack. They take care of you. You have a mate. She never leaves you." His gaze turned toward the mountains. "Until she dies."

There was more to that story, but he didn't give me a chance to ask. Not that he'd have answered.

"Becoming a human for only one night means they have nowhere to go. They wander the earth, naked and confused. Different."

I could see where that might suck.

"What's the purpose of one night as a human?"

"A coyote shifter is more than a beast because it takes

on certain aspects of the human side. Those aspects are regenerated every month beneath the moon."

"Full moon."

"New moon, when it's dark and easy to hide." He contemplated the rabbit. "A coyote shifter has the speed of a coyote, but they're larger than most and much, much smarter. They understand how humans think, because they are human."

"Once a month."

Sawyer dipped his chin. "To the Navajo the coyote is a bad omen. They're a symbol of black magic."

I let my gaze wander over his tattoos. "Then why don't you have one? Aren't you the black magic king?"

"So they say. I could never bring myself to become a coyote." He tilted his head to the side and slightly up, peering at me through the curtain of his long, black hair. "I was a boy once; I learned all the legends. I believed what I was taught. They said that Satan rode a coyote as he spread evil across the earth."

"I thought Satan was a Christian boogeyman."

"So did I, until I learned that the legend of the fallen angels is fact." He let his hair fall back across his face as he stared at the fire once more. "Now I think he's after everyone."

"Satan's running around loose?"

"Hard to say. But his underlings certainly are. My mother was one of them."

Despite myself, I took a step forward. Sawyer tensed. He didn't want my sympathy. In truth, I didn't want to give it to him. I was still understandably pissed off about the drugging-me-and-fucking-me incident. But we'd get to that.

"Did you know we'd meet coyote shifters?"

"How could I?"

A better question would be: How couldn't he? He knew everything else.

"It just seems to me that a gun would be a good idea. Boy Scout law, be prepared. It's a good law."

He leaned forward, putting his weight on his knees, before meeting my eyes. "This was a vision quest. That means we go into the mountains with only water and clothes. No weapons, no food."

"And what?" I threw out my hands. "Wait for the Great and Powerful Oz to help us?"

He sighed. "I'm supposed to be teaching you."

My eyes narrowed. "Is that what you call it?"

He held up his hand, and I stifled all of the angry words within me at the expression on his face. When he looked like that, even the wind died.

"There will be times when you only have yourself and what power comes from within. You can't depend on conventional weapons when dealing with the Nephilim. Most of them are killed by one thing, and it isn't often a weapon forged by modern man since the Nephilim pre-date Christ."

When the only weapons were swords, knives, and the ever-popular cross and nail.

"In the case of the coyote shifters," Sawyer continued, "being killed by another shifter is the only thing that works, which makes them damn dangerous. They'll keep coming and coming until whatever they've been sent to eliminate is dead."

Since what they'd been sent to eliminate was me, I remained silent. I was lucky to be alive, and I knew it.

"How did they know where we were?" he murmured. "That's what I can't figure out. I cloaked our whereabouts."

"You're no slouch in the power department," I agreed.

"I'm not," he said without a trace of false pride. "Which means that whatever is sending these beings— the chindi, the coyote shifters, the Nephilim that are finding and killing the others—is extremely gifted."

"So maybe Satan is riding the coyote."

"Maybe he is."

Chapter 26

Silence fell over the clearing. It didn't last long.

"You drugged me so I'd sleep with you."

His eerily light eyes flicked to mine. "Make no mistake, you'd have slept with me eventually. I just hastened the occurrence of the inevitable."

"What was the rush? Haven't gotten any in a few centuries?"

His lips curved. "Oh, I've gotten plenty."

The way he said it made me think he'd had better, and I wanted to smack him. Last night had been the best sex I'd ever had. Which only made me . . .

Pathetic? Confused? Furious? Tempted?

"That was rape," I lashed out.

"I didn't force you to do anything you didn't want to do. The *ya' lid* is a Navajo herb that releases your true desires." His voice lowered until I had to strain to hear him. "From deep down where those desires live."

Because his words made that deep-down part of me throb, I snapped, "So *you* say."

"You want to believe I raped you, believe it." He stood and caught me by the forearms, hauling me against him. "That won't change what happened and why."

I struggled, but I shouldn't have bothered. He'd let me go only when he was finished with me.

"I'm a catalyst telepath," he said.

I stopped struggling, my brain searching for the knowledge I'd obtained long ago. "You bring out abilities in others."

"Yes."

"How?"

His brows lifted. "How do you think?"

Sex.

I heard the word in my head as clearly as if he'd said it.

A vague sense of disappointment washed over me, followed closely by embarrassment at my stupidity. Had I really hoped he'd drugged me because he couldn't wait another instant to get between my legs? Apparently I did, deep down where all those secret desires lived.

"So you whore for the federation?"

I had expected him to pale, let me go, maybe slap me in the mouth. I did not expect him to shrug and say, "Someone has to."

This time when I struggled, he let me go. "What ability did I need in such a great big hurry? Shape-shifting?"

He frowned, opened his mouth as if to say one thing, then shut it, shook his head and said another. "Ruthie gave you her gift, which was clairvoyance, the ability to clearly see."

"The future? The past?"

"The identities and supernatural natures of the Nephilim. However, you were partially blocking the talent. Or maybe your innate psychometry was. Knowing by touching is your gift. But you had to be able to hear, to see another way. You needed to open yourself."

"Sheesh, could you play a new tune?" I muttered. He ignored me.

"I'd hoped I could get you to open without sex, but you were being as stubborn now as you were when you were here the first time."

"Excuse me if I'm no good at being open." I made quotation marks in the air around the last word. I did have a few trust issues. Considering Sawyer, considering Jimmy, who could blame me?

"Does Jimmy know how you—" I paused, uncertain how to say it.

With his usual intuitiveness, Sawyer filled in the blank. "He knows what I do."

I expected fury, hot and bubbling. Instead my eyes stung, shocking me. I turned toward the clear, calm waters of the mountain lake and waited until the uncommon urge to weep passed. It didn't take long.

I thought about what had happened today, and a prickle of unease came over me. Shape-shifting was a Nephilim trait, at the least a breed. I had no idea who my parents were, but maybe Sawyer did.

"What about the shifting?" I faced him. "Where in hell did I get that?" I braced myself to hear that I was descended from a werewolf or worse. As usual, I was wrong.

"You're an empath."

I'd never been particularly empathetic. People's emotions usually annoyed me. Especially my own.

"Not in the usual sense," Sawyer continued. "True empaths have the ability to put themselves into another's shoes. They feel what that person feels; they empathize. But you put yourself into another's shoes literally. You can take on their supernatural abilities."

I blinked. "Because you can shift, so can I?"

"Yes," he said simply.

I rubbed my forehead. "This is gonna suck."

"I'd think you'd be happy about it. You'll be the most powerful seer on the planet."

"Goody," I muttered, dropping my hand. "I'm going to explode with power if I get some from every supernatural entity I see."

He was shaking his head before I finished. "You'll only take on a power once. If you have it already, you won't absorb more of it. And you don't get their power by seeing them."

"How then?"

He lifted his eyebrows and spread his hands.

"Touching?"

He shook his head again, but the curve of his lips told me what I needed to know, and my heart thudded so loudly my chest ached.

"Fuck me," I muttered.

"Exactly."

Silence settled over us once again as I tried to absorb this new knowledge. I breathed deeply until my heart slowed.

"Just so I'm clear," I said, "I absorbed your abilities when you screwed me."

He didn't blink at the dual meaning to my words. "Yes."

"And you knew this was going to happen?"

"I was fairly certain."

"How could you be fairly certain?" My nose wrinkled, and my voice mocked on the last two words.

"I can recognize psychic talents in others."

"How convenient."

He wasn't bothered by my scorn. I suspected he'd had enough of it heaped on him over the centuries to become immune. It wasn't as if he cared what I thought. It wasn't as if I mattered to him beyond a means to the end of saving the world.

If I wasn't involved in this mess—if I hadn't been literally screwed for the greater good—I might think him heroic. But I *was* involved, and what I thought was that he was a manipulative asshole.

"Take it back," I said.

"No."

"I don't want any of your abilities."

"I don't care."

We went silent. What else was there to say?

"Do you know who my parents are?" I blurted.

He blinked, once, slowly. "Why would I?"

"I got my abilities from somewhere, I just figured . . ."

"That you were a breed? Or perhaps they were?"

I shrugged.

"Could be. I'm afraid I don't know."

"Who would?"

He looked away, then quickly back. "I don't know that either."

Was he lying? Who could tell? Certainly not me.

I got back to business. According to Sawyer, I should now be able to do what Ruthie had—know the Nephilim's human face, understand what they were so that I could give orders to kill them. I should receive this information . . . on a wing and a prayer? I wasn't sure.

"Will I hear a voice from God?" He cut me a quick, disgusted glance. "I'm serious. How does this work?"

"Close your eyes." I did. "Now, open," he whispered.

Images of the last time he'd said that word tumbled through my mind. His mouth on my breast, his tongue against me, his body deep inside, pushing, pulsing, making me—

My eyes snapped open. Sawyer stood too close, body aligned to mine. I could feel his erection, straining toward me through several layers of clothing. For an instant I swayed forward, brushing us together. My breath caught, my body tightened. His pupils dilated, the black driving out every vestige of gray.

"What did you see?" he asked.

I needed to break the connection, but that would only prove to him how much he affected me. So I stayed right where I was.

"Nothing."

His palms cupped the curve of my waist, pulling our lower bodies into alignment. "Maybe we need to try again."

He flexed his hips, sparks flared at the edge of my vision. My head began to drop back; his mouth began to descend. All I had to do was let him . . .

I brought my knee up. He countered the move easily. Although his preternatural speed was supposedly only available in animal form, he was unnaturally quick as a human.

He still held my waist. Our faces were so close our breath mingled. "Don't touch me." I lifted his hands, stepped out of his embrace, then dropped them as if they were crawling with lice.

He continued to watch me, his eyes still spookily black despite the blazing light of the sun.

"I want to leave New Mexico," I said. "Today."

"Until you can do what you're supposed to be doing, you'll stay right here."

"You already did your thing." *Me*. "And I'm still blocked."

"They say the sixth time's the charm."

"Tough. Find another way. You can't sleep with everyone who comes here for help."

"I can't?"

I narrowed my eyes. His face gave nothing away; it never did, and I wondered—

Was that why Jimmy hated him so?

I jerked my mind from the thought, and turned away, but Sawyer followed. "Ruthie gave her life so we could win this war."

"She gave nothing; her life was taken from her."

"I don't think so. Ruthie would have known her time was coming. Being Ruthie, she would have known exactly how and when. She could have prevented it if she'd wanted to."

I spun back around. "Why didn't she?"

"Her death was a declaration of war."

"The prophesy," I murmured. "The final battle."

"Yes. But in dying she made a declaration of her own. It was a great joke, really."

"Yeah, I was laughing my ass off when I found her in a puddle of her own blood."

His lips tightened, but he went on. "The leader of the darkness thought he was making us weaker by taking our leader, but instead he made us stronger."

"How so?"

"By dying, Ruthie became eternal. She guides us through you. And you'll become more powerful than she could ever have been."

I didn't feel powerful. I felt, again, like a failure. However, this time, failing wouldn't just get my partner killed; failing would probably end the world as we knew it. But, hey, no pressure.

I took one step away from Sawyer, needing space, a little time, only to freeze at the sound that swirled around the clearing.

The furious hiss of a rattlesnake.

I looked down. One was coiled near enough to strike. Where had it come from?

"Get back." Sawyer was all business again. His erection appeared to have deflated at the sight of the rattlesnake. Understandable. I thought I might wet myself.

"Can't," I murmured, trying my best not to move anything but my lips, and those not too much either. The word came out both shaky and muffled.

The sound of cloth sliding across skin caught my attention. Sawyer had dropped his breechclout and wrapped his hand around his limp penis.

Now? I thought incredulously. But a single touch and he shimmered, then shifted. His body was there one second and gone the next. Like Wile E. Coyote who drops off the cliff—now you see him, now you don't. The only thing left in the suddenly vacant air was a little swirl of current.

I lowered my gaze. Two rattlesnakes slithered toward each other far too close to my feet. I tensed, unwilling to move and draw attention to myself, even when one of them scooted over the toe of my boot.

I'd never seen a rattlesnake, let alone two. I was a city girl. Did snakes fight? What would I do if they did? What would happen if the Sawyer snake lost and the winner came after me?

I'd hide, but where? Inside the hogan, I'd be trapped.

The water? Not much better. I was pretty certain snakes could swim.

Up a tree? Perhaps. Unfortunately, all the trees were on the other side of the snakes.

The two met, rising up, bodies bobbing more like cobras than rattlesnakes. Their triangular heads shot at each other. I flinched. But instead of striking, they wrapped their necks around and around, twining together for an instant before breaking apart.

I wasn't sure which one was which, until the sun seemed to spark off the nearest, making it shimmer shining silver. The next instant it grew, lengthened, rose toward the sun and burst free a man.

"It's for you," Sawyer said.

Chapter 27

Sawyer grabbed my hand and dragged it to his penis.

"Hey!" I pulled back. "Do I seem like I have a burning desire to jerk you off?"

His eyes flared, the most anger I'd seen from him in ages. "He wants to tell you something."

"Who is he?"

"A snake."

"Just a snake. Nothing extra?"

"No."

"Then how can he tell me anything?"

"That's why you need to shift. The only way to talk to the animals is to become one."

"I don't want to talk to him."

Impatience flashed across his features. "Grow up. This is your life now. Deal with it."

He snatched my hand again, and from his grip, I knew he wouldn't let go regardless of what I said, or how I struggled.

I loosened the tight fist I'd made the first time he'd grabbed me. As much fun as it might be, I couldn't slug him. At least not right now.

He looked me up, and then down. "It'll be easier without the clothes."

I was starting to see why he favored a breechclout most of the time.

I sighed; he let me go. I stripped, then met his eyes. "This is the only way?"

Stupid question. I'd touched the wolf tattoo the first time I'd shifted. Sawyer had touched himself to become the snake. To become one myself, touching was involved, and since I didn't have a tattoo . . .

He gave a sharp nod, face set, as if he didn't want me to touch him any more than I wanted to. Because of that expression, I probably grabbed him a little too hard, squeezed a little too much.

How many times did I need him to show me that he'd only been with me because he'd had to be? What difference did it make? It wasn't as if I loved Sawyer any more than he loved me. I'd only loved one man in my life, and he was as untrustworthy as this one.

I gave myself up to the chill, the heat, the wash of silver flowing through me, the pull of another entity that came from outside myself as well as within.

Beneath my fingers, Sawyer's skin warmed; I could feel his pulse in my palm, beating in tandem with mine. I stroked him and heard the warning rattle of his snake.

Light exploded, blinding me. The wind blew past me as I fell from a great height. I tried to catch myself, but I no longer had arms or legs. Instead the ground met my belly, my back bent in ways my back had never bent before.

I saw the world from a different angle, in an entirely different way. I couldn't hear, not really.

Did snakes have ears? I didn't think so.

Instead, I sensed vibrations, movement, a wash of heat across my face. Something warm-blooded and small just there. My head swiveled to the right. Beneath that bush, a mouse quivered, black eyes wide, nose twitching in terror, and I liked it.

Nearby something much larger and equally warm loomed. Sawyer. A man. Not prey. No. He was the only one like me in the world.

I relished the power to mete out death with one swift attack. I wasn't angry; I was just . . . me. My nature was to watch and wait, to sense, to strike when striking was necessary.

But I also knew, in that other part of me, that I was more. I was Elizabeth. I was a woman most of the time.

The sensation of movement drew me in another direction, but no warmth there. Cold-blooded, then. The rattler that wanted to talk to me.

How did I talk to a rattlesnake, even when I was one?

My companion coiled his body round and round, the movement mesmerizing. The triangular head lifted, darting forward until we were eye to eye.

Seer.

The word appeared in my mind, a thought not my own. I waggled my own three-sided head.

Listen and understand.

Listen? A bit hard without ears, but I got the concept. There was some kind of telepathy involved here. Maybe all animals had it.

Telepathy? the voice whispered. *What is this?*

Sharing of thoughts.

Yesssss. I come to share with you the thoughts of all earth's creatures.

All?

The snake zigged one way, then zagged in the other. *All who matter. Those who follow the path of good.*

Snakes follow the path of good? Wasn't there a little incident in a garden?

The bone-chilling rattle sounded. I wasn't afraid. I had a rattle of my own. Just thinking of it made my tail buzz, and I got a head rush very much like adrenaline.

Not all snakes follow the dark man. Are all women as foolish as Eve?

Point taken.

Our rattles stopped buzzing.

You must fight the fight, seer. Only you can thwart the coming end times.

Why me?

Who is to know why this one is chosen and that one is not? You have the power, and you must use it.

What if I don't want to?

Then you must live with that choice, or die from it. Only those who truly embrace what they are, who commit to the fight, can succeed.

And if I can't? If I fail?

All will suffer. Not just humans, but beasts as well as breeds. The horrors to come will be as nothing you have known or imagined. You must do whatever it takes to become who you were meant to be, and then you must do whatever necessary to win. There will be sacrifice and pain. There will be choices.

Choices. I'd never been good at them.

The rattlesnake's head lowered. Its body swirled, round and round, unwinding from the coil, then sliding rapidly across the dirt until it disappeared beneath the bush where the mouse had been.

A scratch, a scramble, then a sharp squeal. Silence.

The temptation to follow, to see if perhaps there was more than one mouse, was nearly overwhelming. But there was also that large, warm-blooded presence nearby.

Sawyer. He waited.

I imagined myself myself, and I was.

Well, not quite like that—shazam, I was me. But first hot, then cold, silvery light all around. Up I went; there I was.

Sawyer sat cross-legged next to the fire. He'd removed

the rabbit. The scent was heavenly. My stomach contracted so tightly I sneezed. Or perhaps that was just the chill on my naked skin or the remnant of my blood having cooled. Quickly I dressed.

I joined Sawyer, and without comment, he handed me a plate of meat. I was so hungry I didn't mind the lack of utensils. I shoveled it in with my fingers, barely chewing. I couldn't recall anything ever tasting so good.

When I was finished, he took the plate, rinsed it in the lake, and began to pack what was left of his things.

I wasn't sure what to say, so I fell back on the easy questions. "What's the point to snake shifting? I mean, I understand the power of a wolf, a mountain lion, the shark. But—" I waved vaguely in the direction of his crotch.

"Did you feel the warmth of prey wash over your face?" he asked. "Did you know, despite the lack of sound, where everything was?"

"Yes."

"Rattlers are pit vipers; we have pits below our nostrils to detect warm-blooded beings. Even in the dark we will find our prey. We can slither into places no other beast can, often undetected, and survive where warm-blooded animals cannot. Just by rattling our tails, we make all living things run."

It creeped me out the way he said *we,* but I was also oddly pleased. I felt connected to him. There *was* no one like us in the world.

I shook off the pull of that connection. I didn't want it.

"Is there a way to make all these powers go away?"

"All of them?" Sawyer sat next to me on the bedroll. "You don't want the power you were born with?"

"I never did."

"Let me guess. You want to be normal?" I nodded. He sighed. "You aren't. We aren't."

"Couldn't I be?"

"There is such a thing as destiny. You were created the way you were for a reason. You were meant to be who and what you are."

"What if I don't want to be?"

"Did it occur to you that if you don't follow your destiny, if you become the normal woman you think you wish to be, the world you wish to be normal in will no longer exist?"

There was that.

Hell. The snake had said there'd be choices, but in this case there weren't. Not really.

My life had changed at Ruthie's; I had changed, and fighting against that change was not going to bring my other life back. It hadn't been all that great anyway.

Sawyer stared into my face. He must have seen my capitulation, because he stood. "Time to travel down the mountain."

"But I haven't—"

"You will."

His confidence was inspiring, but I still hadn't had a vision; I wouldn't be able to tell Jimmy or any of my other DKs what they needed to know. I hadn't wanted this power, but since I appeared to be stuck with it, I should at least be able to use it without getting myself and everyone around me killed.

"If you're so smart"—I stood too—"why don't you have the visions?"

"Because you were meant to have them. I was meant to show you the way."

He'd knelt and begun to roll the bedroll into a cylinder. I put my foot directly in the middle and he stopped, glancing up.

"You knew that sex would bring me into my power."

His lips thinned; he sat back on his heels. The

sheepskin, released from the pressure of his blunt, strong fingers, loosened, spilling across his knees in a soft wave.

"You know that I did."

"You do this to save the world."

He frowned, confusion spreading across his time-less face.

I thought of the centuries he'd been alive, the things he'd seen, the people he'd done. I'd been disgusted at first, still was a little, but I could also see how his place in this world might be more difficult than anyone's.

"Sex for most people is about love—" He snorted. "At the least about pleasure, fun, a connection. This has to take a toll on you."

He laughed. "It's not such a hardship. I am what I am."

"But—"

"I'd have fucked you anyway. It's what I've wanted since the first time I saw you."

I took a step back, and his smile was all teeth, his eyes all beast.

"I was fifteen," I pointed out, "and you were, what? Three hundred and fifteen?"

He got to his feet. "You think that matters to a man like me?"

It must have, because despite my being here that summer, just the two of us, he'd never touched me like that. Except in my dreams.

Sawyer's fingers closed around my upper arms. "Don't expect me to be a hero; I'm not capable of it."

"I think you're capable of a lot more than you let on."

To prove his point, or perhaps mine, his mouth swooped down. I didn't try to get away. I doubt I could have, even if I'd wanted to.

His kiss was rough, punishing—him or me? I didn't know. I didn't care. Our teeth clicked; he nipped my lip and I tasted blood. His tongue laved it away.

I opened to him, relishing the violence. It called to me. When he kissed me, I saw worlds, centuries, all that he'd done, everything he knew and everyone. I wanted to lap up the knowledge like a tiger at a jungle river, like a wolf at a mountain lake, like everything he was and everything I could be.

He broke away, staring into my face. "Did you see anything? Hear anyone?"

I scowled. He'd kissed me to jump-start a vision? I wanted to kick him, but that never worked out as well as I hoped.

"No." I shifted in his arms. "Let me go."

He didn't, and I considered kicking him again. My fingers brushed his shoulder where the shark lived and for an instant I felt the water, cool and sweet, all around me. I wanted to dive deeper where the darkness lived, chase things and make them bleed.

I yanked my hand away. He still didn't release me.

"Will I have to touch a tattoo every time I want to shape-shift?"

Not that I wanted to shape-shift, but I was pretty certain I was going to have to. Eventually.

"Either that or get some of your own."

"You're sure?"

"Since I have to touch them, and you've absorbed my powers, it would follow that you'd have to."

The idea of marking my skin as he'd marked his chilled me. But I was starting to understand that what I wanted and needed didn't matter, because if I didn't do whatever I had to I wasn't going to have a world for my wants and needs to exist in.

God, this sucked.

Sawyer released me as suddenly as he'd grabbed me, then knelt. I tensed, half expecting him to press his face to my stomach, or perhaps lower. My body responded, going moist at the thought. But he only caught the edge of the sheepskin and began to rewrap it.

I knelt too, then placed my hands over his. He paused, staring at them. My skin was lighter, but not by much. For some reason our hands looked right like that. A man's hands and a woman's, the way it should be, the way it was meant to be.

In the beginning.

Chapter 28

For a second I thought he meant to say something, but he never did. Instead, he pulled his hands from mine as he lifted the sheepskin and went into the hogan.

He returned moments later, dressed and packed, then disappeared into the pine trees without even glancing in my direction. What the hell did *I* do?

I suspected that my trying to talk to him as if he were a person, to understand him, to sympathize, had freaked him out. I doubted anyone had ever bothered before.

The trek down wasn't any easier than the trek up had been. In areas the terrain was so steep, I slid forward, bumping into Sawyer, who never seemed to slip. He didn't pause, didn't help, wouldn't talk.

Near dusk we reached his place. Sawyer walked straight into the hogan. He didn't come back out.

I went into the house and took a shower until the water ran cold. By then, twilight reigned. Standing in the doorway, I watched the stars arrive. In the distance, coyotes howled. I assumed they were real coyotes, but I couldn't be sure. Unless I touched them.

I cocked my head. Something tickled my brain. The snake had said I must do whatever it took to become who I needed to be. Sex with Sawyer had given me his power of shape-shifting, but I was certain he had others. Maybe I'd have to take them.

By taking him.

I lowered my gaze from the stars to the earth, and there he was, standing at the edge of the trees, naked in the night. Had he been running across the mountain as a wolf, a mountain lion, a tiger? The idea was both frightening and arousing, the depths of his power, the possibilities of it, enticing.

He continued to watch me without moving, as if his stillness would keep me from seeing him. He had to know better. I could not only see him, but hear him, smell him.

The snake had also said there'd be choices, so I made one. When he didn't come to me, I went to him.

The first time had been out of my control. I hadn't known then that the sex was real. I knew now. I chose it; I chose him. There was no going back, no denying it.

Hell, there was no stopping it—or me.

I took his hand. His skin was scalding. I wanted to feel that heat inside of me. I wanted to drown in his scent. Taste of his flesh.

His light eyes glowed moon silver as he lifted his other hand and touched my hair. It was a gesture so unlike him, I blinked.

His arm dropped to his side. His expression remained stoic. I wanted to bring joy to his face, at the least make him lose control just once.

I reached for the hem of my T-shirt, then tossed it aside along with my panties to stand naked beneath the moon. The chill night made my nipples harden. My skin pebbled with gooseflesh.

As if he couldn't help himself, he cupped a breast, his fingers dark against my moon-shrouded skin. I let my head fall back, baring my neck, the ultimate sign of trust. His breath caught. I waited for the exhale and when it didn't come, slowly I raised my face so I could see his.

He held my breast like an offering to the god of the moon, his thumb poised over the nipple as if he fought his own desires as well as my own.

I arched into him; my breath caught as thumb and nipple collided, and the curve of my breast filled his palm.

Still he hesitated, even though I could feel his erection warm against my skin. I imagined sliding to my knees, licking him as I went. He'd taste like sun and wind, salt and water, like man and more. I had to have him for no other reason than that.

"Please."

My voice was hoarse. Probably from the unlikely bend in my neck, which I again offered to both Sawyer and the moon. I began to lift my head, intent on doing what I'd just imagined—going down on him until he was the one saying please. But he stayed me with one sweep of his thumb over my nipple, one squeeze of my breast and the harsh, foreign-sounding expletive that was muffled against my neck when his mouth pressed to the curve.

His teeth worried a bit of skin, the sharpness of the bite igniting me further. My hands grasped his shoulders as he made his way to my breast, caressing, kissing, licking until I thought I might explode if he didn't—

Suddenly he swung me off the ground. I gasped at the sensation. I wasn't small; he wasn't large. But he was strong. I'd known that even before he strode across the yard, kicked back the half-open door of the house, and laid me on the bed far more gently than I'd expected.

What I'd expected was for him to do me in the yard, on the ground, against the wall of the house. Or, once inside, to toss me on the mattress, thrusting into me as he followed me down. The sex would be rough and fast, but fantastic.

Instead, he stared at me as the moon streamed through the window, casting him in ebony shadow. I couldn't see his face; I wasn't sure I wanted to.

"Sawyer?" I held out my hand.

The gesture broke whatever hesitation he'd had. I could have sworn I heard him curse again, but he joined me on the bed, covering my body with his.

However, he didn't take me as I wanted him to, filling my eternal emptiness to bursting, opening my body, mind, and soul. Instead, he kissed me for hours it seemed, refusing to finish what I'd started no matter how much I begged.

I'd never been so aroused, so on the edge but unable to fall just from the touch of a man's mouth on mine. I wondered if he'd been in the desert making magic beneath the moon, casting a spell over this house, over him and me, over us.

He lifted his head. The slight light of the moon glinted in his eyes, sparkled off his moistened lips, leached the color from his face so he seemed poised like a sepia photograph, something out of the distant past, frozen in time, surreal despite the burning heat of his body. Then he closed his eyes, shutting me out even as he joined us together.

The orgasm was immediate and intense; I cried out. Not his name, I wasn't that far gone, but a sound both shocked and satisfied, pure woman touched by man in the darkest part of herself.

Out there something answered. Something wild and free. Something other. And Sawyer lifted his head and cried out too, as he spilled himself into me again and again and again.

I was still shuddering with reaction, still hot both inside and out, when he rolled free, got up and walked away. I was so surprised, I didn't follow at first. Had I really expected him to cuddle?

He wasn't the type. However, pretending for a few minutes was usually considered mandatory. Not that Sawyer had ever cared about rules or common decency.

Annoyed now, I jumped up and went to the door, but he was gone.

I crossed to the hogan, yanked back the woven mat, and stared at the empty room as a long, low, lonely howl rose from the mountain.

I expected a visit from Ruthie but none came. Maybe because I had such a hard time falling asleep. Without sleep, there are no dreams and so far without dreams there'd been no Ruthie.

I kept listening for Sawyer, drifting off, jerking awake at every brush of the wind, every chitter of a squirrel, each creak of the house or a tree. When dawn arrived I was more exhausted than I'd been the night before, and no further along in my quest for a vision.

I was a failure at this seer gig. Not that I'd wanted it in the first place, but since I appeared to be stuck it would certainly be nice not to be the worst seer in the history of the world.

"Come on," I muttered. "Let me have it. I'm ready and I'm willing." But was I able?

I sat up, and the room flickered. Dizziness hit me so hard I wanted to retch. I closed my eyes and—bam—I saw a man.

Or maybe *man* wasn't quite the right word.

Strega, Ruthie whispered.

I could see his face—handsome enough, but thin, the bones of his cheeks and nose prominent, the olive-toned

skin stretched tightly so he had few wrinkles, yet his
seemingly bottomless onyx eyes were ancient.

His hair spilled back from his forehead and down to
his shoulders, ebony waves that reflected golden flickers
of candlelight. Wisps of smoke trailed here and there before vanishing on the currents of air.

He passed his hands, long-fingered and supple, familiar somehow, over a bowl of liquid on the table in front of
him. His lips moved in the rhythm of a chant, though no
sound reached me. The liquid rippled—dark and ruby red
in the half-light. It looked suspiciously like—

"Blood."

He glanced up at the word, cocked his head. Had he
heard me?

My heart thundered at the idea of this . . . strega—
whatever that was—seeing me as I saw him. He seemed
to be casting a spell, which made him some kind of
witch. I'd find out just what kind when the vision ended.

I tried to see everything the vision afforded me. He
wore a business suit—black, with an equally black shirt
and tie. The effect should have been funereal, but was instead elegant. Probably because of the strong, straight line
of his body, the sense that beneath the clothes someone—
some*thing*—powerful lurked. He appeared both ancient
and modern—the candlelight and bowl of blood in contrast to the fashionable suit and silk tie.

The room was modern too, the décor slick chrome
and glass. Some kind of office, since I could see a desk
with neat stacks of papers and a telephone; the table he
stood at was long with chairs positioned every few feet.

Suddenly the strega dropped his hands and moved toward the curtains, yanking them aside. Sunlight spilled
in through the wall of windows beyond which a boom-
ing metropolis loomed.

I knew this place. I'd seen it on the television for days

on end one September in 2001. From this window I could see the hole in the buildings where the towers had tumbled down. And if that wasn't a big enough hint, the Empire State Building rose up just to the right on the opposite side of the street.

The strega was in New York City, and so was Jimmy.

Chapter 29

I came out of the vision with a jerk, tumbling from the edge of the bed and barely catching myself before my face slammed into the floor. Then I lay there, trembling with reaction. Visions kind of sucked.

I managed to get up. I had no time to waste. I needed to call Jimmy. Except my cell phone didn't have a battery.

I threw on whatever clothes were handy and headed out the door. I ran right into Sawyer.

"I need my phone battery. Now."

His gaze sharpened. "You had a vision. What did you see?"

"Strega."

"Witch," he murmured.

"Yeah," I agreed. "The spell he was casting kind of gave it away."

"Spell?"

"Bowl of blood, a lot of hand-waving, a chant I couldn't hear." Sawyer frowned. "You know what that means?"

"No, but I've never known a bowl of blood to be a good thing."

Sawyer left the room, returning quickly with a book so old the paper looked like parchment, the writing on the cover faded and spidery. Trust him not to have an Internet connection for research. No, he had to have a book that appeared as old as his soul, written with a quill.

He opened it, thumbed through, then met my gaze. "This is the being responsible for killing Ruthie and all the others."

I started and reached for the book. "How do you know that?"

"A strega is not only a medieval Italian witch but a vampire, one with the power to control animals. So if he didn't kill her outright—"

"He sent those things to do it for him."

All the pieces were falling into place. We'd already established that whoever had set the chaos of doomsday in motion had to have more power than most Nephilim. A witch from medieval Italy certainly fit the bill.

I skimmed the text, frowned and glanced up. "I don't see any way to kill it."

"Maybe there isn't one."

My heart lurched. "That's impossible."

"Is it?"

"I've got to call Jimmy."

Sawyer tossed me my cell phone battery. I snapped it in, pleased to discover I had service, then punched buttons until I found Jimmy's number. I got voice mail.

"It's me," I said. "Liz. Call me right away."

I disconnected, frowning. "The phone didn't even ring."

"You'll have to explain why that makes you frown. I've never owned one of those things."

"What?" I glanced up. "Oh. The phone goes to the message service without a ring if it's turned off, or out of juice—"

"Or at the bottom of the ocean along with its owner?"

"Why would you say that?"

"Wishful thinking?"

"I gotta get to New York."

Sawyer caught my arm as I tried to rush by. "Don't you find it interesting that the one you're seeking is a vampire?"

"Lately, isn't everyone?"

His fingers tightened. "Listen to me." His voice was a growl; his eyes flickered to beast and back again. "A dhampir is the son of a vampire."

An icy finger trailed down my spine. "Coincidence."

"Is it?"

"Jimmy's on our side. Even you said so."

"Maybe I was wrong. Isn't Sanducci an Italian name?"

"Who knows? Even if it is, that doesn't mean *he* is. Jimmy could be anything. For all we know some social worker plucked the name out of a hat like they did for me."

"You truly think the name Phoenix was random?"

I had, but now I wasn't so sure.

Sawyer waved away my questions before I could ask them. "I told you already, I know nothing about your past beyond what you do. I just find the fact that you were named for a mythical bird that is reborn out of the ashes again and again to be curious."

A lot was, lately.

"If Jimmy were working against us, I'd have known when I touched him." I frowned, remembering the flicker of fangs and blood, his seemingly logical explanation of his subverted vampire nature. "Ruthie would have told me."

"Ruthie's dead. Ghosts don't know who killed them, that's usually why they're ghosts."

"She's not a ghost."

"Then what is she?"

Crap. I had no idea.

"We're back to Jimmy killing Ruthie? I thought we established that was impossible."

"I think we established it was impossible that *I'd* killed her."

"He wouldn't."

Sawyer just stared at me and said nothing.

"I refuse to believe that Jimmy would kill Ruthie."

"Maybe he didn't kill her with his own fangs, but her identity was leaked, as well as the identity and where-abouts of all the others."

"He didn't know all the others."

"Someone did."

"Even if the strega is his—" I swallowed, and my throat clicked loudly in the still, empty morning. "Father. That doesn't mean Jimmy betrayed the federation, that doesn't mean he won't kill him."

"No? Funny that the strega's in New York and so is Sanducci."

"We know why he went there."

"We do?"

"Aaargh!" I yanked my arm free, and he let me. "Stop talking."

"Just one more thing," Sawyer murmured. I glared. "I've never tried the method, more's the pity, but there's a legend that says in order to end the existence of a dhampir—"

I stilled as the skin on the back of my neck prickled. In horror or delight? I wasn't sure I'd ever know the answer to that question. But I held my breath, waiting for him to finish.

"You must kill him twice in the same way," he said.

"What does that mean?"

"I don't know. It's a legend."

"Jimmy said not to believe the legends."

"He would, wouldn't he?"

Sawyer walked out. I took a quick shower, dressed, then packed what were mostly dirty clothes that weren't even mine and stepped out of the house. Summer stood next to her truck.

"Sawyer asked me to take you to the airport."

"How did he ask? He doesn't have a phone."

"He came to my house late last night."

I scowled, remembering how he'd disappeared from the premises. What was it about Summer Bartholomew that made every man run directly from my bed to hers?

I hadn't planned to say good-bye, but now I realized I had a few questions that needed answering. If I left without those answers, I'd always wonder. I headed for the hogan.

"We kind of need to go if you're going to make your flight," Summer called after me.

I gave her the finger and ducked beneath the woven mat.

Sawyer lay on his bedroll. Stark naked, ankles crossed, arms beneath his head, he contemplated the drifting clouds through the smoke hole in the ceiling.

"Do you ever think to knock?"

"Why did you sleep with me last night?"

"We didn't sleep."

I kicked his bare feet with my boots. He didn't even flinch, but he did lower his gaze from the roof to my face. Once that look would have made me grovel; now I just lifted a brow and demanded again, "Why?"

"You seemed insistent on sex." He lifted one shoulder, then lowered it, his skin sliding along the skin of the sheep with a soft, sexy swoosh. "Who am I to say no?"

What had I expected to hear? That he'd been unable to resist me? That what had happened between us last night was more than sex for gain, for power, for the safety of everyone on earth?

Ha. Unlikely. Did I really want it to be?

"The snake said I'd have to do whatever it took to find my power."

"You thought that meant do me? I can't say I minded the freebie, but it wasn't necessary."

He was back to the man I'd hated, the one who had no heart, no soul, no compassion. Had he ever really been anything else? He'd tricked me into having sex with him for the sake of the world. That I'd enjoyed it, enjoyed him, didn't change who he was, even if the sex had changed who I was.

The only difference now was that he no longer frightened me. There was an explanation for everything I'd seen, for everything he appeared to have done. He was a skinwalker, a catalyst telepath, and more. Since I now was too, the magic, be it black or not, didn't scare me. The magic was part of me.

"What do you mean by freebie?" I asked. "Didn't the sex we had last night allow me to have a vision of a Nephilim at last?"

"Hardly." He smiled his thin, knowing smile, the one that always made me want to throw something at his head. "I don't have visions, Phoenix. You got that talent from Ruthie. I unblocked you, and shared my skinwalker powers, the first time I made you come."

"What? Then why—"

Sawyer continued to lounge on the sheepskin, body splayed suggestively, like an advertisement for a porn site. Was he trying to distract me?

"I mean . . . How? What?"

"Which is it? Why, how, or what?"

"Explain," I said through clenched teeth. "Why didn't I have a vision until this morning?"

He spread his hands, the muscles and bones moving smoothly, seductively, beneath his glistening skin. "Those who send the visions must not have had anything to say."

"You asked Summer last night to take me to the airport today. How could you know then that I'd have a vision now?"

"I didn't. But I knew that you would. I've done all I can, and it's time for you to go."

Was it time for me to go because he'd done all he could, or because he'd felt something he didn't want to feel?

Either way, Sawyer was right. I had to go. If I could.

"I have all your powers?" I asked. He nodded, and I got a very bad feeling. "Which means I can't leave the Dinetah as a woman?"

That was going to seriously screw up my life. How was I going to get on a plane as a wolf? Maybe that's why Summer was here. She could book me a cage in the luggage compartment.

"That's not a power," Sawyer said softly, "but a curse."

"You were cursed? By whom?"

"My mother."

"She just keeps getting better and better," I muttered.

"She knew if I was able to leave here, I'd kill her."

"She's still alive?"

"Why wouldn't she be?"

I rubbed my forehead. Ding-dong, I'd really been hoping the Dreadful Witch was dead.

"You could still kill her as any one of your animals," I said.

"True, but it's difficult to travel across oceans and continents that way. Nearly impossible to find someone of her power without benefit of money and opposable thumbs."

"You've tried it."

"Every single year."

Silence descended. What else was there to say? I turned to go. I'd been right in the first place. Why bother with good-bye? Sawyer wasn't the type. Hell, neither was I.

I was reaching for the woven mat across the doorway when his hand slapped against the wall next to my head. "One more thing," he whispered.

I tensed and he laughed, low and kind of scary. I refused to react. Hadn't I just convinced myself I wasn't afraid of him? I wasn't. But I appeared to be afraid of how I felt about him.

I didn't love him, but I couldn't stop wanting him. The sex had been incredible—from the first time when I hadn't known it was real right through the last time, when I'd wanted both power and him. I was downright terrified that if he touched me now I'd beg him to take me again, even knowing that there was no other reason for it than desire.

I'd called him a whore for the federation, so what did that make me?

He leaned forward. Despite my clothes, I could feel the unnatural heat of his skin. His chest pressed to my back; his hand lowered from the wall to my stomach as he slid his cheek along mine.

His face was smooth; I'd never seen him shave. I'd read somewhere that the original Native Americans had very little facial hair, but as they'd interbred with whites that had changed. Considering the aeons he'd lived, I'd guess what I'd read was true.

"You are capable of obtaining powers unimaginable," he whispered. "But have a care. Never have sex with a Nephilim." Sawyer turned his head so that his mouth was right next to my ear. "Never."

His tongue flicked the lobe, and I jumped. He soothed me by stroking his clever fingers across my skin, which wasn't very soothing at all.

I slapped my free hand over his, halting the movement, then slowly turned my head until our eyes met. "I'd think the power of a Nephilim would be all that much stronger."

"There's every chance you'll absorb their evil as well as their magic. Nephilim don't care who they kill, or how many, or what they destroy. They never look back, only forward, focused on themselves always and no one else."

His voice was cool, his eyes gray ice, but I knew he remembered his mother. I leaned in and kissed him, meaning to be gentle, a "sorry for your sucky childhood" without words, but he would have none of it.

Sure he kissed me back, but he made it all sex. Tongue and teeth, devouring me until I forgot what the kiss had started out to be.

He lifted his mouth from mine, but hovered there, so close our breath mingled. Then he kissed me once more, quick and hard, before moving away. "You could be headed into a trap."

"I know." I lifted my chin. "I'm going anyway."

"I know." Sawyer held out his hand, palm down, fingers curled inward. "This is for you."

I reached out, and he dropped a silver chain and charm into my palm.

Ruthie's crucifix.

"Where did you get this?"

He gave me a wicked smile, and then he was gone—out the door and . . . I'm not sure where, just gone, the yard empty, not a sway of the foliage to reveal in what direction he'd fled.

The morning breeze blew across lips still wet from his. My body was aroused from his touch, edgy with a lack of satisfaction.

I guess that had been good-bye.

Chapter 30

Summer sat in the pickup. I didn't want to go anywhere with her, but I doubted there was a Yellow Cab company that serviced the dregs of the Navajo Reservation.

The trip to Albuquerque was long and silent. New Mexico had a definite shortage of airports large enough to service jets.

Summer kept her lips zipped. If I didn't get a flash of her and Jimmy entwined every time I looked at her, I might just like her for that alone. But I did, so I didn't.

The landscape was gorgeous—mountains bleeding into desert, every color found in nature bursting from the land, the trees, and the sky—revealing why so many artists and photographers gravitated here. There was something about the light in New Mexico that made everything seem etched by God.

Though one of the oldest cities in the U.S., Albuquerque appeared to have been plopped down at the foot of the Sandia Mountains on a whim. Ancient Native American culture existed right next to modern high-rises. According to local propaganda, the sun shone on Albuquerque over three hundred days a year. That should be enough to make anyone give the place a try.

We took the exit for the Albuquerque International

Sunport, and Summer pulled over at the curb near check-in. "You're on the three P.M. flight to Minneapolis, with a connection into Milwaukee."

I just smiled at her and shut the door. I could care less which flight I was supposed to be on.

"Hey." Summer scrambled out, ran around the front of the car, and caught me before I could escape into the terminal. A patrol car slowed, the officer rolled down his window, no doubt to tell her she couldn't park there, and she flicked her hand in his direction. Sparkles flew from the tips of her fingers, cascading over the man's face like confetti.

I gaped. I could see them, sticking in his eyelashes, coating his lips and cheeks. He drove on without saying anything.

"What the hell was that?" I asked.

Her eyebrows lifted. "You saw?"

"Oh, yeah. Isn't sparkly dust that makes people obey your every unvoiced command a little obvious on the keep-it-quiet scale?"

She rolled her annoyingly pretty blue eyes. "No one else can see. That you can, is . . . interesting. The only other person I've ever known who can see fairy dust is—" Now her eyes widened. "Oh," she breathed.

From her surprise, I guessed she hadn't been in on the plan to sacrifice me on Sawyer's sex altar.

"Was he—" She broke off, biting her lip again. I could see where the gesture would be enticing. To a man. I wanted to reach out and yank her poor lip free of her tiny, perfect, white teeth.

"Good?" I finished.

She blinked. "I—uh . . . Well, I was going to say—"

"Rough? Gentle? Amazing? Mind-blowing? Totally fuckable?" She winced at each word. I was tempted to continue, but I finished with a simple, "Yes."

Summer opened her mouth, thought better of whatever she'd been about to say, and shut it again. She was racking up smart points by the second.

"Sawyer told me to make certain you got on the plane to Minneapolis."

"Knock yourself out," I said, and went through the door.

She followed, of course. No one was going to be able to stop her. Not when she could shoot magic make-me dust from her fingertips. It might be worth sleeping with her to get some of that action.

Nah. I'd never been attracted to women, even though men were so obviously bad for me.

"You're not supposed to go to New York." Summer's shorter legs worked double time to keep up.

"Are you sure? Because I think I *am* supposed to."

"Sawyer's called some of the DKs he knows. They're going to meet you in Milwaukee so you can come up with a plan."

"I'm not going into Manhattan with guns blasting." I lowered my voice. I was in an airport after all. "I just want to find Jimmy, see what's going on. I hear that's my job."

"Jimmy can take care of himself."

Under normal circumstances, I was sure he could. However, I was equally certain the circumstances in Manhattan were not normal. But since I was in charge, I didn't have to explain myself to Summer or anyone else, so I kept walking.

I wasn't sure why Sawyer hadn't tried to convince me to stay away from Manhattan himself. Probably because I wouldn't have listened. But I wasn't going to listen to Summer either.

I guess she felt that she had to try. Just like I had to try and save Jimmy.

"I can make you," Summer said, still hustling along at my side.

"No you can't."

We'd reached the ticket line. I hoped that the difference between a fare to Milwaukee and one to New York wouldn't be over my credit card limit. If I had to, I'd call Megan for a loan, but I hoped I wouldn't have to.

I glanced at Summer, planning to tell her to fly along, and got a face full of fairy dust. Sparkles flew, clouding my vision; when they hit my face they felt like cool rain after a day in the sun.

Her mouth curved into a satisfied smile. I should have kept my mouth shut, let her believe I was going to use the ticket to Milwaukee, let her leave. But I'd never been very good at shutting up.

Instead, I leaned down, got into her face. "Don't ever throw that pixie shit at me again. Errand of mercy, remember?"

Summer cursed. I was impressed with the depth and range of her vocabulary, which sounded much more foul coming from those plump pink lips than they ever would have sounded coming from mine.

"Nice." I straightened. "You kiss your mother with that mouth?"

"I don't have a mother."

"That makes two of us." I stepped up to the counter, gave the clerk my name, and changed my ticket. Luckily there was a flight to New York leaving only half an hour after the flight to Milwaukee.

Though I hated to do it, I checked my duffel bag. I'd left the gun at Sawyer's, but the silver knife was another story. There was no way I was getting that through in a carry-on, so into the luggage compartment it went.

I headed for the gate, the fairy still at my side. "You have a mother."

I cast her a quick, suspicious glance.

"You'll meet her one day."

A chill went over me. "She's alive?"

"I didn't say that."

"You know who she is?"

"No. But you will." She tilted her head, and I could have sworn I heard the far-off tinkling of tiny silver bells. "You might not like it."

I was sick of useless advice from a fairy. I stopped walking and faced her. "If you're flashing on the future, care to let me know how things are gonna turn out with the doomsday portion of our program?"

"Can't."

"Can't because you don't know or can't because you aren't supposed to tell me?"

"I don't know. The outcome isn't certain. Everything depends on you."

"Terrific," I muttered. But Summer wasn't finished.

"There will be pain, betrayal, all you hold dear will prove suspect. What you believed once, you can believe no longer."

"So, the usual, then?" I paused as a thought occurred to me. Summer was a DK. She'd been killing Nephilim for centuries. She might be more useful than she looked.

"Ever meet up with a strega?" I asked.

She shook her head.

"Come on. You must have."

"They're very rare, extremely powerful."

"Any tips on how to kill one?"

She shook her head again. "There's no known way to kill a strega."

"Bullshit."

She blinked. "If I knew of one I'd tell you."

"Would you?"

"Of course. You're the leader of the federation. I swore allegiance long ago."

"You have to do what I say?"

"Well, I don't have to, as in I'm compelled to, but you are the boss."

"Goody." I rubbed my hands together. "Before I go, do you have any insights on killing a dhampir?" Sawyer's method really wasn't working for me since it didn't make much sense.

Now her eyes widened. "You can't—"

"Oh, I assure you I can. If Jimmy's in any way responsible for Ruthie's death, he'll answer to me." I snapped my fingers. "Death of a dhampir. Spill it."

"I never— I mean I didn't because I wouldn't—"

"Make some sense, Summer."

"I never researched that because I wouldn't hurt him."

"Even if he was going to rip out your throat, drink your blood— Wait a second. Do you even have blood?"

"Jimmy's not like that. He kills Nephilim, not people."

"So he says."

"You don't trust him?"

I laughed in her face.

She bit her lip. "I should go with you."

I paused for a minute, imagining what it would be like to locate Jimmy with Summer in tow. It might be amusing enough to put up with her, but I doubted it.

"I don't need your help."

"You do, but I can't fly."

"I thought you could, even without the wings."

"I can't fly on a plane. I mess up the controls somehow."

Then I definitely didn't want her on my plane.

I walked off, leaving Summer on one side of the metal detectors while I made my way to the other. She could have gotten through without a boarding pass, but why bother? We'd said all we had to say. If I were lucky, I'd never have to see her again.

Of course, lucky didn't seem to be in my repertoire very often lately.

That was proved to me when I boarded the plane. Since I'd purchased my ticket all of two hours ago, I had a seat between a woman who'd never seen a cupcake she didn't like and a grungy teenage boy who appeared to have given up showers until Tibet was free.

I wished for some of Summer's fairy dust so I could inspire in them a burning desire to sit anywhere but here. Perhaps back at the terminal.

The flight to New York was excruciating, but like most things in my life, it ended. As the plane banked over La-Guardia, the lights of the city sprinkled the night like that fairy dust I'd wished for. Water sparkled on either side of the runway as the pilot landed the jet with a teeth-jarring thump, then slammed on the brakes so hard I was grateful for the seat belt that kept me from kissing the back of the seat in front of me.

I tried Jimmy's number the instant the words *You may now use your cellular phones* left the flight attendant's mouth. I got voice mail again.

"Shit."

The cupcake lady scowled even as the smelly kid winked. I flipped my phone shut and got off the plane as quickly as I could, my unnatural haste making me blend in with everyone else in the terminal.

I retrieved my bag, stopped at an ATM—then winced at the remaining balance on my bank receipt. This seer gig was costly, and it didn't seem to pay very well. If I managed to succeed, at least I'd still have a day job. If I failed . . .

I shrugged and tossed the receipt into the nearest

trash bin. If I failed, money wasn't going to mean diddly anymore.

Outside the airport, I got in the cab line and climbed into the vehicle indicated when my turn came. The weather here was reminiscent of home, the night clear and crisp. I was glad I'd brought along one of the flannel shirts Sawyer had given me.

The cabby's name was unpronounceable. He was either from the Middle East, India, Pakistan, or some other country whose name I should know but didn't.

I'd been in New York twice and never gotten a cab-driver who was actually from New York. Both times I'd come for work—once for a conference on the urban po-lice force and once for a workshop on new methods for finding missing persons. I'd been sent because I was so good at it. Locating Sanducci should be a—

"Piece of cake," I murmured.

"You would like cake?" The cabby met my gaze in the mirror.

"No. Sorry."

"To where?" he asked.

Horns honked behind us. People in the cab line glared. Soon they'd be making rude hand gestures and cursing in several languages. This was, after all, New York.

"The Empire State Building."

I had to start somewhere.

I tried Jimmy's cell several times between LaGuardia and Fifth Avenue. He never picked up. Like all the other instances, the phone never rang, just went directly to voice mail.

The cab let me off at Fifth Avenue and Thirty-fourth Street. Even though it was long past the time when peo-ple with day jobs should be in bed, the sidewalks bustled.

During business hours, tourists would stream into what was now the tallest structure in Manhattan. I'd never been to the observation deck. Not only was there a never-ending line for the privilege, but it cost money. I had better uses for mine.

The building from my vision—a towering monstrosity made of glass and what appeared to be black marble—sat across the street. The sides reflected the city and its lights.

The edifice seemed almost as tall as the Empire State Building, but it was hard to tell from the ground. Guess I'd just have to check it out from inside.

That proved to be a little harder than I'd thought.

"Do you have an appointment?"

The security guard looked like something out of a graphic novel—as wide as he was tall, no neck to speak of, muscles straining the seams of his black rent-a-cop uniform.

People moved in and out of the revolving doorway—men, women, young and old—they all resembled lawyers on speed. Everyone was in a huge hurry and they were all dressed for court. Dark suits, briefcases, shiny black shoes.

Did I have the right place?

My eyes met the guard's, and Ruthie whispered, *Vampire*.

Guess so.

I smiled, trying to appear stupid, which wasn't as hard as it should be. "I just wanted to see from a higher window. The skyline, you know?"

The guard scowled and jerked his head—no mean feat considering the lack of a neck—in the direction of the Empire State Building. "Opens again in the morning. Pay the price, chicky."

Chicky? Maybe I had scored pretty high on the dummy scale.

"What is this place?"

"Whaddya think it is? Office."

"Who owns it?" I breathed, widening my eyes in fascination.

Too bad I hadn't stopped and changed into a tight, low-cut dress and some do-me shoes. Too bad I didn't own any. Still, I had the feeling this guy would have been more forthcoming if I'd shown a little skin.

As I'd expected, he didn't bite—at least not on my simpering question—just jabbed a strangely skinny finger, considering his barbell-induced body, at the exit. "Go."

I went. I wasn't getting anywhere through the front door.

Which was why they'd invented back doors.

I allowed the crowd to carry me along, then slipped free and headed down a damp, disgusting alley. I didn't plan on doing anything right away. I just wanted to check the place out. What harm was there in that?

No one lurked in the alley but me, so I tried the back entrance. Locked.

I leaned against the wall, wishing I had a cigarette, just for show. Sooner or later someone would come out.

Quicker than I'd expected, the door opened, and one of the suits strode away without even glancing back. I caught the edge before it closed and slipped inside.

I wasn't going to stay long. I stuck out like a sore thumb in my flannel shirt, dirty jeans, and boots. If no-neck saw me, there'd be hell to pay. Around here I had a feeling hell would be just like . . . hell.

Inside, the walls were brilliant white, the fluorescents so bright they nearly blinded me on the reflection. If I worked here for any amount of time I'd need sunglasses—or new corneas.

All of the activity seemed focused at the front—in

and out, a constant stream. Back here there was only me. I took that as a sign I was supposed to do exactly what I was doing. Recon.

The first floor told me nothing except this was a very busy place. The elevators were right behind the guard; I ignored them in favor of the stairs. Slipping into the stairwell, I stowed my duffel in a shadowed corner, removing only my fanny pack, which contained my cash, credits cards, and ID, and the silver knife; then I hustled up the first flight.

The second level contained offices, as did the third. I discovered the hard way that no one cared I was here when I opened the fourth-floor door and bumped into an Oriental woman wearing a suit the shade of charcoal. She nodded and moved past me as I paused to listen to Ruthie's whispered, *Vampire.* I sensed a theme.

Several other employees—also vampires—saw me and didn't scream for a guard. I supposed that once I'd passed security, I was considered A-okay.

I wandered upward, discovering law offices, just as I'd suspected, but also financial services and investment bankers. Pretty much any kind of job you'd imagine a suit would perform was contained within these walls.

By the time I got to the fourteenth floor, I was starting to get wigged about being trapped. If security, or the strega, caught me here, I'd be running down thirteen flights of stairs to escape. Not pretty or practical.

I decided to let fourteen levels of recon be enough. However, when I opened the final doorway, I gaped at a completely different hallway.

Dim lights, muted gray walls, mahogany doors, black tile. Most disturbing of all, no people.

I couldn't resist. I started opening the doors. Each room was empty. No desk, no phone, no windows. Nada.

Now I couldn't just leave. I hiked up to fifteen and discovered more of the same.

I was kind of surprised no one had come after me yet. They had cameras in every hall. Despite the extreme security of the front entrance, I was less than impressed with it as a whole. It hadn't been that hard to get in and even easier to stay.

As I was making my way back to the stairwell, debating whether I should ascend to sixteen or hightail it to the lobby before my luck ran out, I caught sight of something seemingly discarded in an alcove halfway down the deserted hall.

Leaning over, I reached for it, then snatched my hand back when I saw what it was.

A Yankees cap.

Panic flared, but I talked myself down. Jimmy's Yankees cap was still in a plastic bag, tagged as evidence in Milwaukee. This could be anyone's. Yankees' crap was everywhere, along with I HEART NY. They should just make everything I HEART THE YANKEES and be done with it.

As I stared down at that cap, I convinced myself it belonged to anyone but Sanducci. What were the chances he'd bought another, then dropped it right where I'd find it?

Pretty damn good if he was pulling a Hansel and Gretel.

As if in slow motion, I saw my hand reaching out, getting closer and closer as I bent to pick up the dreaded navy blue hat with the annoying NY. The instant I touched it, I saw him.

Bound and gagged, bare-chested and bleeding in a room very much like the ones I'd just searched.

Chapter 31

I dropped the cap and ran, crashing into the stairwell and heading up. I'd checked all the rooms on the two floors below me, and they were empty.

On the landing outside of sixteen, I paused to catch my breath and forced myself to make a plan. Blasting in there, especially when I had nothing to blast with, would get us both killed.

The only weapon I had was Jimmy's silver knife, so I withdrew it from the fanny pack and peeked into the hall.

This one was the same as all the others—dark and depressing, as empty as the rooms that lined it. I continued upward.

Now that I'd seen Jimmy, now that I believed he was *in* trouble and not one of the sources of the trouble, I couldn't leave. In a perfect world, I'd call for backup and the cavalry would come. In my world, which was so far from perfect the word had very little meaning, the backup was in New Mexico, which meant the cavalry was me.

Jimmy had looked bad—pale, sweating, bruised, and unconscious, with streams of blood trailing down his bare chest. I couldn't risk losing him by waiting even an hour. Not when I was so close.

I kept checking rooms, finding nothing, no one, until I reached the twentieth floor, last room on the left.

I smelled the blood as soon as I opened the door, saw it as soon as I hit the lights. I stepped inside, hesitating only an instant before I locked the door behind me. "Sanducci?"

No response.

Jimmy was tied to a chair. Unfortunately he was tied with chains, not rope. Someone meant business, which I'd already figured out from the cuts across his chest. They healed, even as I watched, but slower than they should have, so I knew that whoever had made them had done so with something that hurt a dhampir more than silver. Whatever that was.

Fury boiled in my gut. Talk about inhumanity, but then I guess that's what we *were* talking about. From the appearance of this room, humanity had died badly over and over again.

The place was both similar to and very different from the others I'd seen. Same shape and size, but outfitted a little better, or perhaps worse, depending on your point of view.

Of course, from the point of view of most sane humans, a torture chamber wasn't a good thing.

The walls were lined with spiky implements, both ancient and spanking new—a scimitar, a mace, knives in every shade of metal, a chain saw, even a flame torch.

No guns, bum luck. I supposed a bullet was too far removed. Whoever this place belonged to—and I was pretty certain I knew who that was—liked to get up close and personal with his victims.

Unfortunately, he wasn't too trusting, because every single weapon was chained to the wall as firmly as Jimmy was chained to the chair.

I went to work picking the lock on the chains with the silver knife. I guess it was good for something. If I could wake Jimmy up, and from the way his head lolled, I wasn't certain I could, we were out of here. I didn't bother to think of how we'd accomplish such a feat; I just knew that it had to be done. I'd carry him if I needed to.

Down twenty-odd flights? my mind mocked.

I ignored it. Sometimes you just had to.

The locks were trickier than any I'd picked before. They seemed ancient. Considering the strega's pedigree, they probably were.

Sweat began to run into my eyes. Impatiently I swiped it out and kept working. Urgency made my fingers fumble. I cut Jimmy, and he moaned.

My gaze went to his face, but he didn't wake up. By the time I returned my attention to the cut, it had already healed.

Reaching out, I traced a finger down a puckered red line on his chest. "What did they do to you?" I whispered.

"Do not sound so sad, Miss Phoenix." I froze as the voice swirled through the air all around me. "I can assure you that he liked it."

I expected the room to be empty, the voice either in my head or spilling from an intercom. I'd discovered the room now locked from the outside, with Jimmy and I trapped in the strega's lair.

This place *had* been obscenely easy to infiltrate, which only meant one thing.

Sawyer had been right.

In the back of my mind, I'd known this was a trap, but I hadn't cared. Still didn't. I'd found Jimmy, which was all that mattered. Together we'd end this.

The owner of the voice stood just inside the closed door. Had he unlocked, opened, then shut it? I doubted that. My money was on his just appearing. Poof.

I didn't ask who or what he was. If his Italian accent wasn't a big enough hint, his olive-skinned, patrician face was. I'd seen the strega before.

Slowly I stood, placing myself in front of Jimmy, the silver knife clutched in a hand gone slick with sweat. I doubted the weapon would do me much good against this . . . thing, but I couldn't bring myself to put the blade aside. At least it was something.

"You arrived so very quickly." His voice was mesmerizing—melodious and foreign. If he hadn't been an evil half-demon bent on making the human race his plaything, I might have been charmed.

"I am impressed. I believed we would have to do more to coax you here. But then love—" His lips twisted with disdain. "It has always been the undoing of the human race."

He'd used Jimmy as bait—no shock there. What I couldn't figure out was how Jimmy had allowed himself to be used. No one had used Sanducci since he was eight.

"You have survived every test I've sent."

My face must have shown my confusion because he laughed, the sound smooth, rich, and somehow wrong— joy sprouting from the joyless, amusement where amusement did not belong. "The berserker. The chindi. The coyotes." He spread his hands. "I did not think they would win, but I had to try."

I remained silent, trying to think, to come up with a plan, but having very little luck. It would be nice if Jimmy would wake up. Even nicer if his chains would just fall off like the Apostle Paul's so he could do something other than die.

"I should have known from the moment I heard your name—Phoenix—that you would rise from the ashes of every calamity."

The strega looked me up and down. The touch of his gaze made me long for a hot shower and a gallon of bleach.

"I am sorry to say you will not rise from this," he continued. "You have great powers, yes. But in the end, you are only human."

I couldn't keep my mouth shut any longer. "We'll win, and you know it."

"Do I?" His lips curved; I caught just a hint of fang.

"Read the Bible lately?" I lifted a brow. "Oh, I forgot. Your hands probably get a little crispy whenever you touch one. I'll give you the Cliffs Notes—good always triumphs in the end. Always."

"Do you really think so? What is the point of a battle if the outcome is certain?" He lifted one shoulder, then lowered it. "Even if I lose in one of the years to come, the longer I win, the longer I stay out of that burning lake of fire I have heard so much about. So do not expect me to just give in."

"Ditto," I murmured.

He laughed again. "Delightful. I do enjoy guts, and not always for lunch." The strega contemplated me with an expression I couldn't decipher, but I thought it might be admiration. "I'd like to make you an offer: Care to join my side?"

My answer was a snort. "I'm not that easy."

"No?" His face turned cruel. "According to my son, you were the easiest he ever had."

I jolted, both at the revelation, which really wasn't much of one, and at the crude dismissal of one of my fondest memories.

The strega's eyes widened. "Hit a nerve? Which one? Where you gave up the prize of your innocence so soon, or where the man you have loved most of your life has turned traitor?"

Just because Jimmy was the strega's son—if that was even true; all I had right now was the strega's word, and a lot of circumstantial evidence—didn't mean Jimmy was on his side. Why would he be? The man had left him in the streets to be used and abused.

Considering the blood, the chains, the just-healed scars, it appeared the strega had continued that policy since they'd renewed their acquaintance. Even if Jimmy had gone off the deep end, pledging undying devotion upon meeting his long-lost daddy, I couldn't see how that devotion would prevail past all the torture.

Of course, stranger things had happened.

"Sticks and stones," I said. "There's really nothing you can say that's going to make me leave him behind."

"Leave him? Just where is it you think you are going?"

"After we kill you, maybe we'll take a vacation."

The strega started laughing again. I really hated that laugh.

"He has wondered about me nearly all of his life. Did you really think he'd kill me once he found me?"

"How did he find you?"

The strega lifted one shoulder. "I let him."

"You knew he'd come to New York once he heard the seer was killed," I guessed.

My only answer was a slight tilting of his lips.

I could easily determine what had happened next. Jimmy had done what Jimmy did best; he'd gone searching for a vampire, and this vampire had allowed himself to be found. Jimmy had been trapped as neatly as I had.

The strega moved so fast all I saw was a blur, straight toward me. I gave a little squeak, then he was gone.

I whirled. He held a knife that glinted golden in the harsh overhead lights against Jimmy's throat. If what the strega said was true, if Jimmy hadn't killed him when he had the chance, if he'd been won to the strega's side somehow, I should just let the medieval vampire witch do his worst. But there was always the chance the Nephilim was lying.

A damn good chance.

"You do not believe he's one of us now," the strega said. "You think that if you can have a moment with him, you can bring him back. But life doesn't work that way, Miss Phoenix. You of all people should know better."

There was very little I hated more than when evil vampire witches were right.

"He has two natures, vampire and human. Until recently he's lived as one of you; he had no idea who he was. But since we shared blood, he's become more like me. For me he would do anything. Which is why I conceived him in the first place."

Understanding dawned and the strega smirked. "Your face is so wondrously expressive. Yes, I planted him in his mother's womb so that he could be positioned right in the middle of the federation. A talent like his would never go unnoticed. It was only a matter of time until he was right where I wanted him to be."

"Why now?" I asked. The strega lifted a brow. "He's been your creation from day one, so why declare war now and not three years past or maybe ten in the future?"

The strega's mirth faded and an expression of annoyance took its place. "I've been trying for years to get into his head. Spells and charms. Nothing worked. He's much stronger than I thought."

For an instant I felt a sense of pride that Jimmy had resisted. I opened my mouth to say so, but the strega kept yapping.

"Destiny works both ways, seer. Everything came together. My son inside the enemy camp, those with the talents I needed willing to join under my banner, and several very good years in the stock market." He shrugged. "Even doomsday costs money."

"What if serendipity"—I couldn't get the word *destiny* out of my mouth in regard to so much blood and death—"hadn't arrived before Jimmy died?" He was on the cutting edge of the battle, after all, had been for years. Sooner or later, everyone's luck ran out. Just look at mine.

"Seer." He shook his head and made a "shame on you" sound by clicking his tongue against his teeth. "You think Jimmy's an only child?"

Before I had time to curse, the strega sliced Jimmy's neck with the golden knife.

I took a step forward, and with an absent flick of his free hand, the strega threw me into the wall without even touching me.

My back hit with a thud, my head with a crack. The silver knife skidded across the floor, but I barely noticed as I slid into a dizzy heap. I blinked hard, trying to make the Tweety Birds quit chirping so loudly while they whirled round and round my head.

The strega leaned down and lapped the blood from his son's skin. Jimmy moaned, the same sound I'd heard when I'd accidentally cut him, a sound I now recognized as ecstasy, not pain. I turned my face as my stomach rolled.

"He isn't human," the strega whispered. "He never was."

My nausea receded; anger took its place. "He's more human than you think."

"I've awakened his lust for blood and pain. He cannot fight it anymore. He doesn't want to."

The strega suckled Jimmy's neck. I wanted to gag again.

"If he's on your side and all our plans are crap, why didn't you just kill me the instant I walked in here?" I asked.

Lifting his head, the strega licked his lips. "He is my son, and the one thing he's asked of me in return for all he's done . . ." He straightened, petting Jimmy's sweat-matted hair fondly. "Is that I give him you."

Chapter 32

His words caused a spark of hope. My mistake.

"You think he's still Jimmy?" The strega sneered. "That he begged me for your life? Watch." He lifted the gold knife and sliced his own arm.

Note to self—pure gold doesn't make a strega burst into flames. Too bad. That would have been a bonfire worth watching.

The strega waved his bleeding arm in front of Jimmy's face, and like a baby desperate for nourishment, Jimmy latched on.

"The more he drinks, the more vampire he becomes. Soon there will be nothing left of the human at all."

"I don't believe you," I said.

The strega removed his arm from Jimmy's mouth. It came away with a sucking sound that almost made me hurl. Jimmy fought against the restraints as the strega chuckled and patted him on the head. Then Jimmy's eyes snapped open, and I saw the truth.

No one was home.

He recognized me because he said, "Elizabeth." Except Jimmy never called me that.

Why hadn't I listened to Sawyer and avoided this trap? Would I have, even if I'd known?

No. Because Jimmy, back when he'd been Jimmy, would never have left me here alone.

"She came, Father," Jimmy whispered. "Just like you wanted." He jerked against the chains. "Let me go now."

The strega's long fingers, which should have had razor-sharp, scraggly fingernails but were instead manicured and buffed until they shone, stroked Jimmy's hair again. "You don't want to kill her right away. What fun is that? Besides, the blood of a seer—" He licked his lips, the gesture so suggestive, so . . . hungry I had another "settle down" talk with my stomach. "Ambrosia," the strega finished.

His gaze met mine, and the smirk was back. I clenched my hands to keep from launching myself across the room and smacking him. He'd only smack me back, and he wouldn't even need his hands.

I put aside thoughts of killing him. I didn't yet know how. But I'd spend every moment I had left trying to figure it out; then I'd do it.

I dragged myself upright, thrilled when my legs didn't wobble. Having a plan, however vague, always helped.

Jimmy's dark eyes followed my every movement, like a dog with a juicy steak, or perhaps a wolf that's just seen something small and tasty skitter free of cover. For the first time I was very glad of those chains.

His eyes had an odd flare of red at the center, making me think this body was just a Jimmy-shell, a home for something else, and that scared me more than anything had in a long time. Because if that were true, then where was Jimmy? Could I reach him if he were truly gone?

The door opened, and a man and a woman, black suit and gray, tromped in.

Vampire.

I was beginning to think that Ruthie's whisper was stuck.

"They're *all* vampires?" I asked.

The strega contemplated me for several seconds, as if trying to decide if it would help his cause or hurt it for me to know what I was dealing with. He decided, as I already had, that it didn't make much difference what I knew. I'd never leave here alive.

"They are," he agreed. "My personal army."

"They look like lawyers," I mused, "which I guess makes sense. Bloodsuckers."

He dipped his head in an Old World gesture rarely seen in this one. "We fit in well here, and Manhattan has always been the best place for those of our kind. So many people, so little time."

Sawyer had said that New York was a place where the Nephilim thronged. I suspected a vampire, or a thousand, could survive in the big city virtually undetected. Who would notice a missing street person here, a tourist there? And so what if they did? I doubted anyone would ever find the bodies.

The vamps suddenly lifted me right off my feet.

"I can walk," I protested. They didn't speak, didn't even glance my way. They were a little robotic.

Vampire robots. The movie would probably be a blockbuster. People were such sheep.

I winced at my thoughts. For the vampires, people *were* sheep, or maybe cattle. Definitely food. I did not plan to be the next course on anyone's plate.

As the vampires hustled me from the torture chamber, which appeared to have been staged for my benefit, or perhaps Jimmy's pleasure—his moaning at the pain of the cuts was pretty damn creepy—I searched for any weakness in their defenses.

I didn't find one, unless you counted the ease with which I'd gotten in, and since they'd been waiting for me, had obviously *let* me in, only making a token resistance at the front so I wouldn't bolt, that didn't count. They had played me just right, no doubt because Jimmy had told them how.

Into the elevator we went. Boy vamp swiped a key card, girl vamp pressed *P.*

Penthouse. Swell. The first time I'd ever be in one and I really didn't want to go.

The elevator opened, and instead of lifting me and carrying me, they just shoved—both of them at the same time, as if they could communicate telepathically, or perhaps they only had one brain between them. I flew off my feet, landing on my hands and knees in the middle of the room.

"A simple *this is your floor* would have been sufficient," I muttered.

The only answer was the soft swoosh of the doors, followed by the muted whine of the elevator descending.

I glanced behind me. They'd both left. Scrambling up, I examined the call button. It required one of the key cards to activate. I wasn't surprised.

Penthouse? Prison?

Potato? Pot-a-toe?

I faced the wall of windows. Since this was the tallest structure in the area, except for the Empire State Building, I didn't have to stare into another building full of workers scurrying ratlike through a maze of cubicles.

Out there I saw only navy blue night, a few distant stars not overshadowed by the lights of Broadway, Fifth Avenue, hell, every avenue.

For a minute I missed Friedenberg so badly I ached with it. I had a very bad feeling I wasn't ever going to see home again.

The rest of the place was pure penthouse, and when I say that I mean decorations by Larry Flynt.

The color scheme was black, accented by glass and

chrome, just like the building itself. The sofa was black leather, shiny but soft, with a control panel on the arm. One touch and the thing sprang outward, unfolding into a bed. A second button and music swirled around the room. Barry White. Oh, brother.

The kitchen appeared as if it had never been used, and why would it have been? The entire building seemed to prefer its nourishment straight from the vein.

The bathroom was electric-white ceramic tile with a thin thread of black running through. The tub was huge, big enough for two, with buttons to control the jets and once again to cue Barry.

When I turned on the bedroom lights, I winced at the explosion of color after so much black and white. Red, red, everywhere—the walls, the bedspread, the carpet. My head began to pound just looking at it. How could anyone sleep in that room?

I had a feeling no one did.

Was this seduction scenario for me? Why? I didn't get the impression that the strega, or the new and not-so-improved Jimmy Sanducci, bothered with such trivialities. They took what they wanted; then they disposed of what was left.

I drifted into the living room, hit the button to turn the couch back into a couch, then sat down. I tried the remote for the huge plasma television mounted on the wall. All I got was porn.

With a sound of disgust I jabbed at the off button, then laid my head against the buttery leather. Seconds later, I was talking to Ruthie.

Chapter 33

I ran through the open gate and up the walkway. This house was sanctuary, at least in my head.

Ruthie waited at the kitchen table with two cups of tea. The children played in the yard, their happy voices spilling through the open window.

"Why didn't you warn me?" I asked as I sat across from her.

Ruthie's finely arched brows arched even further. "About what?"

"Jimmy's gone to the dark side. I think—" I took a deep breath, let it out, then swallowed. "I think I'm going to have to kill him."

"Could be." Ruthie sipped her tea. "Could be."

"I'm *supposed* to kill him?" My voice was too high and broke on the word *kill*. Can you blame me?

"No, child, you're supposed to save him. You're the only one who can."

"Sawyer said you could have saved yourself. That you knew the Nephilim were coming for you."

Ruthie took another sip. "So?"

"Why would you do that?"

"Death was my destiny."

"Death is everyone's destiny," I snapped. "I needed you."

"You have me. It's much better this way. You'll see."

I sighed. If it was better or worse, it didn't matter. Ruthie was dead, and I was trapped with Jimmy the dhampir traitor. What was I going to do?

"Remember the most important thing in this war," Ruthie murmured as if I'd asked the question out loud. Maybe I had.

"Kill them before they kill you?" It seemed like a good rule.

Ruthie didn't speak at first. I could tell by the way she took her time that she was counting to ten while she did it. She'd counted to ten a lot around me in the past. She'd no doubt count to ten more in the future. If there was one.

"The most important thing to remember, Lizbeth, is that love is always stronger than hate." I opened my mouth, and she lifted one finger. "You loved Jimmy once; you love him still. There's power in that, such strength."

"Jimmy's gone."

"No, he's not. He's lost. All you have to do is find him."

"How?"

"You'll know when the time comes."

And then she was gone, and I was back in the *Penthouse* penthouse, but I was no longer alone. I knew that as well as I knew the scent of Jimmy's skin.

I took a deep breath. Cinnamon, soap, and water. Still the same. How could that be?

Someone had turned out all the lights, and the only illumination came from the reflection of the city below us.

He slid out of the shadows, his hair wet and slicked away from his face. The blood was gone; only a few thin slices of white remained on his chest where the cuts had been. His loose black pants rode so low I expected them to fall off. I could see his hipbones jutting just above the waistband. He looked even thinner than he had when he'd shown up in Milwaukee. I suppose an all-liquid diet could do that to a man.

How long had he been here? A few days at most. Didn't mean he hadn't been running himself ragged, forgetting to eat, ever since Ruthie died.

In another life, another world, with another me, I might be compelled to feed him. Unfortunately, in this world, what he wanted to eat was me.

I cringed at the double entendre and put it straight out of my head. Panic right now would get me nowhere.

I didn't remember coming to my feet, but I had. Good. I didn't want to be trapped on the couch, with Jimmy looming over me. Not that I wasn't trapped in this room and in the biggest pickle of my life.

He moved so fast, I had no sense he was coming until he was there, so close his body brushed mine, our faces only centimeters apart. I couldn't help it, I took a step back. My legs hit the couch, and I almost went down.

He grabbed me by the arms, and now our bodies weren't merely brushing, but plastered together like lovers.

I lifted my gaze. He smiled. For an instant, in the half-light, he resembled the Jimmy I'd always craved. Then he tilted his head and the strange red flare in the center of his eyes was visible again.

"Let me go."

He didn't even acknowledge the words, just continued to stare into my eyes as if searching. But he was the one who was lost.

"So." His fingers tightened, the pressure, the pain,

causing me to come up on my toes, rubbing my breasts against his bare chest. "Didn't take you long to fuck the skinwalker and have a vision. I figured you'd be there a few weeks at least before he managed to loosen you up."

I tensed at the crudeness but refused to look away. "Was that necessary?"

"I hear that it was. What I want to know is, was it good for you?"

I couldn't resist. "Better than you."

He let me go so abruptly I fell onto the couch with a little bounce.

"Never use his name again." Jimmy's voice was a low, rumbling growl. Not human, not beast, but both.

"I didn't," I pointed out.

If Jimmy was completely absent, if he was possessed, or no longer human, then why was he feeling the very human emotion of jealousy? If he didn't love me just a little, somewhere in there, then why would he care so much that I'd slept with Sawyer?

As bizarre as that spark of jealousy was, it gave me hope. If he could feel that, he could feel more, and if I could get him to remember the love, we might just have a chance.

Love is always stronger than hate, Ruthie had said, and once before, a good memory of a time when our lives had been filled with love had brought him back from a lesser darkness.

I needed to believe what she'd said was true. It was all that I had.

He stalked back and forth in front of the wall of windows. It occurred to me that while he knew I had come into the fullness of Ruthie's powers, he was unaware of the empathy that made me as powerful as any breed. He couldn't know. That talent might save my life.

I forced myself to stand again, to move away from the couch and closer to him. "The strega said you asked for me." Jimmy stopped pacing. "Why?"

"You thought I wanted to save you from death at his hands?" The amusement returned. His moods changed so quickly, I had a hard time keeping up.

I had thought that, for the single instant it had taken me to figure out how foolish I was. "Actually, I thought you wanted to kill me."

"Eventually."

He moved again with that preternatural speed, so that it seemed he was standing by the window and then, faster than my eyes could track, he was grabbing me, hauling me against him, pressing his nose to my neck and inhaling deeply.

"What's happened to you?" I whispered.

He lifted his head, but he didn't let me go. "We are an ancient race."

"*You* aren't," I interrupted. "You're more human than Nephilim."

He ignored me, continuing with the litany he seemed to have memorized, or perhaps had had implanted in his brain. "We will own this world. Humans will be our slaves, our food, whatever we wish. I wanted you to be my first."

"I *was* your first," I whispered.

Something flickered in his eyes. Memory? I hoped so, but it was gone so fast, I couldn't be sure. Then he leaned closer, his lips hovering over my own as he whispered, "My first slave."

I jumped, even though I had to have known that was coming. "You think I'm going to wash your shorts and scrub your toilets?"

His mouth curved, so close to my own I felt the

movement, but didn't see it because I could look nowhere but into his endless eyes.

"Not that kind of slave," he said, and kissed me.

He still tasted like Jimmy, kissed like Jimmy, and my body knew him, even as my mind screamed, *Monster!*

His hands were rough, holding me to him even though I wasn't struggling to get away. When his mouth left mine, he pressed open kisses across my chin, down my neck. When I didn't tilt my head to give him better access, his hand left my hip, capturing my face, fingers bruising as he held me still, inhuman eyes burning with lust.

"You will be my slave for sex. Whenever I want it, however, wherever. You will wear nothing night and day." He placed a hard, closed kiss on my mouth. "I want to walk into this room and have you ready all of the time."

"I bet you do," I managed, even though he still held my jaw far too tightly for easy speech.

"I'll suck you dry slowly. Who knows? You may even find a way out of this with enough time. Keep me satisfied, I might keep you for centuries."

"Yeah, that'll happen."

He leaned forward and caught my lip in his teeth, biting down until the pain began before releasing it. "You'd better hope it does, Elizabeth."

I hated it when he called me that. What I wouldn't give now to hear *baby* just once.

Jimmy released me. "Take off your clothes."

"Not."

He didn't bother to cajole. Instead he fisted a hand in my shirt and yanked. I was drawn forward with such force I stumbled. The seams split, the shirt practically disintegrated. Ruthie's crucifix spilled free and brushed against his hand.

A hissing sound, the scent of burning hair. Jimmy jumped back, hissing himself, as smoke rose from his skin.

I was left standing in my bra and jeans, mouth wide open. The icon hadn't bothered him before.

If I'd needed any proof that Jimmy had changed, that he was becoming less and less human and more and more vampire, I had it.

"Didn't care for that, did you?" I murmured.

His hand snaked out, and he yanked the cross and Sawyer's turquoise from my neck, then tossed them across the room. The chain made a tinny, slithery sound. The cross and the stone bounced like gravel. All three disappeared beneath a huge breakfront of cherry wood and glass. I was going to have a helluva time fishing them out.

"Don't think you can use that against me." Jimmy held his hand up in front of my face. Despite the sizzle and scent, there wasn't a mark on him. He'd already healed. "You can't hurt me; you can't kill me."

I glanced at the bank of windows, then at him in contemplation. Would he fry like bacon beneath the dawn's early light? Once again my face gave my thoughts away.

"The sun won't do a thing. My father is a daywalker, and so am I."

"The others?"

"A few daywalkers to keep things running smoothly. The rest only awaken at night. Peons." He shrugged. "They have their uses."

That explained why everyone had been rushing in and out of the place after-hours as if the clock read ten A.M.

"An entire building of beings that only work at night and no one's noticed?"

"Of course. People are breaking down the doors to hire us. No one else keeps those hours. We fulfill a service for all the scurrying nine-to-five drones."

"The vampire legion actually works for a living?"

"Someone has to. At least for now."

No matter how supernaturally powerful they were, there was still the problem of cash flow. Amazing.

"Enough," Jimmy snapped, and tore off my bra with a sharp tug. My breasts spilled free and his eyes, if possible, became even darker.

"I've been waiting for you," he murmured. "Dreaming of you as I touched all of them."

My eyes narrowed at the word *all*, but I let it go. I really didn't want to know.

"Why me?" I asked instead.

He shook his head as if coming out of a trance. Sheesh. Get a grip. My breasts were good, but not *that* good.

"I crave you. Father says your seer blood will give me more strength than the blood of a dozen others."

I thought if he called that thing "Father" one more time I might just lose my mind. But the longer he talked, the more I learned, and the less sex we had.

"Is that what this place is all about?" I indicated the fold-out bed, the all-porn, all-the-time television.

"My father's idea." I winced at the word; I couldn't help it. "Sometimes it's fun to seduce them. Sometimes it's fun to just take them."

He was speaking of people, of women, as things. Not that a lot of men didn't, but Jimmy never had. Ruthie wouldn't have allowed it.

"You'd like his suite." His lips curved. "I'm sure you'll see it. If Father wants a little seer sex, I don't mind. Maybe we'll have you together."

Do not gag. Do not gag.

"You're suddenly so pale, Elizabeth." Jimmy laughed. "You're a slave now. You'll do anything I want."

"And if I don't?"

"You die, and the whole world dies with you."

Choices, choices.

Sleep with Jimmy, try to make him remember who he was, that he'd loved me once, and maybe, just maybe, discover a way out of this mess.

Or . . .

Attempt to kick his ass, die horribly, and fail at the big mission.

Let's see . . .

I picked door number one.

Chapter 34

I couldn't make this too easy for him. Jimmy would know something was up. So when he reached for me again, I ran.

He let me. Where in hell was I going to go? The only exit was by elevator, and I didn't have a key.

Every door in the place closed but had no lock. What good would it do me to barricade myself in? He could knock anything down with one well-placed kick.

To make things look good, I picked up a chair and tossed it at the wall of windows. Since Jimmy had taken a seat on the couch and watched me with some amusement, I knew it wouldn't work.

Sure enough, the chair bounced back at me so fast I had to scramble out of the way.

"Done yet?" he asked.

I didn't have to fake my rapid breathing. Even though I knew what would come was inevitable, that I'd chosen it or perhaps it had been chosen for me long ago, I was still nervous. He wasn't the man I'd loved. He wasn't really a man at all.

I raced into the bedroom, thinking I'd toss something heavy at the window, just for show, but there wasn't a window. The draperies covered a wall. Behind me, the door clicked shut.

I whirled just in time to see Jimmy punch in a code on a keypad, which I'd taken to be a security control. I guess it was, since bolts thunked home from somewhere inside the heavy portal.

He hooked his thumbs in the waistband of his loose trousers, pulled them outward until they cleared his erection, then dropped them to the floor.

"Your turn," he said.

I scrambled for the bathroom, but he caught me before I took two steps and tossed me with an absent flick of his wrist toward the bed.

I landed in the center, bouncing once. Before I could lift my head from the mattress, he'd torn the button and zipper of my pants apart.

I struggled, which only made him laugh. Struggling seemed to be what he was after.

Considering what he'd been through as a child, Jimmy had never been one for bondage games. In the bedroom he'd always been gentle, almost reverent. Probably one of the reasons the notches on his belt were legion. Women ate that stuff up. I had.

He held me down easily with one arm while he yanked off my boots, then my jeans, and tossed them to the floor. I'd barely lifted my shoulders from the bed when he trapped me beneath him.

His erection throbbed against my belly as he dragged his palm up my thigh, over my hip, the curve of my waist, then cupped one breast and stroked the nipple, which tightened on contact.

His head lowered; his hair sifted across my chest. The scent of cinnamon and soap wafted over me and memories flickered.

I drew in a sharp, loud breath as he took me into his

mouth and suckled, tongue pushing the bud against his teeth again and again and again. The sensation was so familiar, so glorious, my fingers were reaching to twine in his hair before I remembered and forced my arm to drop back to the bed.

I kept my gaze focused on the ceiling as he nuzzled my breasts while suckling, teasing. I shuddered as goose-flesh rose across my skin.

I waited for him to sink his fangs into me, then realized he had none, or at least none that I could see. What did that mean?

He lifted his head, ran a hand over my arm, chafing until the pebbled bumps went away. "You were always so sensitive right here."

He ran the tip of his tongue from the slope of one breast to the other, rolling a lazy lick around each nipple as he passed. My molars ground together as I tried to keep myself from arching into him, from opening my legs and wrapping my ankles around his back as I urged him to plunge deeper, take me harder. Despite my body's response, I wasn't ready.

"No more fighting?" he asked.

"I'm not going to give you the satisfaction."

His lips curved. "Struggling won't give me satisfaction."

I lifted a brow. He laughed, flexing his hips until his erection seemed to make a permanent dent in my skin. "Well, maybe a little."

Annoyed, I raked my nails down his back, and he caught his breath, eyes flaring red. "You want to hurt me?" he asked. "Go ahead. I seem to have developed a taste for it."

I had a flash of him tied to the chair, moaning in ecstasy when the strega had cut him. Pain would only send him farther away from me. To get him back, I was going to have to appeal to the gentle side he'd once shown. I had to make him remember the love.

Because, despite everything he'd said and done, a friendship forged in the fires of our childhoods, a love found amid so little love, meant something. It had to.

"What will give me satisfaction, Elizabeth"—he licked the side of my neck, pausing to nibble at my ear, before whispering—"is making you beg, then making you come."

He seemed to have the whole sex-slave gig backward. If I was the slave, shouldn't I be making *him* come? I decided not to point that out just in case he had a strategy for changing my entire personality from aggressive to passive in one easy lesson.

I closed my eyes and concentrated on the feel of his body against mine, the scent of him. Those things hadn't changed.

His skin was soft at the hip, his long artist's fingers still clever, the hair on his thighs tickled mine. His feet were knobby and large. He loved it when I ran my big toe along his arch. The back of his neck, beneath the fall of his hair, was still tense. When I touched him there, he sighed and rested his forehead against mine.

If I wasn't looking at him, if I couldn't witness the strange flashes of red at the center of his eyes, if he didn't speak and call me by the wrong name, if he didn't talk like a porn star in a bondage flick, I could remember how it had been between us. I could remember how very much I'd loved him.

I lifted my mouth and brushed my lips along his. For an instant he responded, kissing me the way he always had. Then he jumped as if he'd been poked with a stick and pulled away. The movement ground our lower bodies together, and I winced.

"Open your eyes." I hesitated. "Do it, Elizabeth."

I bit my tongue to stifle a nearly irresistible urge to knee him in the groin. I doubted that would even hurt him anymore.

"You won't like what happens when you disobey me."

"I'm not going to like what happens when I obey you either," I muttered.

"Oh, no. You will like it. I promise."

He was probably right.

His face was so close I could see only myself in his eyes. We'd been just like this so many times, all I could do was remember. Couldn't he?

"Jimmy," I whispered, and touched his face.

For an instant I thought I'd reached him, wherever he was. He smiled softly and started to kiss me.

Then his damned eyes flared red, and he lifted his body, plunging into me with a single furious stroke.

I arched off the bed, which only made his thrust deeper. I cried out, the sound not one of pain but surprise and breathless wonder. His laugh wasn't his own—deeper, crueler, not a laugh of joy or amusement, but of dominance. He'd won and he knew it.

Even though what he was doing felt exquisite, I struggled to escape. But there was nowhere to go. I was trapped between him and the bed.

"Hold on." He slowed his thrusts, making me gasp, making me want. "Not yet."

My hands, which had clutched his shoulders when he attacked, no doubt leaving half-moon fingernail marks in his skin, now slid lower of their own accord, clasping his buttocks, urging him on. I had no will of my own, and I both hated and loved it.

I fought the tide of eroticism. With us so close physically, now was the time to try and reach him emotionally.

Think! my mind shouted. *Remember!*

I closed my eyes again and reached for our past.

The first time we'd kissed, the first time we'd touched, the first time I'd known that I loved him. I let those old feelings flow over me.

My hands no longer clutched but caressed. I rubbed the small of his back, holding him still within me. My other hand twined in his hair, stroking, soothing. Turning my head, I kissed his cheek, his eyelids, his forehead.

"We were so good together," I murmured. "Remember how it felt to be in love?"

He sighed, his breath cool against my burning skin. He kissed me and for a single instant I tasted the memories—grass, heat, sex, love.

I wrapped my arms around him, my legs too. "Jimmy," I whispered against his lips. "Jimmy."

Then he was gone.

Not physically. No. We were still twined together, his body deep within mine. But mentally, emotionally, he disappeared between one breath and the next. Everything went cold, including me as he lifted his head.

"Remember," he growled, in a voice that wasn't his, "the hate. I went from your bed to hers. You saw her, Elizabeth. How could I resist?"

He was talking about Summer. Not that there hadn't been more women than her. But she was the one who mattered the most. The one I'd seen him with in my head the last time I'd touched him with love. He had to have known I'd see, so why—?

He took my arms from around his neck and drew them above my head, circling both wrists with one hand, holding me captive though I didn't try to fight. His bringing back that memory seemed to have drained everything from me—except the lust. That appeared to be getting stronger with every thrust.

Faster and faster. Deeper and harder. My body betrayed me.

Damn body.

I fought the orgasm; the orgasm won. I came screaming, not his name. Not anymore. I screamed in fury and he laughed, scraping his teeth down my straining breasts, suckling me just short of pain, drawing the orgasm out, never coming himself so that he stayed hard.

Then, when I went limp, he reached between us and used his fingers to arouse me again. The slide of his hand, touching me, touching himself, he seemed to get larger, stretching me until my head thrashed even as I opened my legs for more.

"I wish I had time to go down on you, but I don't think I can wait. I love the taste of this." He rolled his thumb over me. "I love how it swells against my lips, how it feels when I flick it with my tongue."

"No," I whispered, but I shouldn't have bothered. I had no choice, and by now I didn't mind. An orgasm like that is addictive. My mind might murmur *no,* but my body kept shouting *yes.*

My skin hummed. It only took a few more thrusts for him to at last give in to the inevitable, and as he came, so did I.

With Sawyer I'd seen the universe, felt the power all the way back to the beginning of time. He'd poured heat and magic into me when he'd given me himself.

I felt the same heat, sensed the lightning, but what I saw was darkness, what I felt was madness, a duality that didn't quite make sense.

Jimmy's head was bowed, his hair shading his face and mine; the only sound in the room was the syncopated rhythm of our breathing.

"Don't ever try that again." Without warning, he shoved his forearm against my neck. I couldn't breathe.

"I remember everything, Elizabeth, and it doesn't matter. All I want is to fuck you until I'm tired of you, then drink from you until you die."

He lifted himself off the bed, using the arm at my neck for leverage. For an instant I thought he planned to break my windpipe. I choked, then coughed when the weight disappeared.

He was gone before I could say anything, do anything, though what I'd planned to say or do I had no idea.

I sat up, rubbing my throat, which felt swollen and tender. I was going to be sporting a huge bruise. Luckily I didn't have any pressing appointments.

Had I absorbed Jimmy's dhampir powers? I didn't feel any different. What about his sudden case of the vampires? Would I absorb that too? I had no irresistible craving for blood. No urge to sleep in a coffin. No aversion to garlic. I checked my teeth. None of them were pointy, but then neither were Jimmy's.

I laughed at my thoughts, most of which were based on Bram Stoker, and my throat screamed. I stumbled into the bathroom. A quick glance in the mirror revealed an ugly pressure mark across my windpipe, already deepening from scarlet to eggplant.

I dialed the shower to "burn me, baby," and climbed in, then stood under the stream until the water turned tepid. When I climbed out and dried off, I caught another glimpse of myself.

The bruise was gone.

Chapter 35

I appeared to have absorbed Jimmy's dhampir ability to heal. I had to assume I had his strength, speed, and superior sight as well.

The powers I'd gained from Sawyer were restrictive. Speed in animal form, healing only after shape-shifting, and shape-shifting only if I touched a tattoo or wore a magic robe.

I fingered the pristine skin of my throat. "This works much better."

When I went into the bedroom, my clothes were gone. "What the—"

Clutching the towel, I hurried into the living area. Empty. So were all the closets, all the drawers. Of clothes, at any rate.

Someone had been in here while I showered. That almost gave me the creeps more than the red flare in Jimmy's eyes had.

"If he expects me to prance around naked for all the security cameras to see, he can forget it," I muttered, grabbing a dry towel and fashioning a very short sarong.

My gaze swept the bedroom, the bath; then I moved into the outer rooms and did the same. I didn't see a camera anywhere, but that didn't mean there wasn't one.

In the living area, I went down on my knees in front of the breakfront, but the heavy piece of furniture skimmed the floor too closely for me to reach beneath it and feel around for Ruthie's crucifix and Sawyer's turquoise. I could see them easily, even though the area beneath held no light whatsoever.

Supersight? Check.

With another furtive glance at the empty corners of the room, I reached out with both hands and yanked on the side of the wooden structure. It skidded across the floor as easily as if it were on wheels.

Frowning, I tilted my head. No wheels that I could see. I inched my fingers beneath the bottom and lifted. The breakfront levitated several inches as the muscles in my arm flexed.

"Ooookay," I murmured. "Supreme strength working just fine."

Now that I'd moved the furniture, the turquoise and the crucifix, as well as the chain they'd hung on, were accessible. I snatched them as quickly as I could, my arm a blur even to my own suddenly superior eyes. I braced for the burn upon contact with the crucifix, but nothing happened.

I contemplated the tiny silver charm with the image of a crucified Christ. It had burned Jimmy but it hadn't burned me.

Sharing blood with the strega had aroused Jimmy's vampire nature. Before that, he'd been a dhampir only—more human than vampire. So, it followed that unless I shared blood with another vamp, I'd enjoy freedom from fangs too. To say I was relieved was an understatement.

I dropped all three items into the nearest drawer. The chain was broken and the turquoise only infuriated Jimmy. I could infuriate him just fine on my own.

The elevator opened. I spun around, sliding the drawer

shut as I did so. Maybe they'd seen my Superman show on the hidden security cameras. That wouldn't be good. If the strega discovered that I absorbed supernatural powers through sex, I had a very bad feeling I'd be flat on my back in his bed sometime today and a part of his caval-cade of evil by tonight.

Two of the vampire minions entered—different from the last ones—both men this time, one Asian, one black.

Vampire, Ruthie said.

I'd have known that without the ghost whisper. Their suits, around here anyway, were a kind of vamp uniform. Also, all the guard vampires appeared as if they'd been bench-pressing trucks in between steroid cocktails.

They snatched me by the arms and lifted me off my feet just like last time. My towel slithered downward, exposing me inch by inch before dropping to the floor with a soft, terry-cloth thud.

I wasn't so much concerned about my nakedness—I didn't have any choice and the goons didn't notice—but I was concerned about my obvious healing capabil-ities. If I'd had a scarf available, I'd have wrapped it around my neck. But since I didn't even have the towel any longer . . .

I kicked my legs. "You mind?"

They didn't answer, just hauled me bodily into the elevator.

"Where are you taking me?"

They didn't blink.

"Do you speak English?" Nothing. "Do you speak?"

The elevator opened directly into another room. If Larry Flynt had decorated the *Penthouse* penthouse, this place had been fashioned by the Shah of Sand City.

Pillows on the tile floor, gurgling fountain, the walls covered by gossamer fabric that billowed slightly with the swirl of current from the air ducts.

Women as naked as I lounged on the pillows—
blondes, brunettes, redheads with skin in shades from
gold to copper and ebony. On closer inspection, I saw
they weren't quite as naked as me. They all wore chains
around their waists.

My eyes narrowed. They weren't fancy golden belly
chains either, but heavier, with links large enough to
hook a leash onto, definitely too solid to break by hand
or even with a hammer.

"Why don't you just put a collar on them?" I murmured.

"That would 'cramp my style,' as you say."

At the strega's words, the steroid twins let me go, and
my feet hit the ground without warning. I stumbled, but
managed to keep from taking a header off the marble
steps that led from the elevator into the harem.

"Your style?" I faced him. "You call this style?"

"I enjoyed it when I traveled through what you now
call the Middle East. Comfortable for them and much
easier on me. When I want a snack, there they are."

He snapped his fingers and the nearest woman hurried
to his side. He tilted her head; old bite marks marred her
once perfect skin. I understood what he'd meant by a
collar cramping his style.

I turned away, but not before I saw his canines
lengthen into fangs. It appeared vampires could retract
them when not in use. Handy for keeping that secret
identity a secret.

Though I'd averted my eyes, I couldn't shut my ears
to the sound of sucking. Each and every one of the remaining women watched with rapt attention, as if they
wished with all their soon-to-be-lost souls that they'd
been chosen. That almost made me as nauseous as the
noise.

"Enough," the strega said.

Out of the corner of my eye, I saw the girl collapse to the floor. One of the guard vamps made a move to catch her, but he missed, and her head cracked against the marble. She lay very still.

The strega began to curse in Italian. The vampire paled, which was interesting since I'd always thought vampires pale to begin with. Just another myth. In truth, vamps looked just like you and me as long as they kept their fangs in their mouths.

The boss beckoned the visibly trembling minion. When the man reached his side, the strega looped an arm around his shoulders, which was quite an upward stretch considering the vamp's size.

"You knew she was my favorite." The strega sighed. "Blood as rich as wine. What a waste."

With his free hand, he pushed a button on the wall. The heavy, dark curtains covering the bank of windows parted and sunlight streamed in.

"No, master," the vamp whispered. I guess he *could* talk.

Before the words had left his lips, the strega shoved him into the light.

Bam, instant fire hazard.

The harem jumped up from the cushions, clapping and cooing in appreciation of the flames. I was starting to wonder if being drained of blood was draining them of their brains too.

Heat washed over me in a wave. The flaming outline of the man suddenly disintegrated into ashes, then fell to the floor with an audible *whoosh*.

"Take it away." The strega waved a hand at the pile and one of the women snatched a nearby DustBuster—the proximity making me think the sunshine sentence was a common method of punishing mistakes—and in seconds any trace of the evidence was gone.

"That too." The strega indicated the fallen snack. So much for favorites.

The remaining guard lifted her limp body and carried it into the elevator.

The strega circled me like the predator he was. "I don't understand the attraction."

Reaching out, he swept a finger down my neck, and I tensed. No one had mentioned my sudden ability to lift heavy furniture as if it were a lamp, which made me think that security cameras must be off limits in the private suites of the damned.

"You have nice skin, interesting eyes, but other than that . . ." He shrugged.

The way the strega eyed my jugular, I had a bad feeling I'd been called here for a sample. Instead, he turned and headed for a door on the other side of the windows. "Come along. I want to show you something."

I doubted I wanted to see anything he had to show me so I stayed right where I was.

My only warning was a giggle before one of the women shoved me in the back. She wasn't that strong—constant and extreme blood loss does that to a person—but she surprised me enough that I took an involuntary step forward before spinning around, hands clenched into fists. There was only so much I could take, and I'd just reached the limit.

"Seer," the strega snapped. "Do I need to come and get you? You won't like it; I promise."

"Maybe she will like it, master," said the half-wit who'd pushed me. "Make her bleed. Let us watch."

"Yessss," agreed the others.

Sheesh. Stepford Harem. How redundant.

I shot out the heel of my hand, putting a lot of body into it, and caught the big-mouth idiot in the chest. She landed on her ass in a pile of pillows and strega snacks.

A lot of shrieking and crying ensued. But no one came after me. I think I'd made my point.

The strega considered me as I crossed the sun-drenched tile floor. Had I hit her too hard? Did he suspect that I'd left the realm of seer strength and had crept into that of dhampir?

"Perhaps we shouldn't kill you after all," he murmured. "You'd be such an asset to my team."

"We've been here and done this. I'm not going to pull an Italy. When I pick a side, I stay there."

His face darkened. Ruthie had always called my compulsion to needle people who shouldn't be needled "poking the bear." I couldn't help myself. Whenever I was in a situation where I felt inadequate or threatened, I tried to gain confidence and courage by twisting the knife where it hurt the most.

Damn, I wished I had my knife; I'd make that analogy literal.

I thought the strega might knock me across the room, and I could guarantee I wouldn't get up as quickly as the dumbass I'd smacked down. I'd be lucky if I got up at all.

"Why does everyone bring up the Second World War?" he whined. "It wasn't as if Italy had any choice but to join the Nazis. We were surrounded."

My eyebrows lifted. "You were there?"

"Where else would I have been?"

Italy during World War II hadn't been a picnic. I'd think that someone like him would have ditched the place. Then again, amid chaos, any chaos he chose to cause would have gone unnoticed. Back then, the strega had been biding his time, waiting for . . .

What? The perfect moment to take over the world? What if he'd decided the Nazis were the best bet for that and put his power behind them? I guess we'd all be speaking German.

The strega went through the door and I followed. "What do you think?" he asked.

We'd entered a war room. There was no other word for it. A huge map of the world covered one wall. In each country—north, south, east, west—pins had been stuck. The map was a rainbow of dots in red, green, blue, and yellow.

Several vamps sat at computers, wearing headsets, clacking away as they spoke to unknown informants. Phones rang. Faxes buzzed.

"Red is for DKs," the strega murmured, "blue is for seers."

Frowning, I leaned closer. Just north of Milwaukee someone had stuck a single blue pin. Guess that was me. Right next to the blue pin was a green and a yellow.

"What about those?"

"Yellow signifies a DK we've eliminated."

"Springboard," I murmured.

"Very good."

I didn't have to ask about the green pin.

That one was for Ruthie.

Chapter 36

"How do you know all this?" I demanded. "Obviously Jimmy told you about Ruthie—"

I frowned. Had he? Jimmy loved Ruthie as much as I did. The strega hadn't begun controlling him until they'd exchanged blood, which hadn't happened until Jimmy had come here.

From the way the strega was smirking and pointedly not answering my query, I wasn't going to learn the truth from him about anything.

I reached up and yanked the Ruthie pin free, then met the strega's gaze, daring him to make me put it back. He shrugged.

"Everyone knows we took out your leader." He reached into a desk and removed a purple pin, then stuck it into the hole left by the first one. "That color makes more sense."

"Take out one leader, another just rises up." Hey, maybe they had named me Phoenix for a reason. "You can't win."

"I already have. You aren't going to be able to pass on your power, seer. Your world is mine."

Dammit. Hadn't thought of that. Guess I'd just have to kill him and anyone else who got in my way.

I spun away from the map, and the huge painting positioned high on the opposite wall captured my gaze. A medieval knight on crusade—armor, charger, army, with someone carrying a flag that very clearly had a cross emblazoned in the middle. The picture was so out of place I moved closer. The man in the painting bore more than a passing resemblance to the strega.

Had he been a crusader? If I remembered my history, the timing was right. Encompassed by the medieval era, the Crusades had lasted from the eleventh to the thirteenth centuries, and Christian warriors from all over Europe had served.

However, the strega was a Nephilim, which made him evil; he was the offspring of the fallen angels. I doubted he'd suited up for Christ.

Someone ran a hand down my back, and I jumped. I'd forgotten I was stark naked. Amazing what a person could get used to when their life was on overload.

I turned, fists clenched again, only to slam straight into Jimmy. He reached out and swept a finger down my neck. "Not a mark."

I tensed, at the touch and his words. "Seer blood." I shrugged, knocking his arm away with my shoulder. "I heal pretty fast."

"You always did," he murmured, playing with the ends of my hair. He was really starting to get on my nerves. "You are going to be so much harder to kill than I expected." He leaned over and licked my neck. "Thank you."

The sensation of his tongue on my skin made my stomach skitter, not with disgust but with lust. What had he done to me? The temptation to turn into his arms, to yank off all of his clothes and have sex with him right here was nearly overpowering. I shook my head, hard.

"You feel it too, don't you? The burn." His palm covered my stomach. His erection poked into my backside. "You're mine now in a way you'll never be anyone else's. I'm having a chain made for you." He caressed the curve of my waist. "Then you'll fit in with all the others."

The need to slug him returned, but I managed to refrain. There would be time for violence later. A lot of it, I hoped.

"You like my portrait?" the strega asked.

"What's with the warrior-of-Christ getup?"

Jimmy's hand slid from my stomach to my breasts. My elbow jerked involuntarily.

"Gark," he said as it connected with his gut.

I thought he might force the issue. I really didn't want to have sex on the war room floor in front of his psychotic daddy and a quarter of the vampire legion. I needed to control my impulses—both violent and lustful.

After several seconds, he lifted his hand and began playing with my hair once more. I decided I'd let that pass. The lesser of two evils.

"In the beginning," the strega began, and I took a deep breath, ready to tell him to skip the lesson; I certainly didn't want to hear Bible stories from that mouth. However, he didn't continue with Genesis. "There were Grigori. The sons of God who mated with the daughters of men and produced Nephilim."

"Rerun." I made a whirling motion with my forefinger. "Fast-forward."

The strega didn't appear too happy at my interruption but he did move on. "In the Bible the Nephilim were referred to as giants, and they were."

I frowned. "Giants? I don't remember that."

"Has the name Goliath slipped your mind?"

"He was a Nephilim?"

"Of course. As were many of the other races listed in the Old Testament. For instance, the Raphaims of Genesis were descendants of Rapha, which, in Hebrew, means fearful. In many translations, the word *giant* was replaced with *Nephilim* as if the two were interchangeable."

"I'll take your word for it." My Hebrew was iffy to nonexistent.

"In the Old Testament days, giants were common, but as centuries passed, we needed to blend in better."

"Why?"

"We had ninety percent of our number erased by forty days and nights of rain; there was no telling what might come next if we weren't careful."

"What did you do?"

"We became the giants of each time. During the era of the Greeks and the Romans, we were gods." I snorted and he cast me a quick glance. "You've never heard the tales of Greece and Rome? Those stories of the gods who mated with humans."

"I've heard them. Myths."

"Remember the Titans?"

My eyes widened. For an instant I thought he was talking about the Denzel Washington movie, and I had a little brain freeze as my mind scrambled for the sense in that.

"A race of godlike giants who ruled Greece in ancient times," he explained. "The more famous gods of Greece are descended from them. Gods who had amazing supernatural powers."

"The Greek gods weren't real."

"No? What about the pyramids? You think human hands could build something like that? You had help, seer, from the Nephilim. Giants of stature and strength. Only they could have performed such a feat."

"There are pyramids all over the world."

"As there are Nephilim everywhere." He waved away any further protest and moved on. "In the time of the

Crusades, we joined in. We were the very best of the best, warriors who never died."

"I'd think you would have joined the—" I tried to remember what the "other side" was labeled during the Crusades. "Infidels. Cut down on the competition."

"Humans aren't competition, and religion is irrelevant to us." He pointed at the map. "There are seers and demon killers everywhere. The way they worship, whether they refer to their deity as God or Jehovah or Allah has no bearing on their being called to the fight."

"Angels, fallen and otherwise, are Christian beings."

"The angels fell long before Christ."

Rats. Good point.

"The Old Testament happened," he continued. "It's history, not myth. As we are."

"How are you blending in these days?"

"Captains of industry, lords of the boardroom, leaders of governments worldwide." He bowed and swept out his arm before straightening. "Wherever there's a success story that pushes the boundaries of believability there you will find us."

"Make hay while the sun shines," I murmured.

"Precisely."

"Get ready for the rain."

His smile faded. "I do not know where your arrogance comes from. You are in our power. You are his slave. You do not even have clothes to cover yourself. You have been stripped of everything."

Not everything, I thought. I had powers they didn't know about. They had to be good for something or why have them? Why give me this gift if it couldn't be used to win the war?

I was going to figure out how to bring the strega down, and Jimmy too, if he didn't snap out of it, or I was going to die trying.

But I guess that had been the plan all along.

One of the minions handed the strega a phone. When he began to chatter in Italian, I lost interest.

"Let's go." Jimmy took me by the arm and led me from the war room to the elevator. "You need to rest."

"Is that what you call it?" I muttered.

"Wouldn't you like some food?"

"Not hungry." My stomach growled.

"Making yourself sick isn't going to change anything."

He was right. If I wanted any chance of getting out of here, I had to eat, to sleep, to find some freaking clothes.

The elevator opened on the penthouse. The table was set for one. Steak. Baked potato. Spinach salad. Cabernet. Was I was being fattened up like the proverbial sacrificial lamb?

Yes.

Nevertheless, I made myself sit at the table and consume everything on the plates; then I sat back, swirling the wine in my glass, sipping slowly.

The sun fell, casting shadows across the towering buildings of Manhattan. Up here, it was hard to believe millions of people scurried around down there. Up here, it was hard to believe there were any other problems in the world but my own. But then my problem *was* the world and how to save it.

Jimmy lounged on the leather couch, bare feet on the coffee table. His shirt was unbuttoned, hanging loose, framing his beautiful chest. All the cuts made by the strega were gone, his skin smooth, toned, and tanned. Perfect.

I glanced away and took a gulp of wine.

"You want me," he said.

"No."

"I can smell your desire, Elizabeth. You can't hide it."

I met his eyes, tried not to flinch from the obvious difference in them, in him. "You're delusional."

"Our slaves become slaves to that craving. Eventually you won't run even if I let you. You won't be able to leave me. You'll call me master, and I won't even have to ask."

"I don't think so."

He smiled. "You'll see."

"Just because my body responds doesn't mean I want you."

"No?" His smile grew. "What does it mean?"

Though I was tempted to throw the rest of my wine in his face, I managed to drink some instead before trying to reach him one more time.

"If I don't look at you too long, or listen to you too hard, I can remember what it was like. I loved you then." I took a deep breath and admitted the truth. What could it hurt? This wasn't Jimmy anymore. "I loved you more than anyone in my life. Next to—" My voice broke, but I forced myself to continue. "Next to Ruthie."

"Love is irrelevant."

"Love is everything."

He came off the couch in one swift movement, startling me so much I sloshed wine over my fingers. The Cabernet dripped onto the tabletop, so closely resembling blood beneath a full moon—crimson, almost black—that I had to set the glass down and glance away.

Jimmy hauled me up roughly by the elbows. Lucky I'd set aside the wine. "I told you not to talk about the past."

"Loving you is definitely past," I muttered.

"Good," he said, and kissed me.

He was holding me too tightly, kissing me too hard. I could do nothing but stiffen and struggle. Not that struggling did me any good. He only held me tighter, kissed me harder.

He lifted his head. His eyes, onyx with a pinprick of ruby, stared into mine. "Kiss me back."

"You can't make me respond."

His fingers clenched on my arms, and I fought a wince. "I bet I can."

He let me go without warning, and the chair I'd been dragged out of hit me in the knees. I plopped into it. He punched several buttons on the wall—and I do mean punched—his fist shooting forward, the plastic crunching in protest.

The heavy drapes slid over the windows. The lights went out with a muffled *thunk*.

Across the room, more plastic protested, followed by thuds and swooshes from the area of the couch. I stood, though, as usual, I had nowhere to go.

"Come here." His voice whispered out of the gloom; he sounded so much like himself my breath caught.

I could see pretty well in the dark these days. Not great, not everything, but considering there was *no* light and I could easily distinguish Jimmy's outline as well as that of most of the furniture in the room, I was impressed.

He scooted across the distance between us—quick as a wink, literally. I didn't have to fake my gasp of surprise when he touched me. Speed like that was a shock even when you were expecting it.

"Kiss me back," he repeated.

Goose bumps rose all over me. The last time I'd heard that voice in the darkness, I'd have done anything.

Last time.

He caressed me with a gentleness that left me breathless. How could he not remember how it had been between us and touch me like that?

He couldn't. Because he *did* remember; he just didn't care. However, considering his order to kiss him back, this setting of seduction, maybe he did.

His lips brushed mine like a whisper. My mouth parted on a sigh. He tasted the same, smelled the same too. Shouldn't he smell like a vampire? Rotting flesh, graveyard dust, something bad. But all I could smell was Jimmy.

I wanted to bury my face in his neck, draw in that scent so deeply I'd never know anything else. I wanted to brush my fingers through his hair, coast the tips along his eyelids, feel the flutter of his eyes beneath, his lashes against my skin.

Instead of tossing me onto the bed, he sat, pulling me between his legs, rubbing his cheek along my bare belly, resting his forehead between my breasts. My arms cradled his shoulders; my hands cupped his head. My heart gave one heavy thud and began to race. I couldn't think when he was touching me like this.

His breath puffed across my skin, cool like a spring breeze. It felt so good, so right, as did his hands at my hips, his lips along the underside of my breast.

When I couldn't see the occasional flare of red at the center of his eyes, when he didn't speak and say horrible things, I could forget what had happened to him, to me. I could pretend it was then and not now.

In the dark, in my arms, I could pretend he was still Jimmy.

Chapter 37

I curled into him, pressed my lips to his hair and just held on. Amazingly, he let me.

I'd tried to talk to him of the past, tried to get him to remember love, but that had only made him retreat more deeply into the creature he'd become.

But what if I showed him what we'd had? What if I could make him remember himself, remember us, by loving him?

I was afraid. Not so much that he'd figure out what I was doing and kill me as he'd threatened, but that I'd be captured more thoroughly by my feelings than I'd been by this building of marble and glass. If I let myself love him, would I ever be able to get over him again? Would I be able to kill him if I needed to?

If I didn't do something and quickly, I'd be dead or wishing I was. I had to take the chance no matter the cost.

His lips moved against my skin; he whispered words I couldn't understand, softly, like a prayer. I knew that couldn't be true.

"Shh," he murmured, as if soothing me, and kissed the well between my breasts before rubbing his face over me, as if memorizing the plane of my soul.

He mouthed my nipple, no tongue, no teeth. He didn't

suckle; he didn't kiss; just a quick caress and he was gone, trailing those lips—so deliciously cool amid all this heat—over my stomach, my hip, then lower still. He rubbed his face in my soft curls, trailed a thumb over my center; then before I could protest, or agree, he fell back on the bed, taking me along.

My gasp of surprise turned into a tiny squeak when he rolled, pinning me beneath him. I expected a change— the gentleness gone, the monster returned. He'd roughly thrust; he'd make me come. I wouldn't be able to deny him any more now than I had before. But he surprised me. He forever surprised me.

His chest pressed into mine, naked and slick, like fine marble. If I turned on the light would I see the trace of veins beneath the surface—blue beneath pale brown, instead of black tracing white?

He lifted his head; I captured his face in my hands and kissed him. Sweetly, like the first time. Tentatively. Mouths only, tongues later. Much later, when I couldn't wait any longer for a taste.

The first touch of my lips and he opened. I didn't delve inside. Instead I made my way downward, savoring his jaw, his neck, his chest. When I couldn't go any lower, a tiny shove at his shoulder, and he fell back; he let me take the lead and the top.

His nipples pebbled beneath my tongue; my fingers traced the ridge of his ribs and belly. I forgot he was different, that I was, and concentrated on the things that were the same.

He still liked it when I rubbed my mouth over the fluttering muscles in his stomach. He still moaned when I reached into his loose cotton pants and closed my palm around him. He still gasped when I eased the elastic waistband clear and swirled my tongue over his tip.

If I were a slave he'd grab my head, push himself into

my mouth, and make me stay there while he pumped harder and faster, while he grew larger and larger, the tight, slick heat making him spurt.

Instead he let me do anything that I wanted. Did he trust me that much? Probably not. He merely trusted that there was nothing I could do that would hurt him— at least not permanently.

In the old days, we'd had to sneak around. Ruthie would have killed us if she'd caught us together. So there'd been a lot of back-seat sex, quite a few blow jobs in the closet. One of the few times we'd ever done it on a bed had been our first time.

Ruthie had taken the little ones to the zoo; Jimmy had come home a day early from the farm, and I'd just gotten out of the shower.

Afternoon sun through the window, just-cut grass on the breeze, my body wet, my skin flushed. Jimmy had walked by my bedroom, his footsteps slowing, the door creaking back. His shirt unbuttoned, the top of his jeans too. I can still feel the jab of lust that had hit me when I'd seen the paler skin beneath the sweat-darkened jeans and licked my lips, wondering at the flavor.

We'd come together like thunder in the middle of a summer night. He'd tasted like danger. Hell, he still did.

While I'd been reminiscing, he'd lost the pants. He no longer bothered with underwear or socks, which only made things easier for me.

I took him all the way in, then let him slide almost all the way out, swirling my tongue around the tip, then down to the base; my palm cupping him, at first gently and then more firmly still.

His fingers clenched in my hair, then released just as quickly. He didn't want me to stop, didn't want me to slow. He wanted this, and he wanted it my way.

Increase the rhythm, the pressure, a scrape of the teeth, so close, a few more strokes and he'd be mine.

But he wouldn't give in; he wouldn't give it up. Instead he entangled our legs and did some fancy wrestling move, flipping me onto my back and sliding between my thighs.

"Hey." My protest was cut short by his mouth. He kissed me as if he wanted to crawl inside me forever. He hadn't kissed me like that since we were seventeen.

The memory made my eyes sting, and I nearly panicked. I couldn't lose control. I had to keep trying to reach him, and the only way to do that was to let him in completely, to become as captured by the past overwhelming the present as I wanted him to be.

Our lips fit together like the last two pieces of a puzzle; our tongues met like rain across a wind-washed desert—moisture and heat, desperation, salvation.

"Touch me," I said.

Love me, I thought.

We kissed for what seemed like hours; maybe it was. I'd never gotten tired of kissing him back then. Sometimes that was all that we'd had.

They say you never forget your first love or your first time. When they're one and the same, you dream of it, dream of him, for years, maybe forever. I don't know.

Now I had him in my arms again. His mouth on mine, his hands, both rough and gentle, wandered everywhere. I needed him inside me. I had to see if the dreams were even close to the reality.

I opened myself, welcomed him in, the slick slide, the way that he filled me, familiar. Though I no longer recognized him in the light, I knew him in the dark. There he wasn't a monster. There he was only a man.

He leaned his forehead against mine, took a deep breath as if to speak.

"Don't talk." I crushed any words with my mouth.

Oh, God, please don't talk.

We continued to kiss; I wouldn't let him go. With one hand at the nape of his neck I held him to me, the other at his hip showed him the rhythm. Slow and deep; I didn't want it to end. Not yet. As long as we were like this, in the dark, the bad things couldn't reach us. I was still me; Jimmy was still Jimmy; we were together again as if we'd never been apart.

But nothing good lasts forever. I knew that as well as anyone, probably better.

I pulled him to me too fast, let him in too far, and he tensed, his whole body straining to hold back, but he was unable to.

Once he lost control, so did I. The waves of sensation washed over us both. He plunged in one last time and stilled. The tiny movement, the release so deep within, made me gasp and wrap my legs around him, tilting upward, trying to draw him closer. It had always been like this—never long enough, never deep enough, never, ever enough.

His mouth left mine, trailing over my chin, down my neck to my breast where he gently kissed first one slope and then the other as the last shivers died away.

My chest ached from holding in what I felt. How could he touch me like that and not feel it too?

We'd made love like this half a dozen times before, and every time we'd lain in the same way afterward. His mouth at my breast, tracing the fine blue lines with his tongue, my fingers caressing his face, his back, his arms.

We'd whisper secrets, dream of the future, profess a love that would last forever. I'd believed it then; I believed it again now.

His breath on my neck was soft as he nuzzled me, but his tongue was hard, insistent, as he traced first the hollow and then the slope. My nipples tightened. I still wanted him.

I lifted my arms, tilted my head, arched, and he grew hard again while still inside me. I knew that I'd reached him, that he would come back to me. Together we'd escape. We'd save the world, exact vengeance for Ruthie.

"Jimmy." I put all the love, all the trust, into the response of my body and the whisper of my voice. With that one word I asked him for the truth.

He answered by sinking his fangs into my neck.

Chapter 38

The arch of my body went from pleasure to pain. I tensed, tightened, gasped, and I swear as he began to suckle my neck, he came again in a rush that made me dizzy.

Or maybe that was just blood loss. He *was* sucking on me like a dehydrated kid with a straw.

I would have fought back, but I couldn't move. The first strike of his fangs had paralyzed me.

The betrayal was almost more than I could bear. He could have drunk from me the first time we'd been together, I'd expected him to, but he'd waited until I was at my most vulnerable. Then he'd struck like the evil thing that he was.

My hands fell away from his neck; my body went limp as my eyes fluttered closed. I could see us below me, as if I floated somewhere near the ceiling.

My eyes weren't closed but wide open and staring. I tilted my head. I looked a little dead.

From this angle, with his mouth at my neck, our legs entwined, his body growing slack within mine, the view was quite pornographic. If I weren't careful I'd end up starring in one of the videos on the huge wide screen in the living room.

Aw, hell, was I already? I wouldn't put it past them.

I continued to watch, both fascinated and repelled as he drank from me. His back was so beautiful, all muscles and sleek, tanned skin. I reached out to touch, but I didn't have an arm. My arm was on the bed with the rest of me.

I'd given him my heart, my soul, my body, and when I'd trusted him the most, he'd hurt me.

Talk about déjà vu.

I forced my attention back to us. I was getting pretty pale. He needed to stop that before he—

I went dizzy again. The world spun, and I fell from the ceiling, slamming back into myself with a thud and a gasp.

Jimmy lifted his head, but before I could see his face, his eyes, his no doubt blood-drenched lips, everything went blessedly black.

I dreamed of New Mexico. Oh, come on! Why there?

"Is this hell?" I asked.

"Hardly." I'd know that deep, mesmerizing voice anywhere, even without the hogan, the bonfire, the sweat lodge, the ramada that seemed to rise straight out of the ground in front of me. The mountains were there too, looming shadows stretching into an everlasting sky.

Sawyer stepped out of the night. Naked, with the moon cascading over his skin, turning his tattoos an eerie midnight blue.

"You dream, Phoenix."

"Get the hell out of my head."

"I'm not in your head, you're in mine."

"Sheesh. Sleeping with you was like a virus. What else did I catch?"

His lips compressed into a flat, thin line. "You didn't catch it from me."

"I had it all along?"

"No."

Jimmy. Hell.

"You *had* to sleep with him?" Sawyer asked.

"Yeah, I kind of did."

Sawyer's gaze touched my face, then darkened. "I will kill him."

"The line starts behind me."

Silence fell between us. The only sound was the crackling of the bonfire.

"He kept his dream walker power a secret from us all," Sawyer said. "If I'd known, I would have figured out how the Nephilim had gotten their information and staked him twice when I had the chance."

"What?"

"Only Ruthie knew the names of all the DKs and seers," he said slowly, and the light dawned.

"He walked in her dreams."

Sawyer nodded once.

"She didn't know?"

"A dream walker can wipe all trace of the walk from the victim's head. At the least, the person might remember dreaming of them, but not what the dream was about." He spread his hands. "Happens to all of us."

More than I liked. Especially now that I knew someone might have been trolling the halls of my mind while I slept.

"Jimmy didn't know he was doing it," I said.

"No?"

"No. His father, the strega, said that once he and Jimmy exchanged blood"—Sawyer made a face; I had to agree with the sentiment—"then Jimmy's vampire nature emerged and he changed sides."

"You believe this?"

I shouldn't believe anything the strega, or Jimmy, for that matter, said. Except—

Quickly I told Sawyer about absorbing Jimmy's dhampir powers, but not his vampire nature, which led me to believe that in order to attain a taste for blood I'd have to actually . . . taste blood.

"Also, if Jimmy was on the strega's team all along he would have killed me, you, Summer, hell, everyone he could. Why wait?"

Sawyer nodded thoughtfully. "I agree. Somehow the strega was able to entice Sanducci to dream-walk and pluck the information from Ruthie before she died without Sanducci knowing it. Perhaps the spell you saw in your vision—the bowl of blood—had something to do with it."

I recalled the strega saying he'd done everything to get into Jimmy's head—spells and charms—but nothing helped. He never had revealed just what had given him the access he needed to set doomsday in motion.

"How does the dream walker power work?" I asked.

"You must go into a deep trance, access the realm between life and death, where dreams exist; then you can walk among them."

"I wouldn't know a trance if it bit me on the ass."

"It bit you, all right. Tonight, Sanducci nearly killed you."

"That's how I got here?" Sawyer nodded. "Next time I'll take the bus."

I paused as several separate thoughts suddenly collided to provide a single answer. "Jimmy said he'd been sick. The worst he could ever remember. The strega was trying for years to get into Jimmy's head and couldn't."

Sawyer's face smoothed out in understanding. "None of his magic worked, but when Sanducci became ill, he existed in the realm of the dream walker. The strega was able to get past his defenses, then somehow entice him to walk in Ruthie's head where every bit of information he needed was there for the taking."

"Even so, Jimmy wouldn't have told him the information. Not then anyway."

"I'm sure it was a simple matter to draw what he wanted from Sanducci when he was still too ill to know what he was doing. The strega is, after all, a very powerful witch."

In the end, it didn't really matter how the strega had gotten his information; what mattered was that he had it and he was using it.

"So," I continued, "why your dreams?"

Those tight lips curved. "Yes, Phoenix, why mine?"

"Because you know so damn much about every damn thing?"

"Testy?"

"Do you know where I am? Do you know what's been going on?"

"Yes."

"And why is that?" I considered. "Summer's a tattletale."

"She did her job."

"But she didn't know exactly where I'd gone. Neither did you. I only said New York and it's a big city. Come clean, Sawyer. You put a transmitter on me or something?"

"Something." For an instant I thought he meant to leave the explanation at that, but he continued. "The turquoise is more than just protection from a chindi, it's a connection between us."

I scowled. "I never realized you were a Peeping Tom."

"There's a lot about me you don't realize," he said, unfazed as always by my scorn. "We've been trying to help you, but we can't get in. Several have died trying."

"Don't try anymore."

"It's pointless. You'll have to do this on your own."

"I'm used to it. So, tell me, why your dreams?"

"Dream walkers are drawn to the dreams of the one who knows the answer to their most desperate question. It's the way this power works."

"The only thing that would come in handy right now is how to kill a strega, but you didn't know—"

He moved forward, holding out his hands for mine. "Ever since you left, I've been searching for the answer."

My heart jittered. "Did you find one?"

"Touch me and you'll see."

I didn't hesitate, just slapped our palms together and braced for the ride.

The wind hit me like a tornado. I suddenly flew through dark, twisted corridors. Discarded toys, books, papers littered the floor. Doors whooshed by, some had locks, some stood half open, some were torn asunder as if by a huge, supernatural hand.

I came to a stop so fast I stumbled into the door in front of me. Ancient and cracked, the rusted hinges swung inward with an eerie creak.

I stepped inside. Sawyer's voice whispered out of the shadows. "Only blood of his blood will doom a strega."

"Could you be a little more specific?"

I guess the answer was no since I was yanked backward out of the door and into the corridor, where my speed increased until my stomach lurched with a pain reminiscent of carsickness.

Heat brushed my face where before there'd been only a chill; I opened my eyes and together Sawyer and I swayed.

"I've never liked it when people walk in my head," Sawyer muttered.

"Who would?"

"Exactly." Sawyer withdrew his hands from mine and put them behind his back as if to keep me from holding them again. "Remember that," he continued, "and use the power accordingly."

"I didn't mean to use it at all."

"Though dangerous, dream-walking is a beneficial talent to have, especially for a seer, but you'll have to learn to control it."

"I'll put that on my to-do list: don't die, escape evil lair, save the world, learn how to control dream-walking."

He didn't react, which made sarcasm no fun at all.

"What did you learn?"

"Only blood of his blood will doom a strega."

"Sanducci," Sawyer said. "He's blood of the strega's blood, his son. He's the only one who can do it."

I made a choked sound—half laughter, half disbelief. "That'll never happen."

"You're probably right."

"A little encouragement would be nice. Maybe some hints."

Sawyer closed his eyes, breathed in deeply, and when he breathed out, a scalding wind blew across the desert. "Remember all that you have become; take stock of everything available to you. Think of all you have learned, all you have heard." His eyes snapped open, boring into mine, and the wind died. "Do it quickly. Our time is almost out."

"Terrific."

His voice lowered. "You nearly died tonight. Quit baiting Sanducci. If you keep trying to make him remember the life he had that's gone, he *will* kill you before you can kill him."

He was right. I'd felt it in Jimmy tonight, the desire to both kiss and kill me. I wasn't sure how much longer he'd be able to resist doing them both. Probably at the same time.

"Why would the strega even have a kid if that's the only way he can die?"

"He must have decided that the off chance Sanducci would find the stones to kill him was worth the risk of having his son inside the federation. Now that the strega's controlling him, there's no risk at all."

I bristled. "Jimmy's not himself. He'd kill the strega if he was."

"And then all our problems would be over." He took another deep breath, then let it out in a rush before murmuring, "Momentarily. But Sanducci *isn't* himself. If you can manage to end the strega, make sure Sanducci is next. Killing him would be an act of mercy. He'd want you to."

"You never liked him."

"What's to like? He's an arrogant prick who takes whatever he wants and damn the consequences. He was like that even before he lost his soul."

"Glass houses," I murmured.

"I never pretended to have a soul, Phoenix. I never said that I loved someone, and then tore out their heart."

Was he talking figuratively or literally? I put my palm against my chest. I kind of liked my heart right where it was.

Regardless of what he meant, I struck back. It's what I did. "I doubt you've ever loved anyone in your long, lonely, black pathetic life."

Sawyer began to waver. So did everything else—the mountains and sky, the hogan, house, and ramada. They ran downward, like a watercolor left out in the rain. As they washed together into a swirling mass of stormy gray, Sawyer's voice followed me into the void. "You're right."

What came next was a strange, confusing, untenable period in which I wasn't certain what was real and what was not. Night blended into day. Jimmy was always there, an orgy of two.

He took me every way imaginable and some that weren't. Pain and pleasure became intertwined. I was always on the edge of consciousness, the edge of orgasm. When I fell, I fell hard, drifting into the darkness, but I never found the light.

When I dreamed it was of snakes and coyotes, wolves and bears, cougars and cackling witches all overlaid with the sound a straw makes when someone reaches the bottom of the drink yet keeps on sucking.

I would nearly come awake at sharp needles of pain at my breast, my inner thigh, the soft skin on the inside of my elbow. I'd feel his body in mine, driving me toward orgasm, both of us tumbling together as he drank from me over and over and over again.

My life had become death, or perhaps my death was giving him life. I didn't know. I couldn't escape. I was so languid, I didn't want to. The only thing anchoring me to this world was the sharp pull of his teeth and the constant pressure of him inside of me. I needed it and him; I craved it. I had truly become his slave.

I started up with a deep, gasping breath, as if coming from the depths of a lake and bursting through the surface into the sun.

The sun *was* shining. Jimmy was gone. My mouth was dry as the desert I'd visited in Sawyer's dream. My head throbbed. I felt hungover, and I hadn't even gotten any champagne.

I stumbled into the bathroom. I was pale and a helluva lot skinnier than I'd been when I went to bed. My ribs poked out; my stomach was concave, even my arms seemed bony. But my neck looked just fine. Quickly I checked my breasts, my thighs, my arms. Not a mark on me.

How much of that had been real? How long had I been out?

I showered, the hot water soothing the aches but increasing my light-headedness, and I needed to think. So I stepped out long before I was ready.

"Blood of his blood," I murmured. "There has got to be another way."

I didn't know all that I should about the Nephilim and the ways to kill them. Since Ruthie'd died and Jimmy had become evil's plaything I'd been a little busy.

I left the bathroom and walked into the main living area. A harem costume had been draped across the couch. If I wasn't the only one with a sense of humor in this place, I'd think it was joke. But I knew better. Since the pantaloons and puffy sports bra were better than nothing, I put them on.

I felt like an idiot. I did not have the body for a two-piece. My breasts filled out the top just fine, but the rest of me was all muscle, with few curves, and my short hair only made me look like a teenage boy wearing an *I Dream of Jeannie* costume. Which was just too disturbing for words.

Next, I retrieved Ruthie's crucifix from the drawer. Touching it had burned Jimmy. Sure he'd healed, but so far the icon was the only thing that had done any damage at all. The silver knife was useless, but the blessing on this symbol seemed to have some power. At least his frying flesh might distract him long enough for me to . . .

What? I needed some kind of plan.

Sawyer had said to use all I knew and all I had.

Ruthie's crucifix was about it, except for the turquoise. I tucked both into my pocket. Couldn't hurt.

I was just finishing a second cup of coffee when the elevator slid open. No one got off.

This was new. I stepped inside, attempted to push *L* just for the hell of it, but the only button that worked took me to the strega's lair.

I expected to find the harem waiting for me, but the room was empty. Were they all . . . occupied? The thought of walking in on the strega, or worse, Jimmy— even worse, Jimmy *and* the strega—with all of those women nearly made me get back on the elevator. But now was not the time to be squeamish. I needed guts to kill these guys. Seeing them in flagrante delicto was the least of my worries.

The war room was empty. I'd be nervous if the sun wasn't up. I had to assume the majority of the vampire minions were all out cold. Ha-ha.

The strega strolled in wearing a Hugh Hefner robe, loose silk trousers, and slippers. Despite the casual nature of the outfit, or perhaps because of it, he was still the creepiest thing I'd ever seen.

"What happened to the harem?" I asked.

"I ran out."

Unease trickled down my spine as my costume took on a whole new meaning.

"You look well, seer, considering." His eyes danced. The expression would have been joyous on anyone human. On him it made me ill. "Most women would be dead."

"I'm not most women."

"I'm coming to understand that. You have more power than any of the others. I'm glad my son insisted on keeping you alive. Of course it has been touch and go a few times over these past few weeks."

Few weeks?

My gaze shot to the war board, which was awash in a sea of green and yellow.

If I didn't do something soon, we were finished.

Chapter 39

How many of the people represented by those colored pins had fallen right outside this building because of me? The least I could do was try to even the score.

"Where's Jimmy?"

"We've had a slight change of plans."

I didn't like the sound of that. Mostly because I still didn't have a plan.

"Let me guess," I said, stalling. "You want to repent, come over to my side. Forget about doomsday. Let's move right to heaven on earth."

The strega laughed. "I am planning for heaven on earth, but my heaven's a little different from yours."

"Humans as slaves, Nephilim are legion. Blah, blah, blah, blah, blah."

His amusement fled. "I will teach you humility and respect."

"Good luck with that."

The strega grabbed me by the neck and dragged me out of the war room. I struggled to be free, but it was like fighting against an iron collar. I wasn't going to get away unless he wanted to let me go.

He put his lips right next to my ear. "I've got a

fascinating entertainment in mind for this evening. You. Jimmy."

I tensed, figuring he wanted to watch.

"To the death."

"What?" I managed. "He's your son."

"So?"

True. Guys like him usually ate their young. So why hadn't he?

Because Jimmy had been useful. At his feet could be laid the deaths represented by those colored pins. That he hadn't known his brain was being picked wasn't going to matter to the dead.

"The last bit of humanity in him will die with you," the strega said. "I've been looking forward to it."

He let me go with a little shove. I whirled, then froze. Jimmy stood right behind him.

"Kill her," the strega ordered, and Jimmy smiled. "Whoever's still alive at the end of this gets to be my second in command."

"I don't want to be your freaking second in command, you psychotic bloodsucking witch."

The strega's eyes narrowed. "Then die."

Shit.

The strega moved out of the way as Jimmy began to circle.

"Why don't you kill *him*?" I asked Jimmy. "I'll help."

"I . . . c-c-" He clenched his fists. Since he wore his usual outfit, loose cotton trousers and nothing else, I caught every ripple of muscle as his biceps bulged. "Can't." The word seemed to explode past his lips, as if something had been keeping it prisoner and only supreme strength had forced it free. "Without him I'd be nothing."

Without him you'd be you, I thought. But too late now.

With an almost nonchalant movement, he backhanded me. I flew off my feet, missing the pile of pillows by inches and landing on the marble tile so hard I could have sworn I heard my bones shatter.

I'd hoped for a better outcome; I'm not sure why. The strega controlled Jimmy. There was no way Jimmy would be able to break that hold and save us all. I had to accept my failure. I would die here, probably within the next few minutes, and the strega's plan for mankind would succeed.

But I wasn't going to give in without one helluva fight. I wasn't defenseless. I had Jimmy's strength and his speed. He just didn't know it.

Jimmy moved quickly. I saw his shadow coming at me across the ceiling. I lifted my legs, thrilled when they worked without pain, and kicked him in the stomach. He landed on the kitchen table, breaking it into a dozen shards.

I did a kip, from my back to my feet. I'd always been spectacular at them. Jimmy was already up and heading in my direction.

He swung; I ducked and came up with a left hook. He flew again, this time putting a dent in the wall. I started to feel very much like a terminatrix. There was no reason to hide my superior strength and speed any longer. Letting go felt unbelievably good.

Jimmy shook his head as if I'd loosened a few teeth. "How did you—"

I didn't wait for the question I had no intention of answering. I sprinted toward him and planted a kick right in his chest.

Or at least I tried to. He grabbed my foot and threw me heels over head. I hit the ground right next to the shattered dining room table. He was on me before I got my breath back.

My grasping fingers touched wood. He lunged forward, going for my throat. His eyes flared red; his fangs lengthened. His face was no longer the face of a man but a monster.

Intent on his kill, he didn't pay attention to my legs. I twined them with his, yanked, and he flipped onto his back, taking me and the splintered table leg with him.

"Go ahead," the strega urged, his voice the hiss of the serpent in the garden, temptation incarnate, evil down through the ages. "You know that you want to. They all died because of him. She died because of him."

"He didn't know," I muttered. "You made him do it."

"Technically, it wasn't me. I had to hire that out. But . . . she's still dead."

My fingers tightened on the stake.

"Do it," the strega whispered, his excitement shimmering in the air like the sun across the morning dew. "I'll make you my concubine queen; together we'll rule this rock."

I was torn. There was killing Jimmy because I had no other choice or because he really, really needed killing. And there was killing him because this creature wanted me to, because killing him would make me his concubine queen.

Who talked like that?

"To end a dhampir you must strike twice in the same place—once for each nature, human and vampire."

Was he telling the truth? Considering his method and Sawyer's legend were remarkably similar, I had to think so. Since I didn't have a better plan, I tightened my fingers around the wood and plunged the stake into Jimmy's chest.

He gave a gasp that was more like a shriek, and I almost lost my nerve. How could I do this to him? Though I knew in my head I had to, my own heart was aching as badly as his must be.

But I'd gone too far to stop now. Thankfully, when I yanked the stake out, he went limp. Blood pattered onto the floor like rain.

"Once more." The strega had moved closer, but not close enough. "I'll be invincible."

"I—I can't." I made my voice tremble. It wasn't hard. The sight of that hole in Jimmy's chest made me want to do a lot more than tremble. "Not when he's unconscious. It's—"

"Inhuman?" The strega's voice wavered too, but with amusement.

"Unsportsmanlike," I corrected.

"You make it sound like this is a game." He was closer still. "You will be the most wonderful queen. If you just do what you're told."

There was something off in that reasoning, but with him there usually was.

"I can't," I repeated.

He slithered closer; he was right behind me. "Do it, or he'll do you. You'll scream like Ruthie did, but in the end you'll die. Just like she did."

Ah, well, maybe I could.

I lifted the stake, but instead of striking forward, into Jimmy, I flipped it so the pointy end faced away; then I slammed it backward with all that I had.

"Oof," said the strega.

I twisted the stake, ground it in as far as it would go before I stood to face him and pulled it out.

The stake wouldn't kill him, only Jimmy could, but it would slow him down long enough so that maybe I could get away. And if I did, if I could rally those left on my side, maybe one of them would know another way to end this guy.

I also had high hopes of planting the pointy end in Jimmy's chest for the second strike, permanently ending him. But, as usual, my plan didn't work quite the way I'd thought.

The strega staggered backward until his shoulders met the wall of windows. Behind him, the sun set, turning the sky to crimson flame.

He looked down at the gaping hole in his chest. Blood poured out in a fountain, splashing onto the floor and washing over his feet.

"Blood of my blood," he said, in a horrible, gurgling howl.

Then he disintegrated. One minute he was bleeding, the next he was blood, a river flowing across the tile. I'd never seen anything like it. I hoped I never saw anything like it again.

"What the hell?" I stared at the stake.

Blood of his blood, Ruthie whispered. *Abilities shared.*

I glanced at the ceiling. "Today you get chatty?"

But she did have a point, one I hadn't considered.

My empathetic abilities allowed me to absorb the powers of those I had sex with, and one of Jimmy's powers was that he could kill the strega.

Now I had to kill him.

I hurried back, intent on finishing this before I thought too much about what I was doing, but as I leaned over Jimmy, he opened his eyes. He moved so fast, I couldn't get away.

I tensed for the pain as his teeth tore into me, but it didn't come. Instead he wrapped his arms around my waist, pressed his cheek to my stomach, and whispered in a voice so broken I ached: "Lizzy."

Chapter 40

The weapon tumbled from my suddenly senseless fingers.

Jimmy tilted his face, the anguish there almost too much to bear. "Oh, God, baby, it was me. My fault Ruthie died. My fault all of it."

Well, yeah. But since when did he care?

Tentatively I stepped back. He clutched at me like a child. "Let me see," I whispered.

The big hole in his chest had healed, though the skin was still puckered and red.

"It wasn't you." I smoothed my palm over his hair. "You didn't know."

"Doesn't matter," he managed. "She's still dead."

Exactly what the strega had said. The spell over Jimmy appeared to have broken with the death of his father, but what remained?

"What do you remember?"

"Everything. I was trapped inside of myself. I could see myself, hear myself, but I couldn't stop. The things I did, Lizzy."

He was still wrapped around me. I let him hold on. I wanted that connection too. Just because the strega was dead didn't mean we weren't in a lot of trouble. The building was full of vamps, and they weren't going to be too happy to discover the boss man was a big red stain on the Italian marble tile.

"You need to let me go, Jimmy. We have to get the hell out of here."

"Okay." He took a deep breath. "You're right."

He got to his feet, slowly as if he hurt all over. I know I did.

His gaze went to the floor where the strega's Hugh Hefner outfit lay in a puddle of blood. "How did you do that? Only I'm supposed to be able to kill him, and I . . . I couldn't."

"It turns out sex makes me take on supernatural abilities like other people catch viruses."

"Son of a—" Jimmy rubbed his forehead. "You're an empath."

"That seems to be the consensus."

I couldn't stop glancing at what was left of the strega. I hadn't needed Ruthie's crucifix after all. I patted my pocket, relieved to find both it and the turquoise still there.

Or maybe I had. Maybe that blessing had been just the boost I needed to succeed.

For the first time I could remember I wanted to embrace who I was. I wasn't a freak; I was the leader of the light. With the powers I had, and the ones yet to come, I could really help people. And it was so much less stressful to be myself rather than trying not to be.

Footsteps sounded on the other side of the door.

"Trust me," Jimmy whispered.

As the door swung open, he grabbed me by the neck and squeezed. I didn't have to fake the choking sounds that spewed from my mouth. I clawed at his hands without being asked.

"What do you want?" he demanded.

"The master?"

"Not here. I'm busy. Get out."

The door closed. Jimmy let me go, catching me when I would have fallen to the ground.

"Sorry." His lips pressed against my hair. "Sorry. We can't let them know."

"I'm all right." I rubbed my throat. "All in a day's work."

"That should keep them happy for a while. Follow me."

He moved into the next room, a bedroom fit for a fat Middle Eastern pasha. Filmy bed curtains, low, round bed, huge fountain that poured into what looked like an actual restored bathhouse from some country that had once been ruler of the world and had fallen when the outlaw hordes came. There were quite a few. The walls were equipped with cuffs and chains—several pairs. I gave Jimmy a quick glance, but he was studiously avoiding that area, focusing instead on a panel next to the closet.

"What are you doing?"

"There's a passageway." He put his shoulder to it and shoved. The panel swung open and cool, musty air wafted out.

"No one else knows about this?"

Jimmy shook his head.

I took a step toward him and a photo on the nightstand caught my gaze. Because the strega didn't seem the type to keep mementos, I paused to look and then I couldn't breathe.

The woman of smoke. What in hell was she doing here even in a picture?

I snatched up the framed photograph. I guess I hadn't dreamed her after all. Here she appeared even more lifelike since she'd been captured in living color.

"Who is this?" I asked.

Jimmy glanced at the picture and shrugged. "Never saw her before."

A sound from the other room made us both start. "Gotta go, Lizzy."

I nodded, then, as he turned away, I yanked the back off the frame, folded the picture into quarters and tucked it into the pocket of my harem pants with everything else.

Silently we trailed downward. The path was dark, but I could see as well as Jimmy now, move just as quickly too. A short while later we reached a door that opened outward, spilling us into the same alley I'd entered weeks before.

My pantaloons ruffled in the spring breeze. My bare stomach got gooseflesh. I was headed into Manhattan in a harem outfit. No one would probably notice.

"Hold on," Jimmy said, and disappeared inside.

He was gone so long I began to panic. Right before I rushed back in, he appeared, bursting from the gloom in a great big hurry. As soon as he saw me, he caught my arm. "Run."

I didn't have to be told twice. I figured they were on to us.

We found a break in traffic, streaked across the street, ignoring the horns and the curses. When we reached the far side, Jimmy stopped.

"What are you—" I glanced back, figuring the vampire legion was already there and we were dead; why fight it? But the only thing behind us was the traffic, the normal crush of people, and the big, black chrome-and-glass hellhole.

Except there was something off about the glass. The sun was down, so why did every floor flicker orange and yellow, like the dancing light of—

"Fire," I said.

"The strega's final solution."

"To what?"

"Everything. Revolt. Invasion. Capture. He had the building rigged."

"They're going to burn."

He looked at me and the Jimmy I knew—or at least the one I'd discovered since he'd showed up in my hospital room—was back. "Got a problem with that?"

"Not a one."

Chapter 41

We checked in to the first hotel we found. I hit the gift shop, charged a T-shirt, sweatpants, and some flip-flops to the room. I guess, for the time being, I did heart New York.

When I got out of the shower, Jimmy stood at the window. Something about the slump of his shoulders made me uneasy. He should be happy. No more desire for blood. No more controlling freak of a father. We'd gotten out alive.

"You okay?" I asked.

"Let's see." He faced me. Though the red pinprick in the center had disappeared, I still didn't like what I saw in his eyes. "I've killed Ruthie and a shitload of others, ruined any chance we had to win this war, hurt you, debased you, why wouldn't I be all right?"

"You didn't kill Ruthie." I left out the others. I was pretty sure he'd killed a few people since he'd been in the strega's lair. Best not bring that up.

"I may as well have." He turned away again. I wasn't sure what to do.

Love is stronger than hate.

Trust Ruthie to show me the way.

I opened my mouth to tell him, but I couldn't. I'd never been very verbal with my feelings, at least the softer ones. I could shout hatred from the rooftops, but when it came to love . . . I was better at show than tell.

I let the towel drop to the floor. His reflection in the window tensed; his eyes closed. I moved up behind him and pressed my breasts to his back. He never had found a shirt. His skin against mine felt delicious. Would he taste just as good?

I licked his shoulder—definitely delicious—so I nibbled at his neck, inched my palm around his side and laid it against his flat stomach.

"Lizzy," he said, his voice full of warning.

"Make me forget the other times," I whispered. "Love me like you used to."

For an instant I thought I'd gone too far by referring to the strega's high-rise. Then he moaned as if I'd punched him in the gut, turned and gathered me into his arms.

I touched his face, lifted it, met his eyes, let him see that I'd never stopped loving him. I doubted I ever could. Even when a despicable creature had lurked inside, I couldn't give up the hope of reaching Jimmy, of bringing him back. And I had. That alone was cause for this celebration.

His hands skated over me, reverent but sure, tracing the curve of my thigh, the swell of my breast. My head fell back; his lips brushed my neck, his tongue tracing the vein.

I didn't tense; I trusted him completely. He needed me to.

His mouth warmed me from collarbone to belly button. My skin tingled at the scratch of his beard, the flutter of each and every kiss. He was on his knees again, arms around me, face pressed just below my breasts. I rested my hands on his shoulders, kneading the harsh knots beneath the skin until they smoothed, though they never faded completely away.

I took his hand and drew him to his feet, then with me onto the bed. He still wore his loose trousers. I worked them over his hips, following the descent with my mouth. He was hard; I couldn't wait. I made a move to straddle him and he reared up, tumbling me onto my back and sliding into me.

Sure, slow strokes, deep, wet kisses, I lost track of how long we lay together, bodies in tandem, light, tender touches, a murmur, a moan. He never lifted his mouth from mine, even when our movements became faster, more frantic as we climbed together toward that peak we craved.

His hand cupped my breast, lifting, stroking, the sensation shooting from my nipple straight to my center. He framed my face with his palms, brushed our lips together, tentatively met my tongue with his own, delving within as if he couldn't get enough of the taste of my mouth. The last time I'd been kissed like that I was seventeen and so damn in love I thought I'd die of it.

That memory made me come in a rush that left me gasping. As the tremors faded, he pulsed, increasing the tempo, drawing out the orgasm. His forehead dropped to mine for just an instant before he rolled to the side. I caught his hand as he fell away, and his fingers tangled with mine.

There'd been something different about that last kiss, something I couldn't put my finger on, especially since I was drifting toward sleep on a killer combination of adrenaline letdown and afterglow.

I slept without dreams for a change. God, it felt good.

I woke up and knew instantly what had been different about his kiss. The empty bed, the empty room told the tale.

That last kiss had been good-bye.

Epilogue

He'd left a note on the dresser. When I picked it up, cash tumbled out. I was going to kill him again when I caught up to him.

He awakened my vampire nature, Lizzy. I'm not sure I can put it back. You're not safe with me. No one is.

Ah, hell. I hadn't thought of that. I'd figured that once the strega was dead, his influence was too. But fact was fact, and Jimmy was part vampire.

Someone knocked on the door. I wrapped the sheet around me and checked the peephole. Bellboy with a package.

I tipped him a five—just because I was pissed about the money didn't mean I wasn't going to use it—then checked the return name.

Sawyer. My gaze went to the turquoise I'd placed on the dresser last night along with the crucifix and the stolen photo. Figured.

I tore open the wrapping and a gorgeous silk robe tumbled out. All the shades of midnight: blue, purple, black with sparkles of silver. I held it up and blinked in shock as the image of a wolf shimmered—there and then gone and then there again.

A piece of paper fell to the floor. Today seemed to be my day for notes.

Summer says trouble's coming. You'll need this.

Trust Sawyer to remind me that though we'd won this battle, the war still raged. Casualties on both sides were enormous. They'd regroup, but we would too. Jimmy had been wrong when he said he'd ruined our chance to win. He'd handicapped us, sure, but I wasn't going to throw in the towel quite yet.

I stared at the robe, so beautiful, so deadly. Trouble *was* coming; I could feel it, a storm hovering just out of sight, ready to rain hail and thunder and lightning down on the world.

But first things first.

I needed Jimmy, and I'd find him. Finding the missing was what I'd always done best.

I shoved the robe back into the box.

For now, doomsday could wait.

Read on for an excerpt from

Lori Handeland's next book

DOOMSDAY
CAN WAIT

Coming in May 2009 from

St. Martin's Paperbacks

A month ago I put a stake through the heart of the only man I've ever loved. Luckily, or not, depending on the day and my mood, that wasn't enough to kill him.

I found myself the leader of a band of seers and demon killers at the dawn of the Apocalypse. Turns out a lot of that Biblical prophecy crap is true.

I consider it both strange and frightening that I was chosen to lead the final battle between the forces of good and evil. Until last month I'd been nothing more than a former cop turned bartender.

Oh, and I was psychic. Always had been.

Not that being psychic had done anything for me except lose me the only job I wanted—being a cop—and the only man too, the aforementioned extremely-hard-to-kill Jimmy Sanducci. It had also gotten my partner killed, something I had yet to get over despite his wife's insistence that it hadn't been my fault.

In an attempt to pay a debt I could never truly pay, I'd taken a job as the first-shift bartender in a tavern owned by the widow, Megan Murphy. I also found myself best friends with the woman. I'm not quite sure how.

After last month's free-for-all of death and destruction, I'd come home to Milwaukee to try and figure out

what to do next. Three-quarters of my doomsday soldiers
were dead and the rest were in hiding. I had no way of
finding them, no way of even knowing who in hell they
were. Unless I found Jimmy. That was proving more difficult than I'd thought.

So while I hung out and waited for the psychic flash
that would make all things clear, I went back to work at
Murphy's. A girl had to eat and pay the mortgage.
Amazingly, being the leader of the supernatural forces
of sunshine—I'm kidding, we're actually called the
federation—didn't pay jack shit.

On the night all hell broke loose—again—I was actually working a double shift. The evening bartender had
come down with a case of the "I'd rather be at Summerfest" blues, and I couldn't walk out at the end of my
scheduled hours and leave Megan alone to deal with the
dinner rush.

Not that there was much of one. Summerfest, Milwaukee's famous music festival on the lake, drew most of the
party crowd. A few off-duty cops drifted in now and
then—they were the mainstay of Megan's business—but
in truth, Murphy's was the deadest I'd ever seen it. Hell,
the place was empty. Which made it easy for the woman
who appeared at dusk to draw my attention.

She strolled in on dangerously high heels—tall and
slim and dark. Her hair was up in a fancy twist I'd never
have been able to manage, even if my own was longer
than the nape of my neck. Her white suit made her bronze
skin and the copper pendant revealed by the plunging
neckline of her jacket gleam in the half-light.

Megan took one look, rolled her eyes, and retreated to
the kitchen. She had no patience for lawyers. Did anyone?
This woman's clothes, heels, carriage screamed "blood-
sucker." In my world, there was always great concern that

the term was literal. I nearly laughed out loud when she ordered Cabernet.

"With that suit?" I asked.

Her lips curved; her perfectly plucked eyebrows lifted past the rims of her self-regulating sunglasses, which had yet to lighten even though she'd stepped indoors. I could see only the shadow of her eyes beyond the lenses. Brown, perhaps black. Definitely not blue like mine.

The cheekbones and nose hinted at Native American blood somewhere in her past. Though she probably knew the origin of hers, I did not. Who I'd been before I'd become Elizabeth Phoenix was as much a mystery to me as the identity of my parents.

"You think I'd spill a single drop?" she murmured in a smoky voice.

How could something sound like smoke? I'd never understood that term. But as soon as she spoke, it suddenly became clear to me. She sounded like a gray, hot mist that could kill you.

"You from around here?" I asked.

Murphy's, located in the middle of a residential area, wasn't exactly a tourist attraction. The place was as old as the city and had been a tavern all of its life. Back in the day, fathers would finish their shifts at the factories, then stop by for a brew before heading home. They'd come in after dinner and watch the game, or retreat here if they'd fought with the wife or had enough of the screaming kids.

Such establishments could be found all over Milwaukee, hell, all over Wisconsin. Bar, house, bar, house, house, house, another bar. In Friedenberg, where I lived, about twenty miles north of the city, there were five bars in the single mile square village. Walking more than a block for a beer? It just wasn't done.

"I'm from everywhere," the stranger said, then sipped the wine.

A bit clung to her lip. Gravity pulled it downward, the remaining moisture pooling into a droplet the shade of blood. Her tongue snaked out and captured the bead before it fell on the pristine white lapel of her suit. I had a bizarre flash of Snow White.

"Or maybe it's nowhere." She tilted her head. "You decide."

I was starting to get uneasy. She might be beautiful, but she was weird. Not that we didn't get weirdos in the bar every day. But there was usually a cop or ten around.

Sure, I'd once been a cop, but I wasn't anymore. And pretty much everyone, even Megan, frowned on bartenders pulling a gun on the clientele. Of course, if she wasn't human—

My fingers stroked the solid silver knife I hid beneath my ugly green uniform vest as I waited for some kind of sign.

The woman reached again for her wine. Contrary to her earlier assertion, she knocked it over. The ruby-red liquid sloshed across the bar, pooling at the edge before dripping onto the floor.

I should have been diving for a towel; instead I found myself fascinated by the shimmering puddle, which reflected the dim lights and the face of the woman.

The shiny dark surface leached the color from everything, not that there'd been all that much color to her in the first place. Black hair, white suit, light brown skin.

Slowly I lifted my gaze to hers. The glasses had cleared. I could see her eyes. I'd seen them before.

In the face of a woman of smoke who'd been conjured from a bonfire in the New Mexico desert. No wonder she hid them behind dark lenses. Those eyes would scare the pants off of anyone who looked directly into them. I was surprised I hadn't been turned to stone. They held aeons of hate, centuries of evil, millennia of joy in the act of murder with a dash of madness on the side.

I drew my knife, threw it—I ought to be able to hit her in such close quarters—but she snatched the weapon out of the air with freakishly fast fingers.

"Shit," I said.

Smirking, she returned the knife—straight at my head. I ducked, and the thing stuck in the wall behind me with a thunk and a *boing* worthy of any cartoon soundtrack.

I straightened, meaning to grab the weapon and leap over the bar. I had supernatural speed and strength of my own. But the instant my head cleared wood, she grabbed me by the neck and hauled me over, breaking bottles, knocking glasses everywhere.

"Liz?" Megan called.

I opened my mouth to shout, "Run!", and choked instead as the woman squeezed.

She lifted her gaze to where Megan must surely be. I wanted to say, "Don't look at her," but speech was as beyond me as breathing.

I heard a whoosh and then a thud. Like a body sliding down a wall to collapse on the floor. Had the woman of smoke killed Megan with a single glance? I wouldn't put it past her.

I pulled at her hands, tugged on her fingers, managed to loosen her hold enough by breaking a few to gulp several quick breaths.

What in hell had happened? The woman of smoke was obviously a minion of evil out to kill me. Being the leader of the light, in a battle with the demon horde, seemed to have put a great big, invisible target on my back.

However, the other times I'd always had a warning— what I called a ghost whisper. The voice of the woman who'd raised me, Ruthie Kane—whose death had set this whole mess in motion—would tell me what kind of creature I was facing. Even if I didn't know how to kill it—and considering that I'd been dropped into this job with no training, that was usually the case—I still preferred advance notice of impending bloody death rather than having bloody death sprung upon me.

I tried to think. It was amazingly hard without oxygen, but I managed.

The woman of smoke had grabbed my silver knife and her fingers hadn't sprung out in a rash. Not a shapeshifter, or at least not a common one such as a werewolf. When you mix silver and werewolves, you usually wind up with ashes.

Her strength hinted at vampire, though most of those would just tear out my throat and have a nice, relaxing bath in my blood. Still—

I let go of her arm and tore open my uniform so that Ruthie's silver crucifix spilled free. Vampires tended to flip when they saw the icon, not because of the shape, or the silver, but because of the blessing upon it. She didn't even blink.

I pressed it to her wrist anyway. Nothing. So, not a vampire.

Suddenly she stilled. The pressure on my throat eased; the black spots cleared from in front of my eyes. She stared at my chest and not with the fascinated expression I often got after opening my shirt. If I did say so myself, my breasts weren't bad. However, I'd never had a woman this interested in them. I didn't like it any more than I liked her.

"Where did you get that?" Her eyes sparked; I could have sworn I saw flames leap in the center of all that black.

"Th-the crucifix is—"

"A crucifix can't stop me," she sneered and yanked it from my neck, tossing the treasured memento aside.

"Hey!" I tore her amulet off the same way.

The very air seemed to still, yet my hair stirred in an impossible wind.

Dreadful One, Ruthie whispered at last, *Naye'i*.

A *Naye'i* was a Navajo spirit. I'd heard of them before. Several puzzle pieces suddenly fit together with a nearly audible click.

The woman of smoke backed away, staring at the stone I had recently strung on its own chain rather than continuing to let it share Ruthie's.

"You don't like my turquoise." I sat up.

Her gaze lifted from the necklace to my face. All I could see between the narrowed lids was a blaze of orange flame. "That isn't yours."

"I know someone who'd say differently." My hand inched toward the blue-green gem. "The someone who gave it to me. I think you call him 'son'."

As soon as my fingers closed around it, the turquoise went white-hot, and the *Naye'i* snarled like the demon she was, then turned to smoke and disappeared.

WANT MORE OF
ELIZABETH PHOENIX?

VISIT
us.macmillan.com/anygivendoomsday
and sign up to receive the FREE prequel
story *In the Beginning*

Don't miss the next book in
The Phoenix Chronicles,
Doomsday Can Wait,
COMING IN MAY 2009!